IN THE COURT OF KEMET

Also by Danielle S. LeBlanc

Living with Oral Allergy Syndrome: A Gluten and Meat-Free Cookbook for Wheat, Soy, Nut, Fresh Fruit and Vegetable Allergies

Recipes for Unusual Gluten Free Pasta: Pierogis, Dumplings, Desserts and More!

IN THE COURT OF KEMET

By

Danielle LeBlanc

www.DanielleSLeBlanc.blogspot.com

La Venta West, Inc.
Vancouver, Canada

For Alex

LA VENTA WEST, INC., 2014

www.laventawestpublishers.blogspot.ca

Copyright © 2014 by Danielle S. LeBlanc

This book is a work of fiction and, except in the case of
historical fact, any resemblance to actual persons, living or
dead, is purely coincidental.

Print ISBN 978-0-9920802-4-2
eBook ISBN 978-0-9920802-5-9

Acknowledgements

The comments, edits, questions, and conversations of the fabulous writers of the Madison Writing Workshop have greatly contributed to the quality of this book. Working with such talented and thoughtful writers has been inspiring. Many thanks to Ryan LeDuc, all around awesome organizer and good guy, and in no particular order, David Norman, Andrew Stimpson, Matthew Morris-Cook, Melissa Bergum, Rosanne Braslow, Brandon Taylor, Sue Garman, Julia Soriano, Alan Bahr, and Bill Blondeau. I miss our weekly meetings!

Noelle Phillips and her last minute, overnight, power edit/beta reading is much appreciated.

This might sound cliché, but I'm also grateful for my high school English teacher and published author, Dr. Beverley Boissery (a.k.a. Dr. Greenwood), for her support many years ago. It's taken a while to come full circle, but thanks so much for believing in me.

My husband Alex deserves all the thanks in the world for letting me talk through scenes and ideas with him, and for his constant support.

Table of Contents

Quick Reference
for
Ancient Egyptian Words

Bakh: servants
Bakht: female servants
Hem-etj: Your majesty (female)
Hem-ek: Your majesty (male)
Hnr: musicians and dancers
Iteru: the Nile River
Kemet: Egypt
Sekhrey: Captain
Sar: Prince
Mewet: Mother/aunt/close female relation like a mother figure
Nebet-i: My lady
Sephat: city
Shenti: kilt-like wrap skirt worn by men and women, belted at waist
Wa'ew: soldier

Note: The term *pharaoh*, referring to the king of Egypt, was not in use during the First Dynasty, when the novel is set. However, it is used here for stylistic reasons and because it is a familiar term to most.

Chapter 1 – The Court of Thinis

Egypt (Kemet), 2975 B.C.E.

Queen Merneith sat on the raised platform in the courtyard of the Palace of Thinis, absently watching the festivities unfolding around her. In the past she would have savored the evening as a rare moment of peace. The sun was setting behind the date palms and the servants of the palace, the *bakh*, had lit the torches that dotted the courtyard. The flames cast a glow on the etched columns near the platform, causing the images of the gods inscribed there to shift and dance with the flickering shadows. In the distance Merneith could see the sails of a few large fishing vessels bobbing on the life-giving *Iteru*, the great river that snaked through the land of *Kemet* up to the great northern sea. On the stand next to her chair rested a goblet of wine from the far off lands of Palestine, the steady flow of trade with the Canaanite region a symbol of the current peace between the two great lands.

   The evening's entertainment was unrivaled in the land. In honour of Merneith, whose name meant *Beloved of Neith*, the court's official musicians and acrobatic dancers had enacted a battle led by the goddess *Neith*. Five prized Nubian elephants had danced in unison, and a troupe of fire eaters had been sent as a gift from King Alalngar of Sumeria. Alalngar's gift was an indication that he forgave the royal family for housing his exiled nephew, Atab, the handsome prince who happened to be sitting to Merneith's right at that very moment. After decades of struggle, peace reigned not only within Egypt but between Egypt and the lands around her, at least temporarily.

   Sar Atab, the pharaoh's new best friend, Merneith mused, *and yet he did not join the pharaoh on his tour north.* Merneith's eyes floated over the decorated Egyptian women, with their elaborate, braided wigs and thick gold necklaces, bracelets and hair ornaments. Some wore simple white linen shift dresses belted loosely at the waist, like her own. Others wore long rectangles of fabric wrapped beneath their breasts or draped over one shoulder, leaving only one breast exposed. The men in their wrapped linen skirts were almost as ornamented as the women. Some had shaved heads draped with gold chains, while others had long braids wrapped up on the side or back of an otherwise shaved head. Large hoops dangled from their ears, and beaded collars rested on their naked chests. Merneith found most of them to be overdone, vying too hard with one another to appear the most nonchalantly wealthy and powerful.

Sar Atab himself was particularly prominent amongst the men tonight. He had abandoned the white linen wrap skirt most men in Kemet wore, known as a *shenti*, in favour of his traditional Sumerian finery. He wore a purple, knee-length linen shenti with bright yellow tasseled fringe that fluttered when he walked. A long strip of purple linen was draped over his right shoulder and belted at the waist. The draping was decorated with gold-threaded appliques of lions and large winged eagles. Thick black ringlets fell to his shoulders and he wore a golden circlet around his forehead, a symbol that indicated he was still Sumerian royalty, despite his current state of exile.

Glancing sidelong at the prince, Merneith wondered, *what is the pharaoh scheming now? Did he and Atab quarrel, or did he leave him here to spy on me in his absence?* Merneith had been consumed with dread since the pharaoh, her husband, had left five nights ago for his northern tour. Pharaoh Wadj had ordered Merneith to stay in Thinis while he went north for two months, sparking a quarrel which lasted for several days, right up until Wadj had left Thinis. The scheming vultures that circled him now had over sixty days alone with the pharaoh to burrow into his mind. They would do anything to gain his favour and power, and to twist him to their ambitions. She feared what havoc Wadj might cause to their country and their people if she wasn't there to temper his impulsive actions but she felt at a loss as to how to manage his increasingly disturbing behaviour.

Merneith was lost in thought, eyes skimming over the crowd, when she caught sight of a pair of startling green eyes resting on her. Green eyes were unusual in Kemet, a land of predominantly dark-eyed people. Not only were this man's eyes an extraordinary colour, a shade lighter than the leaves of a lotus flower, but there was also a fierce intensity in them that struck her. The shock of the man's stare hit her as if she had walked headlong into one of the etched columns around the dais she sat upon. Merneith flicked her gaze away, pretending to swat at a fly on her leg while attempting to study the man through lowered lids. She found herself fighting to control an unusual constriction in her chest as her eyes traversed the man.

He was taller than most men from the region, broader, thicker, more muscular. He was hard to miss, and Merneith wondered why she had never seen him before. His attire indisputably marked him as a foreigner. He was completely unadorned aside from a simple white linen shenti, laced sandals, and a belted leather sheath that held a wide, curved blade. Merneith didn't know how he could have entered into the courtyard with it, as no guests were allowed to wear weapons, not even ceremonial daggers. His semi-nude state made visible his tattoos, which were of an unusual sort for Kemet. In general, few men in the region had tattoos at all, and certainly nothing of this magnitude, with its thick, bold lines. What appeared to be a forest of mythical creatures in thick black ink ran up over the man's left bicep and shoulder and over to the right side of his chest and upper back. Merneith had difficulty pulling her eyes away from them as she tried to decipher what animals in particular circled his body and where they had come from. They seemed to move and shift, although the man was standing still. She wondered what it would feel like to touch the thick black lines on his chest, to trace the ridges of the raised ink, and the ridges of his sculpted torso.

To her perturbation, Merneith felt an awkward prickle begin to spread upwards through her body, raising bumps on the skin of her thighs, arms, and, ultimately, hardening her nipples. She tried to suppress it, but then gave herself up to the rare sensation. She drew in a deep breath, allowing a quiver to wash over her.

Why not? She told herself. *It is nothing. Just a pleasant breeze in the warm night air. That is all.* Yet she gave an involuntary, guilty glance over to Sar Atab to make sure he wasn't watching her. He was reaching for his wine goblet, so she turned her attention back to the stranger, her eyes wandering up to his face, framed as it was by wavy chin-length hair with skin tanned the colour of faded henna. As she watched him, the man looked towards her again, his gaze flickering between her and Sar Atab. Ultimately, his eyes locked on Merneith's. In that moment Merneith felt as if the desert began to slide away from her on either side. The crowd swirled off as if in a sandstorm and all that was left was this stranger staring her down as his eyes bore into her from beneath thick lashes and locks of dark hair.

Panicked, Merneith flitted her eyes away, pretending to only be scanning the crowd. Her heart began to pound furiously, and she fought to control it. *Why am I reacting like a silly young girl? He is only a man, and a stranger at that. Why should I not look at him? I am queen, I can do as I please.* But in that moment when their gazes had locked she had felt as if she was being *seen* for the first time ever, which made no sense to her because, as queen of Kemet she was, without doubt, the most observed woman in the entire land. Even the goddesses painted on the temple walls were only seen by the elite temple staff, while she spent a good part of the year touring the country.

"He is sexy, no?" A voice slurred in Queen Merneith's ear, causing her to jump and turn to the handsome prince beside her.

"Sorry, *Sar?*" She addressed him with the respectful title of *Prince*.

Sar Atab leaned over the arm of his chair and looked seductively up at her through his long dark lashes. *He must be drunk.* His Sumerian accent was thicker than usual, and his normally eloquent Egyptian was rapidly regressing. He pointed to one of the two tigers padding across the performance area in front of them. "This cat. He move like woman dancing, and his hair… I think I would like to touch it with my face. This is sexy, no?"

Merneith let her breath out in a little laugh, realizing that she had been holding it in fear that Atab had noticed her watching the tattooed, green-eyed man.

"Indeed, dear Atab, I think you are right." Merneith tried to hold back a smile, but could feel one side of her mouth curl up at the irony of Atab's words. "He is very sexy." Her eyes strayed through the crowd again, unconsciously hoping for another glimpse of the foreigner.

A piercing scream wrenched Merneith back to the evening's entertainment. The tiger Atab had pointed to had broken free of its handler, knocking him down with a swipe from its massive paw. The magnificent cat stood in the centre of the date palm lined courtyard, snout raised high, emitting a heavy *whuffing* noise as if sniffing for something. The other tiger strained against its handler. For a moment, the man looked undecided about whether he should hang on or flee. The tiger looked back over its shoulder at him and, as a horrified crowd looked on, the man released the rope, but too late. The tiger lunged at the man and swiped one giant, vicious paw at his side, catching the man's arm and sending him reeling backwards. Chaos ensued as people fled in all directions. Chairs were knocked over, women were screaming, and the guardsmen fought their way against a sea of people shoving and scrabbling past them. In the midst of if, the tigers roared and flashed through the crowd.

Merneith grabbed the arm of the drunken Sumerian and yanked him up with her. She scanned the courtyard for the best direction to run. The palace doors were a long ways off, and people were already knocking one another down in their attempts to get away. She pulled Atab towards the edge of the platform but he stumbled and became tangled in the chairs, pushing her forward in the process. She tumbled down the steps towards the tigers and banged her knee on the hardened earth, rattling her teeth and scraping her outstretched hands as they broke her fall. On her hands and knees she rested, stunned.

Merneith felt a hand clasp around her bicep, jerking her up. The tattooed man towered above her, his face tight and his bright green eyes fixed on the raging tigers behind her. Her knees buckled, and he snatched her up, tossing her over his left shoulder like a sailor slinging a sack of grain. *Oh dear gods, am I being kidnapped?!*

"Put me down!" Merneith beat a futile fist against the man's back, but he bounded towards a small temple behind the platform, ignoring her protests.

Bey, the recently appointed captain of the royal guard, had been watching the queen all evening. *That damnably difficult woman,* he thought as he prowled through the mingling aristocrats. While the night's entertainment was a routine and reasonably small affair by court standards, he had arranged to have his men stationed at various points, both around the performance square and the outskirts of the courtyard. For himself, he had saved the position of being nearest to the queen. The woman kept putting herself in harm's way and seemed in need of constant supervision. She had refused the request he had put to her advisors to discuss increased security with her. He wanted to have guards stationed around her platform for public events. Instead, she had insisted that she be able to move unfettered through the crowd if she chose. With the rumblings of an uprising coming from the *Hor-sekhenti-dju* domain, and the pharaoh's ridiculous behavior, Bey was increasingly uncomfortable with the woman's obstinate desire to be seen unguarded in public. It made his job more difficult, and if something should happen to her, it would certainly *cost* him his job, and quite possibly his life.

Despite his irritation, Bey couldn't help but notice that the queen looked particularly stunning tonight in a simple white linen shift belted at the waist with a thin gold chain. Unlike many of the other women who wore elaborate wigs over their shaved scalps, Merneith's naturally curly hair hung almost to her waist, unadorned save for a few strands of blue lapis lazuli beads woven in. A beaded lapis lazuli collar rested on her delicate collarbones, and thin gold hoops hung from her lobes.

Her black hair and olivine skin were set off by the bright white of her dress, and the soft curves of her breasts and wide hips were emphasized by the loose drape of the fabric. Her hips were remarkable, as Bey had noticed the women of Kemet tended to have narrow hips and thighs, whereas Merneith's were voluptuous and soft. *Hips like that are hard for a man to miss*, Bey thought. *How could any man not want to grab hold of those curves?* He pushed the useless observation aside, as he'd done so many times since he'd arrived at court two weeks ago. No matter what her curves might be like, the woman was making his life more arduous all around.

For a brief moment her eyes lighted on his, and he thought he saw them widen. Then the drunken Sumerian prince leaned in towards her, and instinctively Bey put his hand on his knife, weaving his way through the crowd towards the platform. Bey had been keeping an eye on that bastard since he had come to court. Bey knew that Atab would have traveled north with the Pharaoh under other circumstances, but had hung back because he was trying to extricate himself from an illicit affair with the vizier's daughter. The vizier and his family were going north with Wadj, and Atab had taken the coward's way out and pleaded illness. And yet here he was, drunk and almost falling out of his chair as he batted his eyelashes at the queen.

Bey had met Pharaoh Wadj and the exiled Sar Atab once before on the battlefield while quelling a Libyan incursion. He'd found them both to be arrogant, rude, and inexperienced leaders with no rapport with common military men, or those who didn't fawn on them. He had assumed Wadj's wife, daughter of the previous pharaoh, would be no different. He'd had more experience with pampered, power hungry women than he cared to recount, and had little desire to spend his days babysitting one of them. However, when he was offered the position of captain of the royal guard he'd had no choice but to accept. Turning down the position would be akin to signing his own exile papers, perhaps even his death warrant. Furthermore, in his three years in Kemet he had become accustomed to sleeping on a bed that did not move with a gust of wind across the sea.

That said, the first time he'd seen Merneith he had been struck by her composure and outstanding beauty. If he was honest with himself, he'd felt a stirring beyond the normal desire to bed a woman. Her large, dark eyes had drawn him in, compelling him to search within them for something he thought he could almost see. He found himself wanting to cup her face in his hands, curve it up to his own and delve into her depths, exposing them, exposing her.

For the past two weeks he'd kept an eye on Merneith from a distance whenever she was out in public. When she went to the temple of the goddess Neith to worship, he could see her clearly from the watch tower. When she was at the festival of the goddess last week, he had watched her from the roof of an adjacent building. Once again, he was furious that she had refused his request for security to be stationed around her litter. When a boy had broken from the crowd and run towards her, Bey had a cold moment of dread that something awful was about to unfold. He'd signaled to the guardsmen on the ground to close in around her. Ignoring the guards, Merneith had instructed one of the bakh to give the boy a gold coin, and sent him on his way.

Seeing Merneith smile at Atab, that degenerate Sumerian prince, made Bey tighten his hand on his knife. Atab was a fool, but a dangerous one, a spoiled princeling who had made a measly, failed attempt to usurp the throne of Sumer from his uncle. Atab had been forced to flee or lose his head for treason. He'd arrived in Kemet a year and a half ago, begging Pharaoh Wadj to take him in. The two had quickly become drinking buddies, and their grandiose, drunken power fantasies put off almost everyone around them. They both seemed to believe they were invincible, and Bey knew Atab still thought he could claim the Sumerian throne, although the king had brought prosperity and peace to the region. Bey had heard the soldiers grumbling their concern that Atab would convince the pharaoh to mount a war against Sumeria. After a period of relative peace the soldiers were not interested in a lengthy, potentially deadly and useless campaign.

Bey had also heard rumors that Atab had taken advantage of some of the poor servant women, that he had lured them with the promise of favours, possibly even forced himself on them, then tossed them aside when he had gotten what he was after. Men like Wadj and Atab were one of the reasons Bey didn't miss his old life, the life he'd lived before he'd left his hometown of Ebla in Syria ten years ago to try his fortune on the waters of the Mediterranean.

Bey had had little time for relationships with women since he'd left home and taken to the seas. There had been women, of course, but they had been the type of women one met in taverns in port cities. The sex had been rough, and more often than not it left him feeling wretched and depressed, rather than satisfied. Since settling in Egypt three years ago most of the women he'd interacted with had been the women who followed the militias in the hopes of selling themselves to the men for favors, or the odd sister, daughter, or cousin of other soldiers. Those women, while eager to meet a high ranking soldier such as himself, were often sheltered, simple women who were so innocent and ignorant of the world that he would have felt guilty courting any of them. He had seen and done too much they could never understand.

However, Queen Merneith was the type of woman who, had she been anything other than a queen, his queen, he might once have pursued. Her obstinate nature infuriated him, but he also respected and admired it. That, coupled with her sharp eyes, full lips, and the high jut of her breasts, so visible beneath her soft, white dresses, stirred more than just his lust.

Despite warning himself against her, he had a hard time not envisioning the things he would like to do to her. Yes, he knew she was most likely spoiled and difficult, but the things he saw himself doing didn't involve talking. For a brief moment while watching her on her way to the temple the other week, he had a vision of what it would be like to be alone with her under the desert stars. On a blanket, he had torn open the front of her dress, fully exposing her to streaks of silvery moonlight. He had run his fingers over the small, rigid brown nipples of her full breasts and hardened at the sound of her sharp intake of breath. Tracing her abdomen, his hand had slid down past her smooth belly, gently teasing the soft lips nestled between her legs, slick like dew-dampened lotus leaves, wanting to make her beg him to drive himself into her. The ensuing painful, throbbing erection made him glad that he was alone in the watch tower. *Damn the gods, and their sense of humour. They reduce grown men to boys with hard-ons, at the mercy of the image of women they cannot have.*

It was the image of Queen Merneith writhing naked on her back under the moonlight, and *under him*, that he was trying to push out of his mind when he heard the scream and the tiger's roar. Thankful for his height, he was able to indicate with a quick gesture to his men to deal with the tigers while he pushed against the crowd surging towards him, making his way to Merneith. He saw the drunken Sumerian knock her down the stairs as the tigers turned towards the dais. Bey reached the foot of the stairs and, in a fluid motion, grabbed Merneith and hauled her up and over his shoulder. He knew he was rougher than he should have been, but he couldn't risk delicacies at a time like this, and he needed a free hand to push past the throngs of desperate people.

"Wait! Stop!" Merneith panicked as the tattooed stranger yanked her over his shoulder and dashed from the dais.

The man ignored her, leaping into the open door of the small temple, then setting her down and pressing her into the corner next to the door. The temple was narrow, and there was just room for her to squeeze against the wall with the large man directly in front of her, face to face. In fact, he had both hands pressed against the wall on either side of her shoulders, caging her in, while he peered around her and out the door. He was close enough that she could smell him, his scent heavy and spicy.

"What in the name of the gods do you think you are doing?" She managed to croak at him.

The man turned to Merneith, placing the palm of his calloused left hand on the lower curve of her waist, pressing her further into the corner. Barely audible, he leaned in close and put his lips near her ear.

"Shhh. They will hear." Merneith felt his breath on her neck and another rush of tingling energy surge through her, causing the hair on her neck to rise and her skin to tighten. She felt a longing to push off the wall towards him and involuntarily drew in a deep breath, raising her breasts up and out towards him and lifting her chin slightly, exposing her neck.

The man pulled his head back and looked down at her, a glimmer of confusion in his eyes. Coming to herself and aware that his hand was still on her side, she pushed at his forearm to remove it, staring at him defiantly and feeling both ashamed of herself and angry at his boldness for touching her in the first place. *What in the name of the gods am I doing?* She flattened herself back against the clay-brick wall.

"Who are you?" She hissed.

Again, he leaned in close to her ear, his own neck coming close to her face as his lips almost brushed her ear. "Sekhrey Bey. I have sent you requests. You refused me."

His foreign accent was thick and his r's rolled. A voice that would normally kindle a hunger in a woman, but Merneith recoiled. She was angry and stunned, and forgot to lower her voice. "Sekhrey Bey? I know not of what you speak."

"The pharaoh made me sekhrey two weeks past."

Merneith was taken aback. She had received requests for increased security, but had no idea that a new captain had been appointed. Why hadn't she been consulted? Warned? Notified? She should have met the man before he draped her over his back and threw her in a temple. *Damn Wadj, and damn this new sekhrey.* Wadj was going behind her back now, and who knew how long it had been going on? *What else has he done?!*

The torches outside the temple cast shadows on the now abhorrent stranger's face and across the darkened temple. As Merneith watched him, Sekhrey Bey looked out the door, his jaw clenching. The air around him seemed to crackle the same way it did that one time two years ago when the gods had been warring. The skies had flashed white rods across the desert, causing terrifying rumbling. Then the rains had come for two whole days. Bey's energy coupled with the events of the evening caused Merneith's body to vibrate and she felt her skin prickle again, but this time it was her own fury, rather than desire, that caused it.

Outside she could hear people still screaming and calling one another. Merneith drew in a shaky breath, almost a sob, trembling all over. She was infuriated with Wadj and the man towering over her, and she was anxious for the people of her court. She felt a stinging in her hands and, holding her palms up to her face, she saw by the flickering light that blood was dripping down her wrists from her fall down the stairs. Her knee stung, too and, looking down, she could see a dark patch where blood was beginning to seep through her dress from her knee. Merneith felt a buzzing in her head and black dots appeared in her vision. The last thing she remembered before everything went dark around her was Bey grabbing her arms as she slid down the wall.

Dammit, not now! But it was too late, and for the second time that evening Bey found himself hoisting up the fallen queen. Luckily, however, he could see that his men had managed to surround the tigers and that the surviving handler had wheeled out a cage. The tigers, one limping from a stab wound to the leg, were corralled to safety. Bey scooped the queen up into his arms and strode across the courtyard to the palace entrance.

Entering under the arched entranceway, Bey made his way to a wide padded bench just inside the door and laid out the queen's limp body. Immediately some of the servants and palace women swarmed around the bench, shrieking and beating their chests in hysterics.

"She's dead! Oh, goddess Neith, our queen is dead! Oh dear one!"

Bey growled at them, "She is not dead, but if you want to prevent any further damage then by the gods, stop this nonsense! She is scratched and bruised, and the excitement has been too much for her. I need two bowls of water, cotton to wash her wounds and cotton to wrap them. Cool water for her face, also. Go, now!"

An older woman whom Bey had often seen by the queen's side pushed through the women.

"I will take care of her from here, thank you."

"I am sorry, *nebet-i*," Bey respectfully called her *my lady*, "but I must insist. I have had much experience with this. You may, if you like, soothe her face with some water."

"And you are?"

"Bey. The new sekhrey of the guard."

The woman raised an imperious eyebrow, lifting her chin to assess Bey, but he chose to ignore it and turned his attention back to the queen. He took the queen's soft hands in his own large, tanned, calloused ones and turned them palm up to inspect for grit and stones caught in the grated skin. Then he caught sight of the blood soaking through the white dress. *Damn.* He turned back to the older woman.

"Madame, I must tend to her legs. I will need you to move her dress." For propriety's sake, it would not do for him to be seen lifting the queen's dress, even in the company of her women.

"Of course, *Sekhrey*." The woman gave Bey a curious smirk that he'd rather not try to interpret. She stepped close to him and, leaning over Merneith, shifted the queen's dress up, exposing raw, scraped knees.

He sat back on his haunches, studying her wounds. He was thankful she was unconscious, as the cleaning process was bound to hurt. Both her palms and knees were quite deeply scratched. The knees were free of stones at least, thanks to her dress, but he would have to clean them. Her palms were dirty and covered in grit from the ground. Thankfully the serving women had arrived with the water and cotton strips.

If the woman had only listened to me… He tried to hang on to his anger as he rinsed her hands in one of the bowls of water. Anger was better than concern, and the tight clenching in his chest at the sight of her blood was not a sensation he enjoyed. As a former brigand and mercenary, he'd seen his fair share of blood and was certainly not squeamish about it. He'd even caused a fair amount of bloodshed himself. But spilling an enemy's blood and cleaning the blood of the queen he was supposed to be protecting were quite different things altogether.

He bandaged her hands and moved on to her knee, ignoring the women clustered around him and their lamentations. Bey felt himself in an uncomfortable position when it came to cleaning Merneith's legs. He knew that he was the best person for this, as he had seen more battle wounds than most of the women in the room combined, but it was also awkward to touch the smooth, soft legs of the woman he had envisioned naked earlier this evening. This was not the way he had imagined caressing her for the first time. He preferred his women conscious, willing, and alone, only occasionally in pairs. He prudently washed and bandaged her knees and stood up.

"I will be back in the morning to re-wrap the wounds, and bring some salve to help the healing. In the meantime, she needs rest. Please, I will take her to her rooms if one of you will accompany me."

"Of course, Sekhrey. Follow me." The older woman gestured with another enigmatic smile and raised eyebrow, and Bey couldn't help but feel she was mocking him in some way.

Chapter 2 – The Morning After

Merneith just barely had time to wake and begin breakfast when her aunt Bekeh and Penebui, her younger cousin and closest confidant, descended upon her. Merneith had woken only briefly after the captain had left the palace, and had slept soundly the whole night through afterwards. But the whispers and giggles of the servants as they brought in her breakfast made it clear that her rising had been eagerly anticipated, and the entire palace was already abuzz with talk of the new captain.

Now Merneith found herself stretched out on a gold gilded bench in a corner near a window in one of her private rooms. The bench was raised and curved up on one end to form a headrest, and blue cushions propped Merneith up. Two carved cheetah heads formed the end posts of the bench. Drapes of sheer white cotton hung around the numerous windows, billowing in the rare breeze that cut through the stifling end-of-summer heat. The sunlight slanting through the cotton cast a bluish light on the mud brick walls.

Merneith sipped tea from a mug and nibbled at a chunk of sweet date bread smeared with honey. Despite the comfortable surroundings, Merneith felt like a virtual prisoner of her aunt and cousin. Her stiff knees and bandaged hands made it difficult to do much on her own. Her hands were still wrapped in the cotton that Bey had applied the evening before. She grudgingly awaited his return.

While they ate, Penebui related the previous evening's events with a dreamy look in her eyes. She told Merneith how one of the guards, Ebrium, had warded off a tiger to save Satsobek, one of the noblemen's daughters. In the process, the tiger had bitten, and subsequently broken, the guard's arm. Shortly after, the tigers were subdued and Bey had carried Merneith into the palace, laid her on a bench, and ordered them to bring water and cotton so he could tend her wounds. Penebui filled Merneith in on the latest gossip.

"He was a pirate before he came to Egypt, did you know? I heard it from the maid Sheshemetka. She said she heard he was rather famous around the Mediterranean a few years ago, and was a very successful brigand. His pirate ship was captured by our men on the Iteru delta, and the general was so impressed by him he beseeched Bey to join them. Sekhrey Bey insisted on bringing along his own men as well."

"Well then, that would certainly account for his uncouth behavior, and why Wadj chose him as sekhrey without consulting me. It would hardly do to announce to everyone that Kemet had taken to hiring outlaws to defend us." Merneith knew better than to speak about Wadj like this in front of others, but she was alone with her aunt and cousin, the only two people who knew the true nature of her relationship with Wadj, and the two she most trusted.

However, Merneith also knew it was not entirely unusual for Kemet to enlist pirates and foreigners into their militias. Kemet was one of the most prosperous regions in the world and traded with numerous far-reaching lands, like Sumeria and Canaan. As such, the waters of the northern coast and the Iteru were subject to raiders and pirates. When raiders were particularly good, and could be caught without too much bloodshed, a militia might employ them. The offer was usually profitable, and better than the alternative – a swift death at the hands of the Kemeti soldiers. In this way Kemet effectively rid itself of a troublesome enemy while gaining a crafty or powerful ally. But no thief had advanced as far as the Royal Guard, never mind Captain of the Guard.

Penebui chattered on, ignoring Merneith's spiteful comment. "None of the *bakht* knows much about him, but the cook's assistant, Meritaten, says that he saved her cousin during a battle with some of the desert dwellers in the west. And *Mer*," she used the shortened term of Merneith's name, *Beloved*, reserved for her closest family, "even though you were unconscious and could feel nothing, he was very careful when he cleansed your wounds. We all thought he was remarkably gentle with you, especially for a pirate. He even asked Aunt

Bekeh to lift your dress to your thigh so he could wash your knee wounds, so it was all very proper."

Penebui put up a hand to adjust her long, blonde braids. Merneith always marveled over the girl's looks, so unusual in Kement. Penebui owed her fair complexion, light hair, and blue eyes to her grandmother. The woman had been a slave, captured by Merneith's grandfather, Hor-Aha, during a campaign far north past Canaan. While Merneith's grandmother had been Egyptian, and the Pharaoh Hor-Aha's primary wife, Penebui's grandmother had been one of his favorite concubines. She'd born Hor-Aha a daughter, and when Merneith's father became pharaoh, he married this half-sister off to a nobleman he had wanted to strengthen ties with.

Penebui was born to this nobleman and the daughter of Merneith's grandfather. Five years ago, when Penebui was twelve years old, the girl's mother passed away and Merneith had her brought to the palace to live. This was not long after Merneith herself had been married to Wadj. Merneith and Wadj, brother and sister as well as husband and wife, had become pharaoh and queen of Egypt at their own father's passing.

"Well the dear sekhrey was hardly proper or gentle when he threw me over his shoulder and shoved me in a corner in the temple." Merneith couldn't help but scoff.

"Oh but he impressed us all!" Penebui gave her a conspiratory smile and lowered her voice. "Although I think he frightened poor Sheshemetka a little bit. The sweet little girl nearly went into hysterics when he carried you in, and that set off some of the other women. They were crying and screaming and he became positively ferocious, *Mer*. He told us to stop our nonsense and get moving, and he would let none of us near you to assist except Aunt Bekeh. It was wonderfully romantic." The girl, sitting on the ground next to Merneith, sighed and rested her head on the settee near Merneith's knee. "Where do you suppose Captain Bey came from? Where do you suppose he got those tattoos?"

Merneith was just opening her mouth to utter another scathing comment when her Aunt Bekeh, who had been silently pacing the room, stopped walking abruptly, cleared her throat and cut through Penebui's prattle.

"I think it is time you took a lover."

Merneith's breath caught in her throat. The breeze from the window suddenly felt too cool, sending shivers along her arms and into her chest.

"Sorry, *Mewet*?" Merneith called her "Mother." There was no word to differentiate between aunt and mother and besides, Bekeh was, essentially, the closest thing to a mother Merneith had since her own mother had died when she was four years old. Merneith had always felt that Bekeh would have been better suited to be queen than she. Bekeh was much more comfortable with being royalty, and she always looked the part. She kept up with the popular, elaborately styled wigs that Merneith couldn't stand (they made her head itch), and had an imperious air that seemed to command people wherever she went. Bekeh knew the ceremonies and the social niceties; who should sit where and why, what they should be served and what it should be served in.

Conversely, despite having been born to be queen, Merneith was often mystified by the machinations required to maintain power over others. She had mastered the art of a cool and calm demeanor, and knew well enough to think before speaking, but that would only take one so far when disaster struck. It seemed more cunning was required.

"Come, Mer, you are losing your grasp on Wadj. He did not tell you about the sekhrey, and even now his vile advisors may be conspiring against you to secure their interests." Bekeh continued in a low, intense voice, "If he continues unchecked he will bring our kingdom to ruin. It is clear he is becoming a madman. He is already angering the priests and priestesses of the temples. Amka has told me he spoke with you yesterday about the unrest in his domain. He told me that the people of Hor-sekhenti-dju are upset with Wadj's insistence they worship him instead of the pantheon and their patron god, Gebeb. The priests are angered with Wadj's favours," here Bekeh raised a disdainful eyebrow, "or lack thereof. If they revolt you know very well it could be disastrous."

Merneith let out a long, slow breath as she turned to look out the window and grapple with Bekeh's onslaught. For four generations now Upper and Lower Kemet had been united, thanks to Merneith's great grandfather Narmer. Since that time the people of Kemet had considered the pharaoh to be a semi-divine being, serving as a conduit between the people and the gods. Lately, however, Pharaoh Wadj had begun to think of himself as more than just a conduit, a dangerous notion in a part of the world where people worshiped a pantheon of gods, and where each god had their place and purpose.

Merneith knew Bekeh and Amka the advisor were right. If there was a revolt it could re-kindle all kinds of grievances and give Kemet's enemies to the south, east, and north an opportunity to strike.

Bekeh continued her argument, "A queen needs allies. Sometimes even against her own husband. A well-placed lover could be the means to safe-guarding Kemet's future, and yours as well. Also, you have not conceived an heir, and people are beginning to talk."

That last comment stung a bit. Merneith was both self-conscious and relieved about her state of childlessness. She tilted her head and looked at her aunt. "Do people believe I am the cause of this childlessness?"

"Some do." Bekeh was never one to lie to her, an occasionally painful blessing. "Some think there is something wrong with your body, while others speculate that you have done something to repel the pharaoh. I have heard there is talk amongst the servants, that they know the pharaoh does not visit your bedchambers."

Despite five years of marriage and the expectation that they produce a royal heir, Wadj had never once visited her bed, and Merneith was extremely thankful for that, at least. The two had been assigned to be married ever since they were small children, as was the way of royal descendants. The legitimate daughters of the pharaoh could only marry other royals and Wadj, Merneith's younger half-brother and next in line for the throne, was the obvious choice. They had once been somewhat affable, with Wadj periodically even acquiescing to Merneith as the older of the two. Lately, however, he had become hard, and at times verged on cruel.

Bekeh continued, "But many also believe there is something wrong with the pharaoh, and that is why he does not visit you *or* his other wife. Some also say the gods are punishing him with childlessness for aspiring to be *the* god amongst gods."

"So he does not visit Ahaneith either?" Merneith murmured as she continued to gaze out the window. Two sun-darkened servants were sweeping the remnants of last night's disaster from the courtyard. Their plain linen shentis reflected blinding white light against the backdrop of the rolling sand dunes of the endlessly thirsty desert. Merneith wondered what it would be like to be somewhere far away on the other side of those dunes, as someone other than queen of Kemet.

She turned to her aunt Bekeh. "I had always presumed that Wadj preferred Ahaneith to me. I suppose it is some small consolation that I am not the only one repugnant to him." Merneith raised a musing eyebrow and pursed her lips in a grim smile. "Perhaps she is the luckier of us two, though, if she does not often see him and is not expected to produce an heir." Merneith rarely saw Wadj's second wife, a Sumerian merchant's daughter who had been gifted to the pharaoh a couple of years ago to ensure the signing of a trade agreement. A pharaoh having more than one wife was not at all unusual. What was unusual was that Wadj *did not* have more, or at least a concubine or two.

"Well," Bekeh continued brusquely, "Whatever Wadj's sexual activities are, they are not helping us. But perhaps yours can."

"Please, Mewet, I have told you before that I am not interested in taking a lover. And if Wadj ever found out, it would be the end of all of us, yourself included. He and his advisors may already be looking for an opportunity to do away with me, for all we know. I would prefer not to give them an excuse for it. They would have us all sent into exile, then quietly killed. And my unfortunate lover would have his genitalia most gently removed for him, and his head kindly restructured by an elephant's foot." Merneith cocked her head, raised her eyebrows and stared expectantly at her aunt.

Bekeh narrowed her eyes and moved in close, "I know very well what would happen if you were to be caught. And you needn't behave like a peevish child, it ill becomes you." She continued, now urgent and intense, "But that is precisely why you must ally yourself with someone who could stand with you against Wadj."

"Mewet, you sound as if you think it will come to war!"

"I am not alone in this belief, child. It is just that you refuse to see it as a possibility. You are ignoring the danger before your eyes."

Merneith sighed and raised an eyebrow. "And I suppose you already have an opinion on whom my dearest love should be?"

"Naturally, or I would not have mentioned it. I believe Sar Atab and Sekhrey Bey are both excellent candidates."

Merneith let out an explosive scoff that turned into laughter.

"Are you toying with me, Mewet? You believe that in all of Egypt, my best choices for a lover are between an exiled usurper and a common thief?"

"Do not be simple, child. Sar Atab *will* be king of Sumeria one day, he is next in line. There are those in Sumeria who support his bid for the throne, even now, and when King Alalngar of Sumeria dies Atab *will* be recalled. They may even make peace one day soon, as Atab has made gestures to get back into the king's good graces. He could be a powerful ally in the future. He could also be useful *now*, as he is close with Wadj and could help temper him instead of encouraging him, as he does at present. As for the Sekhrey, he is well positioned *right now*. My sources tell me the soldiers are very loyal to him, and he has even replaced many of the men of the royal guard with men who travelled with him before he came to Kemet. Mer, if you had the militias of the sephats behind you Wadj and his supporters would be utterly powerless."

"And it matters not that I do not wish to open my bed, or my legs, for either man?" Merneith knew she was speaking out of frustration, and the sensation that it was her own body stretched out on a block with an elephant's foot resting upon her. It would be a lie to say that she had never considered what it might be like to have Atab in her bed. When he had first arrived in Kemet, Merneith had found him incredibly handsome and charming. His dark, honey-coloured skin, long lashes and full lips were hard to ignore. And for a time, it seemed Atab had similar feelings about her.

She had put any thoughts of Atab aside when he and Wadj became close. She couldn't tell if Atab had befriended him out of necessity, or out of a shared affinity for one another. Nothing repelled her more than a man who admired her husband. But befriending Wadj hadn't stopped Atab from trifling with her, leaning in close, smiling conspiratorially now and then, and throwing her looks from under his lashes. With Atab she was never sure if it was just a game for him, so she kept him at arm's length with cool smiles and quick comments.

Sekhrey Bey was another matter. She couldn't deny that for a few brief moments last night, she had felt strong desire for a man, something she had not expected to feel again. In truth, she had locked away any hope of intimacy with a man years ago, when it became apparent she would never have the type of marriage or love some women spoke of. Her vulnerability to a total stranger last night angered her, all the more so since he seemed to notice her attraction to him, her brief moment of weakness in the temple, and had pulled away. She had felt as stripped and helpless as a kernel of wheat whipped upwards in the wind.

"There are plenty of women who would be more than happy for such a choice!" Bekeh hissed at Merneith. "If it were not best for your sake to take one of them, I myself would cheerfully accept either one of them in my bed." She softened and cocked one corner of her mouth slightly, "Well, for a time at least. You need not keep the same man forever."

"Now really, this is too much. There must be a way to gain some control over Wadj without sleeping with either

Atab or the sekhrey. And besides, even if I wanted to, who is to say that I could accomplish taking either of them as a lover?"

Bekeh scoffed.

"You are the queen of Egypt. Should you be twice your age with the face of a crocodile, any man would be mad to refuse you."

Penebui, who had been silent for several minutes, piped in.

"It is hardly a secret that Atab desires you, and last night the sekhrey was so protective and so very gentle with you. And he even insisted that he be the one to change your bandages this morning. It was so romantic." Penebui repeated her earlier admiration of the captain, sighed, and continued wistfully, "I hope one day a man feels that way about me."

"Do not be silly, cousin," Merneith scolded her. "He was doing his job. I have no doubt he feels the same way about me that a farmer feels when a desert jackal eats one of his goats. The farmer could lose his livelihood."

"My dear cousin, you are hardly a goat! You are a queen and practically a goddess. Of course he feels more for you than a goat. Now who is the one being silly? And besides, Sekhrey Bey is hardly a common farmer. He is the most exciting and handsome man to come to court in a long time. At least since Sar Atab came from Sumeria."

At that moment a knock came on the large wooden doors across the room, and Penebui jumped up to open them.

"*Hem-etj*," *Your Majesty,* announced the man at the door, "Sekhrey Bey is here."

Penebui opened the door wide and Sekhrey Bey strode through the entranceway. Merneith felt her face flushing. She was unprepared and off-balance thanks to her aunt and cousin's conversation, and she desperately hoped that he hadn't been able to overhear Penebui chattering about him like a lovesick girl. It was embarrassing enough that she had fallen down the stairs in her getaway attempt, and then passed out in his arms. *Gods, how does this man keep doing this to me? I must get control of myself, or he will think I am a fool.* Embarrassment was swiftly replaced by anger as she was reminded of the way he had handled her. If he was gentle with her when she was unconscious, he certainly was not when she was awake. She drew in a deep breath and collected herself.

"Sekhrey." Perhaps she was a tad cooler than intended, but better that than the alternative.

"Hem-etj." Bey stopped a few feet from her bench and knelt on one knee with his head bowed. *Well at least he still affords me that respect.*

"You may approach, Sekhrey. Penebui, Mewet." Merneith gestured with a nod to a pair of couches in the far end of the room. Merneith was afraid if they were hovering nearby she would not regain control of herself, or that they might instigate something. Penebui looked as if she were about to argue, but Merneith raised a warning eyebrow and the girl gave her a quick smirk before spinning off.

Bey nodded respectfully at Bekeh and murmured, "*Nebet-i.*" *My lady.*

"Sekhrey." Merneith found herself irritated by the knowing smile and nod Bekeh gave the captain.

Clearly he intended to keep his word and change her bandages himself. In his hands he carried a package wrapped in linen. Bowls of water and strips of cotton had already been arranged for his use.

"It really is not necessary that you do this, Sekhrey. Any of the women here are capable of changing a bandage." Again, she found her voice colder than intended, but she couldn't seem to help herself. She watched as he unfolded his package. Inside was a brown, sticky looking substance.

"I am sure they are capable, but it is my job to make sure you are not hurt. This here will soothe the pain. Your knee was quite bruised last night, and this will help with the swelling." It was most annoying that he was right; her knee was incredibly stiff, and she'd had to lean heavily on others to get around that morning. "Please allow me to remove your bandages and apply this."

Hesitating, then deciding it was best to acquiesce, Merneith slid her robe up over her knee. She herself was shocked to see how purple and swollen the area around the bandage on her knee had become. As she bent her knee slightly to allow him to unwrap the cotton strips her dress slid further up her thigh. She was acutely conscious of her exposed skin and tilted her knee inwards.

She leaned back on the bench and watched the back of Bey's head as he settled on a stool beside her bench. He hunched over the bowls and bandages next to the bench, shifting with his back to her. She studied the series of thick tattoos that covered his scapula, bicep, shoulder, and chest. She was able to make out a ram and a panther, wrapped around one another amongst a series of thick lines. As he moved it appeared as if the animals and lines flowed with the movements of his thick, tight muscles. Merneith had to confess that, angry as she was with him, his nearness caused a heat to ignite in her that felt almost obscene with her aunt and cousin in the same room. She found herself anticipating his touch with both desire and fear, and her breath quickened. That he had that sort of power over her made her angrier at him.

As Bey reached out to touch her knee, Merneith jerked involuntarily, as if discovering a locust on her leg. Bey swiftly turned his intense eyes to her.

"I am sorry, Hem-etj, but I will be as quick as I can. I will try not to hurt you." Merneith could only clench her jaw and nod once, letting him think it was pain that made her jerk.

As Bey laid his hands on the bandages on her knee, she found herself letting out a deep breath that she hadn't realized she'd been holding. She tried to let it out quietly, but it came out shaky and uneven instead, more like a pained wheeze. *Well, it is a good thing you are not trying to seduce the man; you sound like a dying crocodile.* Bey unwrapped the bandages and reached down for the sticky package. Scooping up a handful, he cupped the back of her knee and Merneith felt a shock as his hand touched her skin for the first time. This time she did gasp. *Get a hold of yourself! What in the land of the gods is wrong with you? He is just a man, like any other.*

"What is that?" She managed to croak. He was slowly rubbing the paste into the skin around her knee. The paste was less sticky than it looked; in fact, it felt silky and soft. Bey's touch was surprisingly gentle, just as Penebui had said it

35

was, and despite the stiffness and enormous bruise, and the roughness of his calloused skin, his touch was soothing. She couldn't help but wonder what it would feel like if he ran his hand up to the exposed parts of her thigh. A wave of shivers ran through her, and she wondered if he noticed the sudden, tiny bumps appearing on her legs. If so, he ignored them.

"It is a honey and herb poultice, to reduce swelling and heal wounds. I would have liked to use it last evening, but I had none. It was very late when I was able to find a merchant with some honey and herbs to make this. It must steep for twenty-four hours to be most effective, but there is no time to wait. So I will apply some now, and leave some for later." He continued to rub her knee with his back to her as he spoke.

"That was not necessary, Sekhrey." *Why does everything I say to him sound so cold? I cannot seem to help myself!*

"It is necessary. Cuts left untreated can become filled with fluid, and rot. I have seen many men lose a foot or an arm after a scratch in battle. You do not want to lose a hand, or this leg, do you?" At this he turned to her with a raised eyebrow while the calf of that very same leg was encased in his hand. Merneith got the distinct impression that he was teasing her.

Merneith arched her own eyebrow in response and felt her lip curl in a slight smile in spite of herself. "No, Sekhrey, thank you. I like my limbs just as they are."

"Then I will finish with the honey."

"Please do."

Bey wrapped fresh cotton strips around her knee and turned to her hands. In order to do this he moved his stool so close that his elbow brushed her hip as he reached for her hand. She tensed as she again had a vision of his hands on her bare legs. She had to be more careful of watching him now that he was facing her. She had to avoid any more visions of him touching her.

"I was very sorry to hear about your man. Ebrium was his name, correct? I hope he will be well soon."

Bey took one of her hands in his in order to unwrap the fabric strips and she felt herself fixated on the sight of her hand in his.

Bey shrugged. "None died, except the one handler, but Ebrium's arm will take some time to heal. He is strong and will recover, but he does not like to be at home too long. I saw him this morning and already he is afraid he will have nothing to entertain his time but women's court chatter." Bey looked up at her through locks of dark hair with a glint in his eyes that could be construed as a taunt. He watched her face intently as he smoothed a scoopful of the honey poultice over her scraped palms.

"Well I certainly cannot blame him for that. I have had more than enough of women's court chatter already since last night. Although I hear you are quite effective at silencing overly excited women." Merneith watched as his large fingers made gentle circles over her palm. Again, she couldn't help but imagine his hands elsewhere, circling and rubbing. And then his mouth…

Abruptly, Bey's jaw tightened.

"They were worried about you. They thought you were dead. If you would *allow* me to place men closer to you, Hem-etj, there would be little need to fear for your safety." By his tone she sensed that it was not a suggestion, but a reprimand for having refused his original request for more security. Merneith felt her earlier anger and resentment rise back up. *How dare he scold me like an unruly child?*

"Thank you, Sekhrey, for your *advice*." This time the coldness was intended. "However, I do not wish to be surrounded at every turn, nor to be trapped in the palace harem like a caged monkey. It is enough that the Pharaoh has gone north without me, so I do not see how I am in any danger. It is unlikely wild tigers will get loose again anytime soon so you need not overly concern yourself with me." She would not live her life like a pampered princess, cooped up inside the harem while the men controlled Kemet without her. And, if she were honest with herself, she wanted the freedom to be able to walk through her own courtyard without the presence of guards everywhere as a constant reminder of who she was. She wanted, from time to time, to feel like a normal human. This man in front of her seemed incapable of understanding that.

"I am sorry, my lady, but it is my job to be concerned about your safety. Given last night's events, and the news from Amka regarding the Hor-sekhenti-dju domain, I must insist that you allow me to increase your security presence." At this he finished with the honey poultice on her left hand and began to bandage it.

"You *insist* that I *allow* you?!" Merneith hissed at him, shocked at his impudence. What irritated her even more, however, was the nonchalant manner in which he looked into her eyes with that damnable raised eyebrow and shrugged.

"My lady, if you do not accept then I will be forced to appeal to your advisors, the pharaoh and, of course, the women of the court, all of whom I am sure will see the practicality of it, and who will require it of you nonetheless. In the end, it will save you hours of *women's court chatter* if you give me your blessing now."

Before she could stop herself Merneith muttered through clenched teeth, "You may have my blessing to visit *Ammit.*"

It infuriated Merneith even more that Bey had the audacity to throw his head back and laugh heartily. "I have heard of this demon of yours. This is the one from the underworld, yes? The crocodile one that weighs men's hearts and eats the unworthy ones while the man's soul is sent into torment?" Merneith was disarmed by the realization that he might not fully understand her insult, or believe its veracity. He had inclined his head and was looking at her with a questioning look. She found herself giving a curt nod to let him know he was correct.

Bey chuckled and nodded. "Well wish me dead as you like, Hem-etj, but you must anticipate my men and I to be a little closer to you from now on."

"And you must anticipate finishing quickly and getting out of my line of sight, *Sekhrey.*" Merneith raised her chin and looked down at Bey through eyes that had become angry slits.

"As you wish, Hem-etj." Bey smiled a wide grin at her as he tied the last knot, bundled up his honey poultice and stood up. "I am glad to see you are in lively spirits after last evening and wish you a speedy recovery." This was more than she could bear.

"And I wish you at the bottom of the Iteru. Unfortunately the gods rarely grant us our wishes. Thank you, Sekhrey, you may take your leave, and swiftly please."

"*Senebti*, be well." Bey bowed, keeping his merriment-filled eyes on hers. Then he stood up tall and turned on his heel. Merneith was left watching his muscular, tattooed back as he strode out of the hall, nodding at both Bekeh and Penebui along the way. She pulled her lips in tightly. *Damn him. And damn Ra for bringing him here. How could he do this to me?* Merneith suddenly felt that she had exposed far too much of herself to Bey, and angrily jerked her dress down to her ankles.

Penebui and Bekeh were both just standing when the servant knocked on the open door.

"Governor Amka here to see you, Hem-etj."

"Thank you." *What now? When will this morning end?* Merneith begged silently. *Can I not have a moment of peace?*

A tall, thin, dark man with tight, curly gray hair strode into the room.

"Hem-etj," he bowed.

"Amka, my dear. What news today?" Amka had been the most trusted advisor to Merneith's father towards the end of his life, and Merneith believed she could trust him still. Unlike many of the others, when she and Wadj had married he had not taken to fawning over Wadj and ignoring her. He, at least, made her feel that her opinion was still valued, and even necessary.

"Likely nothing you have not heard already, as I see your mewet is here." Amka smiled in Bekeh's direction, and it was clear that he meant it as a compliment to her abilities to root out information. Bekeh laughed flirtatiously.

"Amka, you old dear. You flatter me. I am just a simple woman, who hardly concerns herself with political affairs." Bekeh smiled guilelessly.

"Madame, your wisdom in the affairs of politics is like showering petals from the lotus flower. Beautiful and fragrant, a gift from the gods." Amka bowed low with a twinkle in his eyes.

Merneith marveled at the familiar dance the two seemed to have perfected, and wondered if she could ever garner the admiration her aunt effortlessly commanded. Not for the first time, she wondered if Bekeh and Amka had once been, or were currently, lovers. Married life had hardly stopped Bekeh from having her way with men, and now that her husband was gone, she was all the more free to do as she pleased.

Amka turned to Merneith.

"Hem-etj, I am here to discuss the banquet to honour Sekhrey Bey and the guardsmen."

"I am sorry. To do *what?*" *This day continues to improve, does it not?*

"Hem-etj, the captain saved your life last night, and the guards acted courageously. One almost lost his arm. I assumed you would be having a banquet in their honour to thank them"

Merneith sighed. *Damn the gods! Yes, I would be doing that, if I did not just wish the man to have his heart eaten in the underworld.*

"Is that really necessary? It is only a few scratches, really."

Bekeh cut in. "I think it is a wonderful idea, Amka, and you are most certainly correct. Not only is it important to let the guards know we appreciate *all* that they do, but it is most important," here Bekeh looked pointedly at Amka, "that *the sekhrey* know how much we value his loyalty."

"Indeed, *nebet-i*, I could not agree more. It is imperative that the new sekhrey *and* his men feel valued by the queen." Here Amka turned to Merneith, looking expectant. Merneith, for her part, had the distinct feeling that she was on a raft on the Iteru that had spun out of control while traveling towards the dangerous, rocky cataracts below Aswan.

Merneith couldn't help herself when she snapped, "And if I chose *not* to honour the dear sekhrey?"

"I do not think that would be wise, Hem-etj." Merneith could see why Bekeh might take him as a lover; they were both mercilessly blunt and pushy.

Taking her petulant silence as acquiescence, Amka nodded his head and said, "Excellent, Hem-etj, I will begin the preparations for a banquet in three days' time."

"And I will assist. The seating arrangements will be most important. We would not want any man to feel left out, or slighted." Bekeh gave Merneith a slight, pleasant smile with a hard look in her eyes, as if daring her to object.

Instead, Merneith was left muttering as Bekeh and Amka left the room. "Am I the only one who still believes that *I* am queen?"

Chapter 3 – Ebrium

Later that afternoon Bey wove through the narrow streets of the dusty village twenty minutes outside the palace walls, on his way to visit Ebrium for the second time that day. When he knocked on the wooden front door, Ebrium's sister, Akshaka, a pretty young woman with light skin, dark hair, and big blue eyes, opened the door with a grin. She immediately began chattering in Eblaite, the language of their shared homeland of Ebla.

"Thank the dear god Dagon you're here, Bey. He's been nothing but ill-tempered and sullen all day. How on earth did you stand being on a vessel with him for so many years and not throw him overboard? I'm ready to toss him out of the house. Take him home with you, please? Mother is patient with him, of course, but I haven't the fortitude. I don't know how he'll ever marry if he can't sit at home for half a day without turning into a cranky crocodile. Then again, I don't know what kind of woman would take him anyway. Oh, but I wish one would and perhaps we could be rid of him for a time."

Bey laughed and brushed past Akshaka to step into the hallway of the hut. The hard dirt floor was covered with woven papyrus mats that crunched under foot. To the left was the doorway to the kitchen, the women's domain, and beyond that was a bedroom shared by Ebrium's sister and mother. Both of them had come to Kemet from Ebla almost a year ago. It had taken some time for Ebrium and Bey to settle after having been pressed into service in Kemet, but once it was clear where they would be staying, they arranged for Ebrium's mother and sister to make the journey to join them. The greeting room to the right was the largest of the three-room hut. Ebrium ate, slept, and lived in this room, but given his duties in the military and now the guard, he was rarely home.

The greeting room was dimly lit by a small window cut out of the brick that looked out onto the narrow pathway winding past the hut. The room was cast in shadows of dark brown, beige, and grey, with the occasional golden glint as particles of dust floated through a ray of sunlight from the window. Ebrium was splayed out on a wide, cushioned bench pushed up against the wall opposite the window. Thick locks of dark hair draped over blue eyes so like his sister's and so unlike their mother's. Both brother and sister took after their light-skinned, northern-born father. Ebrium's right arm was swaddled and bound up to prevent him from moving it. Like Bey, Ebrium was taller and broader than most men in Kemet. The two large men filled up the small room with both their stature and their presence.

Ebrium's mother, a small, dark woman who looked aged beyond her fifty years, had a black fringed shawl swathed around her head, and rested on a carved wooden chair. She smiled and stood when Bey entered the room.

"Little Mother," Bey said warmly, taking her hand and kissing it, then pressing it to his forehead in a sign of respect. Bey dropped his voice into the colloquial dialect of his homeland, one he'd learned from the servants of his parent's home. It had been so long since he'd spoken formal Eblaite that Bey sometimes doubted he could even speak it anymore. Ebrium's mother had been a servant in Bey's home since he was a boy and he and Ebrium had grown up as playmates. Later, when Bey had left Ebla to take to the seas, Ebrium had gone with him, and the two had spent eight years traveling together until their ship had been captured off the coast of Kemet, and they'd been co-opted into service.

"Bey, my boy. How good of you to come back again." Bey smiled at her, then turned to Ebrium and raised an eyebrow. "I hear you've been giving your sister trouble."

"Pfft, I'm merely helping to prepare the girl for when she marries one day. She's been lucky, so far," Ebrium squinted and raised his good arm to shake a finger at Akshaka, "to have no one else to care for except herself. She's had no younger siblings, and she's lived like an only child without a care in the world. One day she'll have a husband and squabbling children of her own and she won't be able to spend her time gossiping and nattering about what the queen wore last night and how she styled her hair."

"But I hear the queen did have spectacular hair last night, did she not, Bey?" Akshaka turned with excited eyes to Bey, who suddenly felt very awkward. He plopped himself into a chair across from Ebrium and ran a hand over his face. "Amazing that she wears her own hair, and why do the other women wear wigs here, anyway? Did you go to see her this morning? How is the queen? How are her wounds? Is she well this morning? I heard she fainted last night. You didn't tell me that. Shame on you for leaving out all the good details. What good is it having a brother in the guard, and you like a brother, the captain of the guard, when I have to hear the details from the palace kitchen servants at the market this morning?" Akshaka took a swipe at Bey with a cushion she grabbed from a chair.

Bey laughed, then grabbed at the pillow and while Akshaka hung on to it he pulled her closer to him.

"But truly little sister," he leaned towards her and arranged his face in a most serious expression, "the queen's hair was spectacular this morning, it resembled nothing short of a vulture's nest, and last night I could not tell if it were the queen or a black-haired lion on the throne at dinner. Certainly this morning she was as cantankerous as a lion and I barely escaped with my head in place." Bey released the pillow, laughing as he threw up his arms to defend himself from a barrage of soft *thwacks*. Akshaka's assault gave him the opportunity to push away a vision of Merneith's hair last night, adorned as it was with lapis lazuli beads, and what it would be like to tangle his hands into the thick, dark mass of it at the nap of her neck, tugging her head back to force her lips upwards…

"How dare you?! That's the queen you're talking about, and everyone knows she's beautiful." Akshaka panted, dropping her arms, and the pillow, although she was smiling.

"Fear not, little sister, your hair is just as lovely, if not more so, than the queen's." Bey reached out and tugged on a lock of Akshaka's hair.

"Enough, Akshaka, go make us some more tea and leave us to talk." Ebrium cut in. Akshaka threw both men a glare, then turned and stomped into the kitchen, the papyrus mats crackling under her feet.

"But really, how is the queen today?" Ebrium sat up and leaned forward.

Bey blew out heavily, trying to decide what to say. He scrubbed his face with his hands again, feeling weary. Ebrium's mother reached out and rested a hand in the crock of his elbow. He turned to look at her concerned, questioning face.

"No, no, the queen is fine, there is nothing to fear there. She has some scratches but she'll recover, I'm sure of it." Now that he was relaxed, his own exhaustion began to sweep over him. He'd had no sleep since the previous morning, having spent all night searching for a man who carried the honey and herbs he needed to make the poultice for the queen's, and Ebrium's, cuts.

"Dear boy," Ebrium's mother stroked his arm. "You are too good." She reached a gnarled hand up to adjust the scarf wrapped around her head. "But tell me, this was your first time meeting with the queen. How did you fare? What is she like?"

Bey sputtered a laugh. "I was only half-joking when I said that I barely escaped with my head, Little Mother. The woman is…" Bey smiled, then stopped himself and scrubbed his hands over his face again. "She doesn't want more guards. She refuses more security. She doesn't like to be told what's good for her. She argues about everything. She is *difficult…*" *Thorny, complicated, challenging, annoying, fascinating.* Bey tried to find the words to describe her, but there didn't seem to be one word that explained how he felt. He found himself both immensely entertained and irritated by Merneith. Her moods were like that of the desert. One moment she was cool and still, like the sandy flat plains that could occasionally drop down to freezing temperatures at night, while the next moment her energy radiated heat hotter than the sun beating down on the cotton wrap on a nomad's head. Without notice, she could become a *samuum*, one of the cyclonic, poisonous sand storms of the Sahara that choked all in its path.

"When I *gently* insisted on added security, she wished a demon of their underworld to eat my heart out of my chest. If the woman had a weapon handy, and her hands had not been bound, she may well have made an attempt to send me there herself."

Ebrium barked a laugh and raised his tea mug in Bey's direction. "Now *that* is the captain I know. And *that* sounds like a woman after my own heart."

Ebrium's mother gave Bey an appraising look. "But you're smiling."

Bey felt a heat rush to his cheeks. He looked down at his hands, stacked as they were in his lap. *How is it that a man can lead a thousand men in battle, yet be reduced to a guilty little boy by the look of an old woman? And why do I feel guilty in the first place?*

"Oh, my boy." She patted his arm then wrapped her small hand around his large forearm. She gazed over at Ebrium. Both men gave her quizzical looks, and she continued.

"For many years I thought that nothing would make me happier than to see the both of you married. Bey, you've always been like a son to me, especially since your own mother died. I cared not if the girls be Eblaiti or Sumerian or Akkadian, or whatever else. I married Ebrium's father, and he was from the far north, and I never cared what anyone said of it, even though when he died he left us nothing and I've had to work all my life. At least, until you men began to send money, and now that we're here in Kemet I can finally take some rest." Bey recalled those first few years of hardship when he and Ebrium had left Ebla and had struggled to make enough money working on the ships to send something back to help Ebrium's family. Until finally Bey had taken command of a ship and they had become two of the most successful pirates of the Mediterranean.

Ebrium's mother nodded in his direction. "Ebrium I think may now be in a position to marry well, if he sees a girl he likes. Perhaps even a nice, pretty merchant's daughter who can bring some money with her and who will be content with the simple life of a soldier." Ebrium raised a skeptical eyebrow, shaking his head in amusement. Bey pursed his lips to avoid smiling. Ebrium's type of woman was anything *but* nice and simple, but his mother did not need to know that. "But you, Bey," Here she looked sharply at him, "Over time I've come to see that you cannot be happy with such a girl, or such a life."

Bey opened his mouth to refute her, but she cut him off.

"No, don't argue. You don't need to be ashamed of having aspirations, even if you're too good to admit them, even to yourself. You weren't born to a modest family like ours, nor were you born to be someone's servant. And you certainly weren't raised to marry a shopkeeper's daughter. You were meant to marry much higher than that."

Bey winced. Ten years had passed, but he could still taste the bitterness of his own broken engagement in the back of his throat, like a blackened, rotten nut.

"But perhaps it was for the best that Achsah and her father changed their minds. Better she broke your heart than you discover her true nature when it is too late. She was a selfish, spoilt girl, I'm sorry to say. No, what you need is a woman who is your equal, as your mother was your father's. But even though you are a captain here, these people will not see you as equal. It is not like in Ebla, they don't know you. You must seize your opportunities to show them who you truly are."

Bey wasn't sure he grasped where she was going with this. He shook his head, looking to Ebrium for clarification. Ebrium leaned forward, and opened his mouth to speak, but just then Akshaka came back into the room carrying a tray with several mugs on it. Ebrium sat back, and Akshaka handed them each a mug of thick, sweet tamarind tea. As she was setting down the tray a knock came at the door. She leapt to answer it and the other three paused to listen as she opened the door.

"Message from the palace for the soldier Ebrium." A young man's crisp voice filtered into the room.

"Yes?"

"His presence is expected at the palace in three days' time to attend a feast in the guards' honour for their bravery at last night's affair. He and Sekhrey Bey will be the guests of honour and will be seated with the queen and her entourage."

Akshaka gasped in shock. "Excuse me. My language here is not so good. You say my brother and Bey will be honoured at the palace?"

"Yes, Miss. At the palace. If your brother is the soldier Ebrium. In addition, each soldier is entitled to one female guest to be seated at the women's table."

Akshaka breathed in. "To go to the palace?"

"Yes, Miss. To the palace. Do you happen to know where I can find Sekhrey Bey? I was told he might be here."

Akshaka finally came to herself. "Yes. Yes he is here. I will tell him."

"Thank you, miss. *Senebti.*"

"Thank you, *senebti,* be well also."

Akshaka turned to the three watching her from the main room. Her mouth hung open as she absently pressed the door shut.

Bey burst out laughing.

"What?!" Akshaka demanded, indignant. "What did I do wrong?"

"It's not you, little sister." He chuckled. "I'm trying to understand how it transpired that in one moment the queen wished me dead, and in the next planned a party in my honour." Bey reveled in the image of her being harangued into it, and how furious she must have been about it. He couldn't imagine the idea had been her own.

"Oh isn't it wonderful!" Akshaka perched on the arm of Bey's chair. "Of course, Ebrium, you will bring mother, will you not? But, Bey, who will you bring?"

Akshaka leaned over him and Bey laughed again, ducking away from her.

"Little sister, you look as if you are about to burst. I believe you have some ideas already. Who do you think I should bring?"

"Oh dear goddess Isthar, please take me, Bey! Oh what I would give to see the queen in person. And the court! And the nobles! Oh please say you will let me come. Mother, you will let me go with you all, won't you?"

Ebrium's mother smiled but said, "My dear, first you must wait for Bey to ask you."

Akshaka looked at Bey, her blue eyes wide with excitement.

"Ohhh, I don't know, little sister. Perhaps you are too young to be at court?"

Akshaka opened her mouth, looking so crestfallen that Bey actually regretted teasing her.

"Of course, little sister, you may come with me. And who knows, maybe you will catch the eye of some handsome young nobleman, and before long we will be celebrating your marriage?" Akshaka had been like a little sister to Bey since her birth, and he didn't really want to think of her marrying *any* man but he knew that her mother wished it for her and he was glad that now he was in a position to investigate any potential matches.

Akshaka's pale cheeks turned pink. She swatted at Bey's shoulder, but then jumped up.

"Oh! Maybe Ebrium will see Satsobek again!"

"Tssst." Ebrium flipped his good hand up dismissively.

"Eh? What's that?" Bey turned to Ebrium, but Akshaka jumped in.

"The girl he saved last night. She already sent a servant this morning with a message to thank him. I hear she's young and attractive and her father is very well off."

Ebrium clicked his tongue again. "Sure she is. But it was also *her* and not *her father* that sent the note. If the man wanted his daughter to have anything to do with me, he would have been the one to send it. The girl probably sent it without his knowing. He's probably saving her to try and snag one of the princes." Again Bey felt disdain rise up at the reminder of his own broken engagement, but Akshaka's enthusiasm broke the mood.

"Oh! But I have nothing fine enough to wear to the palace! I must go look for something. And I suppose I must practice my manners. And, oh gods! I must practice my language. Oh Bey, please say you will teach me to speak like a noblewoman, and to eat like a proper lady, or else they may all laugh at me as if I were a donkey driver's daughter."

"Hey now, you're hardly a donkey driver's daughter, not that there would be anything wrong with it if you were! It's honest work, which is more than most of those nobles can say. But three days is hardly time to teach you the manners of the courts. Besides, not everything is the same as in Ebla. I myself may look like a donkey's ass at court." Bey winked at Akshaka. "But I will do what I can."

"Thank you, Bey! You really are the best almost-brother a girl could wish for." Akshaka threw her arms around Bey's neck for a quick hug. Bey warmed at the affection and for once was glad for his own past life that now enabled him to help prepare Akshaka, but he also knew that she was too innocent and kind for court life, and hoped that it would only be a brief encounter.

"Hey! What in the underworld am I, then?!" Ebrium called out in mock indignation.

"You are a real brother, which is not the same. You're also a giant brat who has taken the opportunity of having a broken arm to order me around like a serving girl, that's what you are." Akshaka stuck her tongue out at Ebrium, dodged the pillow he threw at her, and ran off into the bedroom, muttering to herself about jewelry.

Ebrium's mother tucked a stray strand of fringe back into her head wrap. "This is the best thing we could have hoped for. You are right, Bey. Akshaka is pretty enough, and may just catch a man's eye. She's a little younger than I would like for her to marry, but this is the best opportunity she is likely to get. We have little enough to offer as dowry for a marriage, but perhaps if a rich man fancies her it won't matter. And you men will be honoured and recognized as you deserve. Ebrium's chances at a good match will most certainly be improved. And you, Bey…"

"Yes. Me. What about me? What were you going to say before, Ebrium?"

Ebrium leaned forward again and rested the elbow of his good arm on his thigh. His voice was hushed as his eyes flickered back and forth to the window behind Bey.

"Bey, brother, this morning we spoke about the unrest amongst the soldiers of the guard, and the militias of the *sephat*, the cities nearby." That morning Ebrium and Bey had discussed the fresh rumours about the potential uprising in the Hor-sekhenti-dju domain. It was obvious to many of the militias that Wadj's power-hungry fantasies were increasingly dangerous. Furthermore, the soldiers had a strong dislike for Sar Atab. They feared that the prince would convince the pharaoh to go to war with Sumeria. To leave their farms and wives in order to fight a peaceful neighbor for no purpose but to put that snake, Atab, on the throne of Sumeria was of little glory to most men. Bey glanced over his shoulder at the window and kept his tone low. Any discussion of attempted overthrow of the royal family was no small matter, whether it be their own plotting or that of Hor-sekhenti-dju's. If they were overheard it wouldn't matter how high ranking they were, they'd all hang.

Ebrium continued. "Your spy, Hadanish, was here after you left this morning, with that other man from the south, Belu. They were looking for you. They've been traveling amongst the militias of the southern sephats. They say many would be happy to see the queen take a greater role in the affairs of Egypt." Ebrium lowered his voice even further, glancing out the window again before looking pointedly at Bey. "And by that I mean they would prefer to no longer have to deal with the pharaoh at all. Hadanish and Belu said that the militias are split. Some want to do away with Wadj and keep the queen, but others don't trust her." Ebrium paused.

"So what do these others want?"

"They want *you*, Bey."

Bey sat back in his chair. "They want what?"

Ebrium's mother stood up and hobbled over to the window, keeping an eye out on the pathway.

"Bey, many of them know *you*, not Wadj. The militia leaders say they're loyal to you, not him."

Bey drew in a long breath, letting it out loud and slow as he scrubbed his face again and scraped his hands through his hair. It was true that he knew many of the militia leaders. He had traveled up and down the great river in the past three years training and working with them, particularly in sea warfare. He knew many of the militia leaders and soldiers were unhappy with the pharaoh, that's why he'd sent Hadanish and Belu to determine if there were any security threats. He'd not expected it to be to this extent.

"This is madness. There are princes with claims to the throne, and while I have no love for Wadj, I certainly would not wish to replace him with myself. I will not be a usurper to the throne. I'm not like Atab, or my brother. Besides, I'm a foreigner. The militias can't want me."

"And not all of them do. They're divided. At least here in southern Kemet. What they want in the north isn't clear yet, Hadanish is trying to find out. But Bey, something's going to happen soon. You know it, I know it, clearly the militia leaders know it. Wadj's the only one stupid enough not to see it. And maybe her lovely majesty doesn't yet realize it. But whether you like it or not, something's coming. It's better to be on the upside of it somehow, isn't it?"

Ebrium's mother laid a hand on Bey's shoulder.

"Unless you can convince the queen to do something," she said near to his ear. "Bey, you need to find out where her loyalties lie, and if she is willing or capable of ruling without the pharaoh. Otherwise, the home we've all just found will end up in civil war. You boys will be in the middle of it, and you might not like the side you're on. If you like her, she must be good, right? Perhaps you can persuade her to listen?"

"Bey, you have to get close to her. You're the only one in a position to." Ebrium leaned back and grinned. "I know you must have some charm in there somewhere. Now's the time to work it."

Bey took a moment to sit back and muse. The lack of a centralized military in Egypt was both a blessing and a curse, he thought. On the one hand, it made it difficult to plan an uprising as militias from different cities and regions had to coordinate together, something not easily done. On the other hand, it also made it difficult to prevent an uprising as the same organizational problem applied to those trying to protect the throne.

Despite being stubborn, the queen was not ignorant. In fact, she seemed far more intelligent than the pharaoh, and there were rumours that the two weren't getting along. It might not be too late to protect her. It flitted briefly through his mind that, if the pharaoh were out of the way, the queen might be in need of male companionship, and wouldn't that fit nicely into the desires of the sephat militias? Well, that and the more carnal desires he'd felt stirring within himself…

Bey cleared his throat. "I'll speak with Hadanish and Belu. But for now, no one has anything planned that we know of, right? This is all just talk."

"Right."

Ebrium's mother announced that she would go and help Akshaka find some jewelry for the palace event, and bid goodbye to Bey, insisting he come back for dinner later. Once she had made her way down the hall, Bey leaned in towards Ebrium once more.

"So what's this about the nobleman Sobek's daughter sending you a note?"

Ebrium, still leaning back against the wall, grinned and with feigned innocence he raised the palm of his good hand up in the air.

"I was merely acting as a brave young soldier should. Can I help it if danger and near death experiences excite some women and drive them to seek out the arms of their saviour?"

Bey chuckled. "No you cannot. But I know you, and I know that we can no longer afford our own such dangerous dalliances. If you get in to trouble with this girl we can't just flee again. Not like that time in *Ya-Pho* with that sword-smith's daughter. We don't even have our own ship here to flee *on*, as we did then."

"Oh brother, as if *I* were the only one in trouble! You act as if you forget that the girl had a sister, and if her father had caught you he would have flayed you just as badly as me!"

Bey snorted. "Flayed? Maybe. Forced marriage? Quite probably!"

"And even as I was jumping out the window that sister was slipping me a note *for you* to tell you she'd always love you, even if you never came back again. And *that,*" Ebrium pointed at Bey, "is how I know you have charm enough in you somewhere to get close to the queen."

Bey heaved in a breath as a somber mood once again descended over him.

"Ahhh. That was a long time ago, brother. I was more impulsive then. Nowadays I find there may be some value to my life." Bey smiled grimly, "and to keeping all my body parts in their place."

"Well if you ask me the queen looks like the kind of woman that, once, you wouldn't have thought twice about going after. By Dagon, if I thought there were any hope of it, I would risk a limb or two to be with her. She's certainly got all *her* body parts in all the right places, after all."

Bey glared at Ebrium as Ebrium feigned an innocent expression. Bey growled, "I am not blind to the woman. I know exactly what she looks like." *Too well. And I can still feel her naked leg in my hand from this morning, so close to her thigh, and I can still see the folds of her dress as they fell between her legs…* "She is more than appealing. That is not the problem. It is her husband, our jobs, and our lives I'm concerned about."

"Psshhh," Ebrium waved his hand in the air, dismissing Bey's comments. He lowered his voice to barely above a whisper. "We've both heard the rumours that Wadj doesn't visit her rooms. It's not clear where his passions lie, is it? He certainly likes to keep handsome young men around him at all times, doesn't he? Even though he could have *any* woman in Upper or Lower Kemet. Besides it doesn't sound as if there would be much opposition to you taking his place in the lady's rooms, now would there? And there would likely be less of a problem if you were to even take his place by her side than if you did nothing at all."

Bey couldn't help but chuckle at the thought of his time spent in Merneith's rooms that morning.

"At the moment, I think the lady herself would oppose my stepping foot anywhere near her rooms again, even if the *militias* are not opposed. I think that means little to her. Even so, we must wade carefully here, brother, lest we drown in this political scheming." Bey glanced over his shoulder out the window again. "Nobody can think that any movements on my part, or our part, are intended to seize the throne. If I fail in getting through to her we must plan and be prepared for what might come after."

"On this part I agree with you, brother." Ebrium raised his tea mug in toast.

"Thank the gods we agree on something today! Now if all is well for the moment, I think I will go home and sleep. Tell Akshaka we can begin her lessons later tonight, when I've had some rest."

"Indeed. Teach that girl some manners, please, so someone will marry her!"

"To be fair, man, she may not be the only one who needs to learn some table manners." Bey raised his eyebrows and shot Ebrium a serious look.

"That's it! Off with you!" Ebrium pointed at the door, laughing.

Bey laughed also and clasped Ebrium's hand before letting himself out the door. As he walked by the window of the greeting room he heard Ebrium call out, "Akshaka! More tea! And I need you to take a message to Baufra to come and keep me company. I won't listen to any more of this chatter about the palace and what you are wearing and what the queen is wearing and whatever some nobleman's cat is wearing. Quickly! Before I lose my mind."

Bey chuckled, but the whole way back to his own one-room hut he couldn't take his mind off the queen and the dilemma at hand. After some sleep he would track down Hadanish and Belu and find out what else they knew.

Chapter 4 – In the Garden

Merneith had a brief respite while her aunt Bekeh was busy planning the banquet Merneith didn't want to have. Although Penebui stayed with her, for a time Merneith feigned dozing while a warm breeze floated into the room, fluttering the white cotton drapes that cast blue shadows on the brick walls and cool, basalt tiled floors. She couldn't sleep; being agitated by both her aunt and Captain Bey was enough to keep her mind busy. She couldn't bring herself to focus on any one thing. The image of Bey, hunched over as he worked the honey mixture into her skin, fixed itself in her vision. She caught herself wondering what it might be like to trace his tattoo with her fingers, to feel the thick raised lines of ink running across his muscled arms and chest, to see close up what animals were buried in the thicket of lines.

Then she remembered his insolence and taunting. *The man needs to be reminded that I am queen. It is bad enough that he has already placed two guards at my doorway, who knows what is next?*

As for her aunt Bekeh's urging to take a lover, she couldn't find a way around it, but she knew there had to be another way. She shouldn't have to strategically sleep with a man to gain allies. *Even if that man might not be so unpleasant to bed.*

As the late afternoon approached she knew she would have to receive those guests who would be arriving to feign their concern for her well-being. She was well aware that most of them would happily gush over whoever threw the most lavish parties with the most food, wine, beer, and entertainment.

Merneith called for a couple of servants to help her hobble on her stiff legs to the palace garden. When two manservants arrived, a host of women bustled in along with them, including three other cousins and two aunts.

"By Neith!" "You must not walk on those poor legs of yours." "Let the men carry you!" The women proclaimed "Do not be stubborn, Hem-etj! You are injured. Look at you! You are too sore to move! Let the men carry you." The two aunts tried to push her back down on the bench.

"No, no!" Merneith batted at their hands. "If I do not walk myself, it will only get worse and I will be more rigid than a granite pillar from Aswan." The women continued to protest but Merneith beckoned to the servants to come near. She hoisted her legs over the side of the bench, then let the men pull her to standing. Each man put an arm under hers and she leaned on them as she tried to make her way towards the door.

"Hem-etj, stop this! You should not be walking." The aunts continued to argue and Merneith finally snapped at them. "I am already up and now you are only making it more difficult. If you are concerned about me then please, get out of my way!" *Damn those tigers and their handlers. If they had just done their job I would not be in this wretched position. First all the damnable chattering in the morning, then Sekhrey Bey and his brazen insolence, and this stupid banquet to honour his insolence, and now I cannot even leave my own bedroom without a struggle.*

The women parted and Merneith was able to limp past them. The men helped support her as she made her way out the door. She wanted to sit in the garden to feel the warmth of the setting sun, and receive her guests amidst the jasmine bushes that lined the garden walls. Perhaps the bushes' soothing scent would help make her more agreeable.

It was then that Merneith first saw the guards Bey had posted outside her door. Penebui had told her earlier that they had arrived, but Merneith had not gotten up yet to see them. They were both striking looking men. While not particularly tall or large, at least not in comparison to Sekhrey Bey, both had lean, muscled chests and copper skin. Both men had white linen scarves wrapped loosely around their heads, underneath which fell long dark braids adorned with feathers. Charcoal smudged around their eyelids served to enhance the white of their eyes and darkness of their pupils. The tattoos on their cheeks and legs suggested they may have come from one of the nomadic Libu tribes to the west of the great desert. Belted at the waist of their white linen skirts were large, wickedly curved blades. The men were now flanking her and her manservants as they made their way down the hall.

"You may tell your sekhrey that I say you need not stand so near." she snapped at them. "I have known these women and servants since I was a child, and had any of them wanted me dead I am sure they would have found opportunity by now."

The two guards looked at one another over her head and finally one of them pursed his lips and gave a short nod to the other. "I am sorry, Hem-etj. But Sekhrey Bey insisted that we stay close at all times."

"Regardless of what I tell you?" She retorted.

The men cast their eyes down. "Yes, Hem-etj."

That insufferable man! But Merneith knew that, even if she commanded the men to move away or threatened them, she would win nothing. The women behind her and the servants would be watching to see how she handled the situation. It was one thing for Bekeh and Penebui to see her argue with the Sekhrey, but if it got around that Sekhrey Bey didn't listen to the queen, she could lose respect and power in their eyes, and appear vulnerable. She couldn't afford that what with the way Wadj's advisors and followers might be scheming against her.

Merneith made her way down the hallway, past multiple other rooms belonging to the women of the harem, and out into the garden. The manservants settled Merneith on a cushioned chair in a corner, under the shade of a grapevine trellis, overlooking the raised pond that was the centerpiece of the garden. In the pond, fish in shades of orange, black, white, and red swam back and forth amidst the blue-tipped lotus flowers and their broad green leaves. The walls that enclosed the garden were painted in bold colours, depicting various stories of the gods, and the occasional lush banquet scene. Tall sycamore figs lined the walls, casting shade and offering clusters of orange-red fruit, nearly ripe for the picking, while jasmine bushes grew in between the tree trunks.

Merneith wondered what it would be like to have just five minutes alone in the garden. Or five minutes alone anywhere, for that matter, other than in her own bed at night. Even without Bey's guards following her, she was never really alone. There were always cousins, aunts, distant relatives, servants, or guests within arm's length. Sometimes, when she was younger, Merneith had faked illness just so that she could have a few minutes of peace and silence in her rooms. It inevitably backfired though, as the result was always groups of fussing women congregating around her, professing their concern that she would get lonely in her sickness-induced seclusion.

For a long time Merneith assumed the women wanted to be close to her for shallow reasons. Perhaps to ensure that she would look favorably on them and bestow them with gifts, or even that they might use their relationship with the queen to influence and curry favour with others. She also suspected they feared they might miss out on some important piece of gossip, or that they might even be the topic of gossip if they were absent. It took some time, and some enlightenment from Bekeh, for Merneith to realize another reason many of them stayed close to her; their anxiety that she might somehow plot against one of them or their husbands. Their constant presence and affection ensured she would have a difficult time doing away with any of them if she felt angered, or betrayed by any of them or their high-ranking husbands.

Merneith gestured for Penebui to sit close to her. They were quickly joined by more palace women who arranged themselves on benches and chairs around the garden. Merneith tried to ignore the two guards who took up positions just behind her chair.

Amongst the first guest to enter the garden was Prince Atab. When he came through the entranceway Merneith noticed that another guard had been stationed by the door, and was watching with raised chin and narrowed eyes as Atab and his small entourage of Sumerian noblemen and Egyptian servants walked the path towards her. *How many guards has that damned man stationed around the palace without telling me? And how did he get them there so quickly? I only saw him this morning. Damn him to Ammit.*

Merneith also noticed that Atab looked remarkably good for someone who had almost been attacked by a tiger the night before. In fact, he looked quite handsome in a white linen skirt that was wrapped and tied around the waist. His olive-toned upper chest was bare save for a strip of white linen draped over his right shoulder that cast half of his lean, muscled chest in shadows. A large flat gold disc hammered with symbols of the Sumerian royal family hung around his neck. The golden circlet of Sumerian royalty rested on his thick dark curls.

"Hem-etj," Atab flashed her a wide smile as his eyes flicked to the men behind her. "You are looking quite radiant in spite of last night's horrible affair." Atab motioned for two of his men to bring chairs for himself and some of his entourage. Merneith noted that he did not bow as was customary when greeting royalty. Despite being a prince and heir to the Sumerian throne, Atab was still expected to pay his respects to Egyptian royalty while he was seeking refuge in their lands.

"Thank you, Sar. I am recovering. I would offer you my hand to kiss, but," Merneith held up her bandaged hands in a casual shrug, "as you can see, you would get a mouthful of cotton, although it is, at least, sweet honey-flavoured cotton, thanks to Sekhrey Bey." She had meant the remark as a reminder of court formalities, as well as a subtle shot at Atab's role in knocking her down the stairs last night and causing her cuts and bruises in the first place. If he noticed, though, he ignored it.

"Thank Enlil you are looking so well. I myself have no recollection of the evening. I am told that I fell and must have been knocked unconscious in the excitement." Atab turned away for a moment to settle into a chair.

Convenient, thought Merneith. *Now he need not suffer the indignity of apologizing.*

"I have heard the new sekhrey was less than decorous in his handling of you. But then I suppose a low-born foreigner cannot be trusted to behave properly in polite company." Atab lifted an eyebrow and pursed his lips in a sardonic smile.

"Sekhrey Bey was quite brave when he saved Mer last night," Penebui interjected, leaning forward as she gripped the arms of her chair. "I do not think he behaved low-born at all. He even came early this morning to check on her and brought something for her hands and knees to help her heal."

"Did he now?" Atab tilted his chin and gave Penebui an implacable look until she blushed and looked away with a confused expression. He turned his gaze to Merneith and asked softly, "Is this so? And how did you find the sekhrey?"

Merneith felt like a fly Atab had picked up by the wings and was inspecting as it buzzed between his fingers. How had she not noticed this ability of his before? It made her angry, and she had no desire to discuss her feelings about Bey with him, whatever they may be. Instead, she said, "It is difficult to say since I was unaware he was sekhrey at all until after he had thrown me over his shoulder. Perhaps if I had met him beforehand I would have been in a better position to judge, instead of just having an informal introduction to his backside."

She had no wish to defend Bey, but found Atab's behavior even more antagonizing than the Bey's. *He is hardly in a position to be judging Bey considering it was he who knocked me down the stairs.* But she couldn't get angry at him, at least not visibly. Court behaviour dictated she be more diplomatic than that. She also felt uncomfortable talking about the captain when two of his men were standing right behind her chair, within hearing distance.

Atab chuckled. "Indeed. Your wit never ceases to amuse me, Hem-etj."

"I am always pleased to amuse you, Sar." Merneith lifted an eyebrow and pursed her lips in mock indignation. *I am thrilled I amuse you. What else is a queen for if not the amusement of her subjects?* But she knew better than to be too sarcastic with Atab. "Did you know before last night that Wadj had appointed a new sekhrey? I assume he was too busy making preparations to travel north to inform me and arrange for the customary ceremony." She studied Atab as he looked down and picked at something she couldn't see on his skirt. "I thought you might be more familiar with the sekhrey than I, and Wadj's decision, since you and Wadj are so close. Why would he have chosen that man in particular?"

Atab leaned back in his chair. A lock of wavy, dark hair fell over his right eye as he tilted his head back and gave her a sidelong look through lowered lids, his lips upturned in a slow half-smile. It was a look of powerful confidence and self-assuredness, something she had once admired in him, had even found sexy, because she so rarely felt it herself. *It was precisely that expression that had attracted me to him when he first arrived. But how do I feel about it now?*

Then Atab shrugged and grinned, revealing teeth so white they shone in the shadows of the grapevines. "I am sure the pharaoh was merely pre-occupied, my lady, as you said. I do recall him mentioning that he was considering a new sekhrey, as the previous one was ailing. I believe I may have met the man once or twice, but, truly, Hem-etj, I know so little of Wadj's affairs. You know he can sometimes be a private man."

Merneith suppressed a snort. Atab's comment was absurd, considering how close the two of them were, but she wasn't sure if he was intentionally affecting innocence to amuse her, or deliberately trying to deceive her. She knew she was not supposed to suspect the latter, and she didn't want to enter sensitive territory with Atab in case he became suspicious of her and reported something negative to Wadj. Atab and Wadj couldn't ever know, or even suspect, that she had been contemplating plotting against Wadj with Bekeh. Or that she had considered Bey as a co-conspirator. Instead Merneith forced a light laugh.

"Now I know you are toying with me, Sar. But tell me, have you had news from your uncle, King Alalngar? How goes it in your homeland?"

One corner of Atab's mouth lifted in what could have been a poorly repressed smirk. "News came this morning, but not from him, from my cousin Serida. My dear uncle has, unfortunately, been ill." Atab cocked his head to the side. "Of course, I can only hope that he will recover so he and I can make peace one day before his death."

Atab's calm expression didn't match his words, and again Merneith couldn't positively discern if he was being sarcastic, truthful, or intentionally deceitful. Atab had tried to take his uncle's throne. If he'd been successful, Alalngar would have suffered an unpleasant death. Atab himself was lucky that his failed attempt hadn't resulted in his own beheading. Merneith doubted there was much love between the two men.

"May the gods be with him and keep him well." This was the only possible response she could give. She couldn't question Atab about how he really felt, especially not in front of so many other people. "How old is this news?"

"The messengers left two months ago." Merneith knew the messengers likely would have traveled across Sumer to the Mediterranean coast, through Syria, then down the Iteru, a long journey at the best of times. "I expect there will be more messengers soon with more news. Before I left Sumer I requested Serida send me regular updates on my uncle's well-being." *Of course you did*, Merneith thought. If Alalngar died without naming another heir, Atab would likely return immediately to seize the throne of Sumer. Although there would doubtless be a struggle with some of the other potential heirs, Atab still had many supporters in Sumeria that might well be able to overthrow any new ruler.

"And if he continues to languish?" Merneith wondered if Atab would return to seek his uncle's good favour, and be poised to take the throne immediately when he died.

Atab gave her another languid smile. "I may have to rush to his side in the hopes that my presence and our reconciliation will nourish him back to health. Although I would hate to leave *your* side, Hem-etj, as your presence has nourished and consoled me these past few years."

Merneith smiled back, knowing it was the expected response. "My goodness, Sar, if you are not careful you will cause my head to inflate like a well-watered camel's back. What shall you do without me to amuse, nourish, and console you when you are back in Sumer? Of course we shall miss you, dear Sar, if you should go. But as royalty we are often constrained by duty, and what is expected of us." Merneith lowered her head and eyes in what she hoped was an innocent look, put on more for the Sumerian noblemen around her than Atab, who seemed less and less concerned with keeping up the appearance of genuine concern, or respect.

The late afternoon wore into evening. Bekeh came to join them, and Merneith called for food to be brought out. Tables were set up around the garden and torches were lit. Roasted fish, bowls of nuts, grapes, and sweet cakes were distributed amongst those present. Atab stayed throughout the evening as Merneith received various members of the Egyptian nobility.

"You poor thing!" They would exclaim when they saw her bandaged hands. "What a horrible thing." "Thank the gods for that guard, what was his name?" "Oh and that one that saved Satsobek?" "My how brave these foreign, barbarian men are!" "Thank the gods for Wadj appointing the new sekhrey, that he was able to save you!" "What a hero the new sekhrey is!" "But my goodness, to throw you over his back like that! How barbarian!" "Is it true he is a captured pirate?" "There is no accounting for foreigners! Where is the man from again?"

"Indeed," Merneith would utter, "Thank goodness for him." "Yes I am grateful." "Thank the gods for Wadj's good decision." "Yes, there will be a banquet to honour the guards." "Yes, in a few days' time, it is being arranged right now." "Yes, of course you are invited." "I believe he comes from a place called Ebla, south from Halab." All the while Merneith couldn't help but think, *Gods, it will be the talk of the land for months to come that I was flung over the backside of a foreign pirate, like plunder from a seized vessel. Ammit take him, I will never hear the end of this.*

Late in the evening Nenofer, a distant family member and a woman whom Merneith admired, came to visit. Nenofer was recently divorced, and although she was still wealthy, she had in fact lost some of her inherited landholdings as it was she, rather than her husband, who had initiated the divorce. "It was worth it to get rid of the man." Nenofer had told Merneith once regarding the loss of land. "While he was not all bad, he was terrible in bed, and I am not so desperate for a husband that I will put up with a man who believes a woman has no sexual desires. There are men enough who can satisfy me without requiring me to play the role of dutiful wife. At present I have several attractive Nubian manservants and I need only pick one to keep me company for the evening." Nenofer was in her late thirties, but with full hips and long dark hair she was an attractive woman. Her seductive, engaging personality attracted men to her, although it intimidated many more women.

The sycamore trees and their leaves swayed in the evening breeze, and the torchlights beneath them cast strange shadows across peoples' faces. As Nenofer floated along the torch-lit pathway her long white robes shone in the garden's darkness. Drained from entertaining and warm with wine, Merneith looked forward to Nenofer as if her presence was like cool water on a warm brow. Merneith held out a bandaged hand and Nenofer took hold of it, kneeling briefly to pay her respects.

"Hem-etj," Nenofer said warmly, taking the chair that Atab had recently vacated after pleading the need to walk and stretch his legs. "My dear, how are you feeling? You must be exhausted and worn out with all of this." Nenofer gestured around the garden, and Merneith knew she was referring to all the people who milled around. She realized that, for the first time since that morning, someone had actually asked her how she was instead of talking nervously at her.

"Thank you for asking. I am as well as can be." Merneith allowed herself to relax into her seat. "The new sekhrey came by this morning and brought some sort of honey mix for my cuts. I believe it may have helped with the healing."

Nenofer looked at Merneith's hands, then up at her. "Ahhh, the new sekhrey. I hear he is quite handsome." The torch light cast dappled shadows across her face, but Merneith could see Nenofer's half-smile and raised eyebrow. *So much for relaxing,* Merneith thought.

Penebui leaned forward eagerly, "He most certainly is! I have been trying to find out more about him all day, but I cannot gather much more than that he is from Ebla and came here as a pirate." Merneith threw Penebui a tight-lipped look and a glance at the guards behind her, sure that the men had heard her. Penebui caught the look and lowered her voice, but only slightly. "It is terribly exciting and mysterious."

"Indeed." Nenofer gave another half-smile. "That does sound terribly exciting. And how did you find him otherwise?"

Merneith was opening her mouth to answer when Bekeh cut in, loud enough that Merneith feared the guards would overhear again.

"We were all impressed by the new sekhrey last night, *and* this morning." Merneith noticed that Bekeh's eyes shifted slightly to the guards behind her and Nenofer's glance followed, then turned back to Bekeh. Bekeh inclined her head towards the guards, and Nenofer gave a slight nod of her chin. Merneith realized that Bekeh had intentionally been loud. She *wanted* the guards to hear her praise Bey, and she wanted Nenofer to know it. "He was quite a powerful figure last night, very much in command, and this morning he was quite considerate. He came, as promised, to tend to our queen's wounds."

"Well that does sound impressive."

"Quite." Bekeh raised her eyebrows in a look of innocence and continued in an earnest manner, "In fact, the Sekhrey has stationed these two intimidating, powerful-looking fellows here to help protect our queen from any further incidents that might harm her. I believe it is a good sign that we can rely on him to continue to protect her interests and well-being."

Nenofer's voice took on a soft tone, "I doubt not the men have our good queen's well-being at heart. I have heard that Sekhrey Bey and his men were quite admirable in their handling of last night's affair." Nenofer heaved in a deep breath that caused her ample breasts to lift up as she sat straighter in her chair, "And that *all* of them are very, very *capable*." She gave a coy look up at the two men standing behind Merneith. Merneith couldn't see their faces, but she suspected they must have looked back at Nenofer, because she lifted her eyebrow and gave a half-smile that turned into a slightly pursed pout, her chin inclined so that her face was angled towards the men.

Is she trying to seduce my guards?! Although it irritated her, Merneith realized it was probably best to let Bekeh and Nenofer talk around her, as she suspected they were playing at some game she didn't want to risk losing, but wasn't adept enough to take part in.

"I am certainly looking forward to the banquet in their honour, and the opportunity to get to know more about the Sekhrey and where he and his men came from." Penebui leaned forward, breaking the mood with her cheerful bubbling. "What do you suppose Ebla is like? Do they have a king and queen also? I imagine they must, would they not? Or are they a city inside a kingdom? What kinds of adventures do you suppose the Sekhrey would have had before coming here? It must have been terribly exciting to be a pirate! Bekeh, please do tell us about your preparations and what we can expect! And please tell me that we will be able to ask the Sekhrey about his adventures."

Merneith breathed a sigh of relief, thankful for Penebui's guileless nature. She sat back and let Bekeh talk. Although she was interested in the banquet in spite of herself, she found her head dropping forward from time to time, and feared that she would fall asleep in her chair. Eventually, she was able to excuse herself and have the manservants assist her back to her rooms, the guards again flanking her on either side. Several maids appeared and helped Merneith prepare for bed while chattering about how lovely the evening was and how beautiful the garden looked tonight with the skies so clear and moon so bright.

Finally, Merneith was alone. Despite her earlier exhaustion, she had a difficult time sleeping. She was restless, but tossing was awkward and frustrating with her sore, bandaged knees and hands. Too much had happened in one day and scenes from the day played themselves over and over in her head. And to top it off, Bekeh and Nenofer flirting with the guards. *What game are they playing at? Are they trying to curry favour with the guards for my sake? Or their own?*

Her mind kept turning over Penebui's earlier question. *What kinds of adventures would the Sekhrey have had before coming here?* She wondered. *What must his life have been like before he became a pirate, and what of it after? What if we had met under other circumstances, would I find him so unbalancing?*

Merneith found herself questioning what it would have been like if she had just been some orphaned fishmonger's daughter in some port city up north, and not a queen. If she had no one to answer to, no husband, no pharaoh, and no subjects. No one would care if a foreign man flung her over his back, and wanting a man would not be punishable by death or exile.

Sometime during these contemplations she drifted off to sleep and saw herself looking out the window of a dusty gray hut near the waterfront, reddish gold light streaming through the window to cast a warm glow in an otherwise gray, one-room hut. Watching the silhouette of Bey's ship dock against the orange and purple sunset, an aching craving building in her core and spreading in tingling waves throughout her limbs. Bey appeared at her door, she let him in, and he grinned that insufferable grin that had annoyed her so much, and then he caught her up, his tattoo rippling as he gripped her body in his arms.

Tumbling back onto a rag-stuffed mattress, stubble scratching her cheeks and neck, warm lips pressed against flesh, with hands hardened from ship wood and rope reaching to push up her robe. She could feel his hardness pressed against her hip and his hand sliding up between her sensitive thighs, her shivering, and the agonizing burning anticipation of his touch on her tender inner lips. He knew he wouldn't be soft and gentle, they would have been apart too long. He pressed his fingers into her, working them through her clenching muscles to curve upwards to her most sensitive spot while she gasped in tormented pleasure and dug her nails into his arms.

69

Merneith woke with a start, sitting straight up in her bed. She wiped away a strand of hair stuck to her sweaty cheek. *When had she fallen asleep?* She swung her legs over the edge of the bed and hobbled to the window, pushing back the curtain to feel the warm evening breeze on her skin. Yes, her skin, which tingled and ached from the dream she'd just had, a dream more heated than any she'd had before. *What in the name of the gods just happened? What is wrong with me? Damn that man.* She tried to push the images of the dream from her mind.

She looked out onto the courtyard, at the servants who were sweeping the stones, their white robes glowing in the moonlight. Some tables had already been moved, and Merneith realized that the preparations for the banquet to honour Bey and the guards were already underway. The servants were working even as she slept. *Just as Bey had last night when he had gone out to find the honey mix.* Just as his guards must be working right now, standing outside her door, working for her sake, to protect her, as were her aunt Bekeh and Nenofer when they were flirting with the men. It wasn't *their* fault their captain made her mad with anger, and perhaps a little bit of something else.

Merneith smoothed her hair and her dress and limped to the large, heavy door of her room, heaving it open awkwardly with her bandaged hands. The two copper-skinned men who stood on either side looked at her in surprise.

"Is everything all right, Hem-etj? What is the matter?"

"Everything is fine, thank you." She hesitated, then tried to soften her voice, "I did not ask your names before."

The men again exchanged a glance, and Merneith noticed that one had three brown feathers in his hair while the other had three white ones. Otherwise, though, the men were almost identical, including their closely cropped beards and the thick tattoos that spiraled up their legs.

The one with the brown feathers spoke first. "Batr, Hem-etj, of the Lawatae tribe of Libu." The braids and feathers swung forward as he bowed his head, and came to rest on either side of his muscular brown chest when he straightened. The one with the white feathers also bowed his head and said, "Makae, also of the Lawatae tribe of Libu, Hem-etj."

"Batr and Makae." Merneith looked from one man to the other, trying to remember which was which but found herself distracted by the thick tattoos on their legs, tattoos that were not unlike the one on Bey's shoulder and chest. The shoulder and chest that, moments ago, she had envisioned herself crushed against, and under.

Batr cleared his throat and said cautiously. "Did you require something of us, Hem-etj?"

Merneith came to herself. "Not tonight. Only to thank you for your services."

The men exchanged another surprised glance, but both bowed their heads and murmured, "It is an honour to protect you, Hem-etj. We are pleased to offer our services to you in any way." Merneith nodded shortly then turned.

Batr called after her, "Hem-etj, can we help you back into your room?"

Merneith turned and gave him a slight smile. "No, thank you Batr, but you may close the door behind me."

Batr returned her smile and reached to pull the door shut.

Chapter 5 – On the Rooftop

As the sun rose the next morning, Bey sat on the roof of his one room mud-brick hut. nAcross from him sat Batr and Makae, who had recently gotten off duty with the queen. The three men sipped tea that Bey had prepared in the small clay oven behind his hut and carried up the stairs to the roof. Most people in the neighbourhood spent the majority of their time on their roofs, as the small, cramped huts trapped heat, whereas the roofs were cooler and there was more room to stretch out.

Across the narrow lane, the family of five that lived in a three bedroom hut was eating breakfast on their roof, and had waved their hellos. The man next door had already gulped his tea and gone off to work at the market, where he swept the grounds and periodically threw out buckets of water to cool the sandy walkways in an effort to make the heat of the day bearable. It was good he had left, as their huts were so close they almost touched and Bey didn't want to be overheard. Bey had told Batr and Makae to report to him at the end of each shift, as he had for all the other guards stationed within the palace.

Bey was on edge. After having spoken with his spies, Hadanish and Belu, he'd been unable to extract much more detail than what Ebrium had related the morning after the tiger attack. His intuition told him that something was on the verge of happening, but for the moment there was nothing he could do to prevent it, or even determine exactly what *it* would be. He hoped that Batr and Makae would have something to either distract him or help formulate some course of action.

The two brothers had already outlined the main events of the day and the queen's initial resistance to their presence. "She was…" Batr paused as he searched for the right word then cleared his throat, "Well, you were right when you warned us, Sekhrey. She was not happy." He gave a slight smile.

Bey exhaled in a low chuckle, nodding. "I am not surprised." Bey was perplexed when Batr described how she had surprised them by pulling her door open in the middle of the night, breathless and with her hair somewhat askew, to ask their names and thank them. *By Dagon, what would have possessed her to do that?* He was first turned on, and then distracted, by the thought of her in a night shift with her hair messed up and breathless... *as if she had just had sex? But with whom? And why go to Batr and Makae right afterwards? No, not sex. There's no way a man could have gotten into that room. What, then?*

Bey listened with interest as the men related what Atab and the other nobles had to say about the tiger attack and his role in it. He nodded at the anticipated insults of his foreignness, although he couldn't help but think, *That spoilt Sumerian bastard*, when told of Atab's snide comment on his method of saving the queen. *It would not have been necessary if Atab hadn't been a drunken fool, and what does he get from discrediting me?*

"And her mewet, Bekeh?" Makae raised his eyebrows after recounting how the two older women had praised the guards' prowess.

"Yes?" Bey prompted.

"She and the other woman, ahh...Nenofer?" Bey nodded. He knew who the woman was.

Makae flicked his eyes over to his brother. Batr dipped his head in acquiescence.

"I... *we* think they may have been..." Makae paused and then told Bey what the women had said about them. He paused and then said, "We thought that perhaps they might have been... uhm..." he stopped and ran his fingers over his lips, seemingly at a loss for words.

"You thought perhaps the ladies were a little bit too interested in you?" Bey tilted his head.

Makae breathed a sigh that sounded like relief. "Yes, Sekhrey. It struck us as... *unusual.*"

In the Court of Kemet

Batr cut in, "Of course we are not familiar with the ways of ladies of the court, Sekhrey, and this may not be unusual for ladies of Kemet, but it is not familiar to us, except from the women who follow the camps at war, and they always expect something in return for their favours."

Makae hurriedly added, "Not that these women are like the camp women, of course. These are noble ladies, not prostitutes."

Bey smiled and nodded. "I understand."

"Not that the ladies were not charming and attractive." Batr raised his eyebrows, put his hands up, as if warding something off, and feigned an innocent look, "And if you thought it would be helpful in some way to get closer to the women, or to respond to their advances, I would not be one to defy an order, sir. I am sure my brother here would also be willing to sacrifice himself for your cause, Sekhrey." Batr gestured to Makae, who dipped his head to hide a smile.

Bey cleared his throat to cover his own laugh. "I do not think that will be necessary, Batr. But I do need you to stay alert, as you have. These details are important."

The men finished their tea and headed off to sleep and prepare for their next shift at the palace. Once they were gone, Bey sat back up on his roof with another cup of tea and watched as the city began to bustle with activity. From his vantage, he could see the thatched palm leaf shelters of the market stalls and the vendors laying out their wares. The noise of barter and livestock began to filter over the rooftops, as donkey-drawn carts laden with produce and bread rumbled along the narrow dirt paths between the tightly packed huts.

Bey mused. *What did Atab have to gain from insulting him, when Wadj was the one who had appointed him? And why would Bekeh and Nenofer flirt with the guards? There was no shortage of young noblemen who would be quite happy to spend time in bed with attractive, wealthy, royal women, so why bother with the guards? What are those women playing at?*

Chapter 6 – The Banquet

Two nights later, Bey was seated between Queen Merneith and her aunt Bekeh on the dais in the courtyard of the palace of Thinis. To his left, on the other side of Bekeh, sat Ebrium with his legs splayed out under the table, hands folded on his belly. To Merneith's right was Prince Atab, and to his right, Merneith's cousin Penebui. Off the corner of the dais steps a small group of Sumerian warriors, part of Atab's entourage and bodyguard, sat at a table.

The sun had set some time ago, and torches flickered around the courtyard, lining the square reserved for performances in front of the dais. Scones of heady perfume burned in bowls in tall holders, sending swirls of smoke spiraling up into the moonlit sky. To the left of the square, seated at rows of tables, were the men of the royal guard and, behind them, some esteemed nobles of the Egyptian court. To the right of the square were the women's tables, the wives of the guardsmen and nobles, and other female nobility.

It was the first time Bey had seen Merneith since the morning after the tiger attack. Merneith's nearness set his nerve endings vibrating. She looked stunning in a soft white linen sheath dress that molded to her supple curves and a beaded collar of dark red carnelian and gold. The white dress magnified her charcoal rimmed eyes and olive skin. Throughout the course of the evening Bey had been having a hard time preventing his eyes from trailing down the length of the thick black braid of her hair that draped over her left shoulder. The length of the braid fell on one soft, perfectly rounded breast, rising and falling with each breath.

But he couldn't let her attractions distract him tonight. Since the announcement of the banquet, Bey had been anticipating the opportunity to gauge Merneith's stance on the pharaoh and the state of unrest in Egypt. With no more information on any potential uprising to the north, or the anti-Pharaoh sentiments in the south, Bey had had little to do the last few days but turn the situation over in his mind, with no resolution. It was really a matter of wait-and-see, and try to keep abreast of any new movements. Not his favorite way to operate, he preferred having a clear direction and course of action. He was left feeling like he had many times at sea when a storm is brewing in the distance, not yet seen. The air has a sharpness to it that puts one's body on alert. He was tense with the anticipation of an onslaught of hurricane proportions, but so far was left floating in calmness.

Tonight he had to find a way to bring up the topic of the general unrest, but without raising any suspicions regarding his intentions. Although he suspected Merneith was far more intelligent and clear-headed than the Pharaoh, he had no way of knowing if she supported Wadj in his grandiose plans to become a living god, or if she was opposed to the havoc his plans were wreaking across Egypt. For all he knew, she just didn't care. But he doubted that. The woman appeared fiery and vocal in her opinions. Then again, he'd been wrong about women's passions before. His own broken engagement was a testament to the lengths that some women were willing to go to in order to maintain wealth and status.

Despite sitting next to Merneith for most of the evening the two had had no opportunity to speak. He'd had no choice but to allow the events of the evening to immerse him. First there had been a ceremony to honour Bey and his men. Then servants had brought around bowls of water for them to wash their hands in, and then had come numerous courses of food and ample amounts of beer.

Bey had been surprised the first time he'd witnessed a banquet at the Egyptian court, almost three weeks ago, mostly due to the extreme drinking that took place. Even the women got drunk, and more than one had to be helped back to her seat after staggering into someone. Once, a lady had vomited near some tables, setting off roars of laughter from the men and squeals of horrified delight from the ladies. Some of the local guards had explained to him that it was considered a sign of appreciation to get drunk at a royal feast, and drunkenness was, in fact, often expected.

This evening was the first time he had experienced this general drunkenness for himself, however. Bekeh had ignored his refusals to drink more beer, and instead insisted that, with the extra men having been called in for the evening's security duty, he was free to relax and enjoy the evening. To refuse would have been an insult, and Bey had lost track of how many times his mug had been refilled with dark, honey-flavoured beer.

Bey was feeling extremely satiated after eating what felt like an entire roasted goat, a river's worth of grilled fish, a flock of grilled geese, multitudes of fresh dates and grapes, bowlfuls of nuts, and finally, the sweet honey cakes which he had just finished consuming. It had been well over a decade since he'd sat down to a meal of more than one course in civilized company, and never to one of such extravagance. The opulence of the Egyptian court truly was incomparable and the beer, the potent perfume, and his gorged belly, all worked to dull his senses and calm the tension of the last few days.

Two pygmy dancers from the south took to the square in front of the dais and began to perform acrobatics. Bekeh leaned towards him. "Have you seen men like them before, Sekhrey?" She nodded her head in the direction of the dancers.

"Only once in a port city in Getulia. I met a man who had one of these little people working for him." Bey's lips compressed in an ironic smile at the contrast between the filthy port city full of thieves and whores compared to the opulent beauty of the Egyptian court.

"Indeed. And are they esteemed there as well? Our people believe they are made in the image of the god Bes."

"I am not familiar with this god of yours. What is he known for?"

Bekeh raised her chin proudly. "Bes was born of the little people of the south, and they are made in his image, so Bes and his people are small. He is the god that protects our women when they are birthing. Bes also drives away the chaos and brings happiness, and so we sing and dance, and make love," here Bekeh raised both an eyebrow and one corner of her mouth in a slight smile, "in Bes's honour. Because you and your men have helped to stave off chaos by saving our queen from the tigers, we thought it best to have the little people dance for you in your honour tonight."

Bey felt the corner of his lip twitch in response and couldn't help but think, *And who will be making love in our honour tonight?* Instead, he said, "Well I know not whether the little man I met in Getulia was made in your god's image, but he was certainly a gifted pick pocket. His size made him the perfect height to reach men's coin pouches and pockets, and he was near impossible to find in a crowd. The man he worked for was no god, and I doubt he brought many people anything but misery, but he was certainly not the type to be trifled with."

Bekeh threw her head back and laughed. To Bey's right, Merneith turned to the two of them with an inquisitive furrow of her eyebrows, but Bekeh leaned in towards Bey again with a penetrating look, placing a hand on his forearm.

"These two dancers were sent by one of our generals to the queen as a gift three years ago when he was touring the south. *That general,*" she tilted her head and gave him a suggestive look, "was also once captain of the guard."

Bey got the impression that Bekeh was weighing him, and that something was expected of him. He just wasn't quite sure what.

Instead he turned to Merneith.

"I am sorry, Hem-etj," he said with a slight bow of his head, "that I have not yet sent small dancing people to you to demonstrate my regard. Please accept my apologies and know that I regard you very highly nonetheless."

Merneith opened her mouth to speak, but Bekeh cut her off.

"All in good time, Captain. There are many ways to show your regard for your queen. Not all of which include gifts." She gave him another cryptic look. Bey glanced at Merneith but she had turned to stare straight ahead. It could have been a trick of the flickering flames, but Bey thought he saw her jaw clenching.

Bey knew he was treading on dangerous ground with the queen, baiting her as he had the other morning when he'd bandaged her cuts. But he took pleasure in being able to provoke her. On the one hand he knew he was being vindictive, forcing her to do penance for making his job more difficult and for not listening to his earlier requests for added security. On the other hand, and this reason he was less willing to acknowledge, he also found her intriguing, and powerfully sexy, when incited. A woman with that kind of temper could be a lot of fun in the bedroom. And a lot of trouble.

The pygmy dancers left the stage and several female drummers and musicians, known as *hnr*, took up positions at the far end. Two women seated themselves on stools and began to beat a slow, pulsating rhythm on large hand drums. One woman wore anklets, several inches wide and comprised of dozens of tiny animal hooves strung together, strapped above her bare feet. As she gently stepped from foot to foot in un-hurried circles the hooves made a light clapping sound, which she variously altered and enhanced by twisting her hips or stomping more firmly. Another woman also stood, a stocky, elderly woman with broad hips and shoulders and a dark shawl draped over her head. From the depths of her warbling throat, she began a mournful song.

Bey felt an unexpected wave of emotion wash over him. The woman wasn't singing in the language of Kemet. She was singing in Eblaite, the language of his homeland.

"What do you think of our singers tonight, Sekhrey?"

Bey turned to Merneith, who was looking at him with a slight smile.

Bey softened his tone as a wave of slightly intoxicated nostalgia washed over him. "Hem-etj, I have not heard such as this for…since I know not when. Perhaps since I was a little boy, and my brother and I would listen to the women sing in my mother's quarters." He paused as the faces of those he would never see again floated out of focus, and then said softly, "I thought never to hear it again."

"The queen herself chose these *hnr* to perform," Bekeh explained with one of her half-smirks. "We made enquiries and found that you and some of your men came from Ebla. One of the *bakht* knew some sisters from a nearby village whose family had come from Ebla many years ago. They perform periodically at weddings and festivals, and the queen was able to procure them on short notice."

"Truly this is a surprising pleasure, Hem-etj. I am sure the men will appreciate this greatly." Looking around at the men of the guard, it was clear that Bey was right. A hush had fallen over several of the guardsmen who had been rather raucous after the copious beer drinking of the evening. More than one had a wistful tear shining in his eye as the woman continued her song of homesickness and loneliness. Ebrium and Bey glanced at one another; a mutual understanding passing between them that recalled a lifetime of shared memories in a brief, simultaneous nod of their heads. As the *hnr* finished their first song, some of the guards leapt to their feet, cheering and clapping and calling out their appreciation. The women took up another tune amidst more cheering.

Thinking of his mother, Bey felt ashamed for having goaded Merneith the other day and at the same time, he seized the opportunity to talk more intimately with her. He inclined his head towards her, "Did you understand their song?"

She turned to him, hesitating, her face guarded. "I am unfamiliar with the language, but it sounded sad."

Bey nodded. "It is about a young nomad girl who is sent far away to marry a man from another tribe, whom she has never met. Her father wants more wealth and obtains a healthy gift for marrying his daughter to the man. The girl's husband and his family are not cruel, but the girl longs day and night to see her mother's face, and to hear the laughter of her sisters. The girl knows she can never see them again, but she aches for them nonetheless." He watched her face intently, waiting for her response.

"Such is the life of a woman, though, is it not, Sekhrey? We are offered little choice in whom we marry, no matter where we come from. Marrying a man for love is not an option, while men are often free to marry whomever they chose, and as many as they choose. Our bodies are bought and sold for the greater good and the betterment of men." Merneith pursed her lips and narrowed her eyes and Bey felt as if he was somehow being blamed for this. *He was in no way responsible for the plight of any woman, and had himself once railed against such conventions.* He felt a coldness in his chest, and the urge to antagonize her came over him again.

"Yet some have choice, but choose unwisely. Some choose comfort and wealth over love." He knew this all too well from his own experience.

"I have never met a woman with such a choice, nor would I understand it if I did," she quipped.

Bey was about to retort when Bekeh cut in. "Please, Sekhrey, do tell us more about you. All we know is your homeland, and we have heard that our men picked your ship up in a storm in the Iteru delta. Do tell us about how you came to be there." Bekeh smiled pleasantly, but Bey thought he saw her flick Merneith a hard look. He also seriously doubted that was all she'd heard about him, but he took the opportunity to take a deep breath and warn himself to control his emotions. *Don't forget your goal tonight.* But he couldn't help it. He *wanted* to make Merneith angry and, now that he was a few drinks in, he *wanted* to lose himself in his own anger, as he had when he'd first left Ebla and took to the seas, spending his free time drinking and fighting in filthy taverns in port cities, and hung over mornings throwing up off the side of the ship. He wished he had drunk his beer more slowly.

"I was a sailor," Bey began. "A *seqdew* as you say in your language, and sekhrey of the ship your men found docked in the storm."

"Pfft!" Sar Atab, who had had been silently drinking most of the evening, scoffed. "Not a *seqdew*, friend, I believe the word you are looking for is *itja*." *A low-class thief.* Bey looked past Merneith to respond to Atab's insult.

Before Bey had a chance to say anything, however, Ebrium, who had drunk even more heartily than Bey, uttered an insult in Sumerian at Atab and added, "You know not to whom you speak."

Atab turned to Ebrium, calling him a 'clever fool' in Sumerian, *"Galam-huru,"* he hissed, then threw out another common insult at Ebrium, "Like a whelping bitch you bite the workmen."

Ebrium clenched his fist and shot back with some of his best Sumerian insults, learned courtesy of a Sumerian crewmate, "He who leaves his mouth open long gets dung in it, like a hippopotamus, and like a hyena you will not eat something unless it stinks."

Bey held up a hand to stop Ebrium, and instead told Atab in Sumerian, "While I may have taken things, from time to time, that were not mine, I never took them from anyone who had less to lose than I. I also believe, *friend*, that it is better to be an *itja* than a *hapiru*." Bey smiled with his lips pressed tight as he called Atab a traitor, the type to sell himself to the highest bidder. *The man licks the boots of Kemet's pharaoh, and he has the nerve to call me a thief and Ebrium a whelping bitch? When we left our homeland, we had no entourage or fancy court to flee to, nor an uncle or pharaoh to support us. Prince or not, the man is a dog.*

"It would serve you well, *Sekhrey*," Atab's voice dripped with sarcasm and disdain, "to remember that I am Sar of Sumeria, and will one day be king."

"You are not *my* sar," Bey kept his voice level, "and whether you will be anyone's king remains to be seen."

"And maybe you aren't the only sar at this table," Ebrium shot out before Bey could throw up his hand again to stop him.

Merneith spread her hands out on the table and cleared her throat. "While this has been an interesting lesson in the Sumerian vocabulary I was clearly lacking in my upbringing, from what I gather I think it would serve you men well to remember that you are *all* guests in *my* court tonight, each one of you." Merneith was now looking with a raised eyebrow between the three men, "And presently, *I am queen*, which I believe outranks all of you, whether you are a seqdew, sekhrey, or sar. Or must I call in the extra guards to protect us all from the current, off-duty guards?" She cocked her head to the left, looking pointedly at Bey.

Bey realized that he was actually clenching his fists under the table, despite his intentions to keep his calm. *Damn Dagon, and Ishtar, and their stupid god Bes and Ammit and whomever.* Bey took a deep breath. He had to get control of himself and the situation. He couldn't allow his distaste for Atab to distract him from talking to Merneith.

"You are right, Hem-etj. My apologies, we are acting like little boys in the presence of beautiful women. Your hospitality has overwhelmed simple men such as myself and Ebrium, unaccustomed as we are to such rich food and drink and fine company. Please forgive us." Although still seated, Bey dipped his head in a small bow. He looked up at Merneith through a stray lock of his hair.

Merneith had lifted her chin and was looking down at Bey with a look he didn't quite understand, but he felt that he was being assessed in some way. She pursed her lips and for a brief moment, he got the impression she was trying to cover up a smile.

She shook her head slightly and said in a light tone, "Let us enjoy the rest of the evening. I for one would like to hear more of this music of yours, and would appreciate it if you, or your rather eloquent friend Ebrium, could translate the words for me."

Bey chuckled and, leaning closer to Merneith, said in a low rasp, "You have no idea how *eloquent* Ebrium can be when he wants to."

The corner of Merneith's lip twitched, "I doubt it not. I suspect, Sekhrey, that you have your moments also."

"I have my moments indeed, Hem-etj." He shot her a half smile, then glanced over at Ebrium, giving a quick jerk of his head to indicate all was well. Atab, he noticed, was clenching his jaw and glaring at the singers. Bey settled himself back into his seat.

Merneith tossed her braid over her shoulder and he caught a hint of the rich, provocative aroma of her jasmine scented hair, and had to push away an image of himself plunging his hands into the thick braid and pulling the strands of hair out and around her shoulders and over her breasts. He pushed the image from his mind and was pleased when

Merneith queried him about Ebla. He decided to take the opportunity to probe her feelings about her husband.

Chapter 7 – Queens and Wives

Merneith had struggled throughout the banquet with the divergent desires to both speak to Bey and avoid him. Her skin tingled at his proximity, as if in anticipation of his touch. As if she could feel his energy in the air, sharp and crisp, raising the hair on her arms and neck as it had when she'd seen him for the first time, and then afterwards when he'd pressed her up against the temple walls.

At one point, she'd even caught herself wondering if, should she desire it, there would ever be a way to get Bey back to her rooms without anyone else seeing. She had no doubt that Bekeh would be more than happy to assist, and probably knew all sorts of methods for sneaking men in and out of rooms. The mere image of them alone together in the cool shadows of her room caused her nipples to harden and she'd become acutely self-conscious.

It was at that point that Bey had broken in to her thoughts and apologized for not sending her small dancing men. She could do little more than open her mouth before Bekeh cut her off with her innuendos. "All in good time, Captain. There are many ways to show your regard for your queen. Not all of which include gifts." Merneith knew exactly what Bekeh was getting at, and wished she hadn't brought it up again. Merneith was having a hard enough time *not* thinking of an affair with Bey without Bekeh implying that he should show his loyalty by *having* one.

Then she'd almost laughed at the way Sekhrey Bey had handled Sar Atab's snide comments. She wasn't blind to the fact that the same insolence that drove her mad was also somewhat amusing when it was directed at the drunken Sumerian prince.

Now her curiosity got the better of her and she was compelled to turn to Bey. "Tell me, Sekhrey, I have heard that in your land, your leaders are not born to be king or queen. They are not chosen by the gods to rule. I do not understand how this system works." Merneith had heard that Ebla had a different ruling system, and the concept was so foreign to her she wanted to know more. Bey was rested one large forearm on the table, twisting his body to face her. Merneith could feel the warm breeze of his movement against her bare arms and neck as he leaned in closer, and his heady, spicy scent washed over her. She drew in a long, slow breath, unable to stop herself from savoring the delicious shiver his smell sent throughout her limbs, hoping he wouldn't notice how it raised bumps along her skin.

Bey smiled, flashing white teeth. "Yes, what you have heard is true. Our leaders are not born into it. They are elected by a council of merchant noblemen for seven-year terms."

"And what happens at the end of this term to these rulers?" Merneith had supposed they must attempt to seize power for themselves.

"Then there is another election. If the people are pleased with the ruler, he may be elected again. If not, another man will be elected."

"And what of his wife?"

Bey hesitated, and the intense look in his green eyes made her self-conscious. She looked down to avoid them. "She will be what we call *maliktum*, like you, Hem-etj. A queen. In fact, Hem-etj, many years ago we once had a *maliktu* rule without a *malik*."

Merneith raised her chin, feeling as if some of the wine and incense from the evening had muddled her mind. "I do not understand."

Bey turned fully towards her now, shifting to sit almost sideways on his chair and lean even further forward, resting a forearm on his thigh. She had to lean closer to him to hear him, and felt a slight thrill at the intimacy as she inhaled another lungful of his rich scent. Merneith noticed that Bekeh, who appeared to be looking away, was sitting rigidly, and Merneith suspected she was also listening closely to them.

Bey explained. "The king died well before his term as ruler was complete. The *maliktu* was quite capable, and the people liked her very much. Rather than calling a new election, she ruled for five years after the *malik* died." Bey's drew in his lips, flicking his tongue over them to moisten them. Merneith couldn't help but watch his lips as he spoke. Anything to escape those piercing eyes that made her so uncomfortable, as if he was pushing aside thin linen curtains to let light into a shadowy room that contained the secret thoughts and feelings she couldn't reveal.

Bey took a deep breath and then turned his penetrating green eyes back to her. "There has long been a rumour about the *malik*. Some say that in his first term, he began to go mad. But the *malik* had made many allies with the noblemen, the merchants, by giving them money from the city's coffers. So the men voted him in again. However, after the election, the *malik* began to talk of doing away with the elections all together." Bey lowered his voice even more so Merneith was forced to lean closer, "He wanted to be ruler for life. He began to withdraw his favours, the common people suffered and grew angry under heavy taxes, and trade in the region became unstable, which harmed the merchant noblemen."

Bey paused and Merneith watched as he drew one corner in to moisten his lips, and then slowly released them. "Some say the nobles plotted against the man and made his death appear an accident, and they chose for the *maliktu* to remain as queen to return stability to the region." Merneith looked up and her eyes connected with Bey's. A shiver ran through her body, causing her skin to tighten and tingle again, and she quickly looked away. He was so close she could almost feel his breath, his voice barely more than a whisper. "Some say the *maliktu* knew what the nobles were planning, and chose not to act."

Merneith realized she was holding her breath, and let it out unevenly.

Bey gave a wide smile and leaned back. "But whether or not this is true, today the people recall her with great favour. She is known for her kind works, and for bringing prosperity to Ebla. She is a legend amongst the women of Ebla also, who admire her for her strength. "

A jumble of questions were just formulating in Merneith's mind, when she was cut off by the call of a royal servant announcing that the guests of the guards would be brought by her table to be introduced.

Merneith was irritated by the interruption, but sat back in her chair as the servants moved away the dinner tables on the dais in front of her. The Eblaiti musicians had moved off the performance square and a lineup of women, the guards' guests, formed at the far end of the square. Merneith could see that two women were led to the front of the line, but their faces were obscured by flickering torchlight and the smoke rising off the incense burners.

After a few moments, a servant motioned for the two women to approach the dais. One walked with a cane but rested heavily on the other's arm. As they neared, Merneith could see that one was older with a long, beaded black scarf draped over her head that cast her face in even further shadow than the flickering oil wicks. But Merneith could see that age had written itself across her dark face, and the folds of her wrinkled lids rested heavy over sharp eyes. The other woman, Merneith couldn't help but notice, was stunning. The girl's skin, framed as it was by straight black hair, was so fair it nearly glowed in the torchlight. *And young*, Merneith thought. *By the gods, her skin is smoother than a baby's bottom. I have not had skin like that in ten years, if I ever even did.* Merneith felt acutely self-conscious sitting next to Bey. Out of the corner of her eye she could see him watching the girl closely.

A servant called out the women's names. "Akshaka, guest of Sekhrey Bey." The beautiful young girl bowed. Merneith felt her heart jump and her chest tighten as her breath froze. *Bey's guest?* "And Ishara, guest of Ebrium." The old lady gave a half-bow, and it looked as if that alone was a painful act.

It took Merneith a moment to gather herself and formulate the expected greeting. "Welcome. I hope you have been enjoying yourself this evening."

The pretty girl, Akshaka, ducked her head in a shy gesture then looked up with eyes as strikingly blue as Bey's were green. "Thank you, Hem-etj," the girl spoke haltingly, and with an accent. "It is our honour for us to be here." She paused and licked her lips, appearing to concentrate. "Please forgive us both, we do not speak the language well." She flicked her eyes to Bey, and Merneith couldn't help but notice he was nodding at her, as if in encouragement.

Is this girl Bey's wife? She is about the right age for it, and pretty enough to turn any man's eye. After all, why would he not be married? He is handsome in his own way, and has been in Kemet long enough to settle. Long enough to order a young wife from Ebla. Merneith forced a tight smile.

"You speak very well. And you are both welcome in *my* court." Merneith hadn't intended to sound so imperious, but the girl was just *too* sweet and *too* pretty. Furthermore, Merneith's body had gone rigid, as if any movement might betray the conflicting feelings rising up into her throat. She was having a hard time pushing words out of her mouth.

"You are overly kind to us, Hem-etj," the girl ducked her head again, her beautiful dark hair swaying forward. The torches flared and shadows danced around the two foreign women. Akshaka looked up, flicking her eyes to Bey again before continuing. "It is our desire to serve you, Hem-etj, and we thank you for welcoming us and our husbands and sons into your land." The girl pursed her lips, and squinted, as if unsure of herself.

So husband it is. Merneith lifted her chin. *And this must be Ebrium's mother.*

"You are welcome. Senebti, both of you." Merneith wished them well, and one of the servants stepped forward to lead the women away as they bowed their heads and thanked her again. Out of the corner of her eye, Merneith detected Bey smiling at the girl. She couldn't bring herself to look at him, and instead went through the motions of greeting the rest of the guards' guests. Merneith was consumed by Bey's story about the Eblaiti queen, as well as thoughts of the pretty young Eblaiti girl who must be his wife. However, once the greeting of the guests had begun, Merneith did not have another free moment to speak with Bey. Not that she would have given the man the satisfaction of knowing he had aroused her curiosity anyway. No. She would not, could not, ask him about Akshaka or the Eblaiti queen. When the last of the long line of women had passed in front of her, Merneith could not remember one single woman's name.

Thank the gods this wretched evening is over. It finally came time for Merneith to rise and take her leave. She once again thanked the guards for their service, nodding both at Ebrium and Bey shortly and bidding goodnight to Atab. She made her exit with Penebui and Bekeh at her side, and the two guards Batr and Makae close by.

Female servants came to prepare Merneith for bed and, once in her night dress, she sat alone with Penebui and Bekeh. The women had pulled their chairs into a close circle. The room was dimly lit by several bowls of oil with burning wicks placed on two short tables near their chairs. Batr and Makae were stationed outside the closed door.

Bekeh had insisted on debriefing after the events of the evening, despite Merneith's protests. Merneith just wanted the day to end. After the initial shock of meeting Akshaka, Merneith's anger at Bey had resurfaced. *The arrogance of him, talking about marrying for love!* He'd had the audacity to tell her a story about a girl taken from her family and sent away to marry while he himself had a pretty young foreign bride that he'd had shipped to a far-away land where she didn't know the language. The girl was practically still a child, barely older than Merneith herself had been when she was married off to Wadj at the age of thirteen.

"I cannot believe Bey is married!" Penebui finally burst out into the silence of the room. "Did either of you know this and not tell me? How did I not hear about this?" Penebui scolded them.

"If it is true, it is insignificant to our plans," Bekeh waved her hand, as if swatting a fly.

"Insignificant?!" Merneith gripped the arms of her chair, leaned forward, and hissed, "For all we know the man kidnapped that girl on some pirate raid."

Penebui's jaw dropped and her eyes went wide. Then a quixotic look came over her and she breathed out, "Do you really think so? What a love story that could be." Merneith threw her a glare and Penebui shrugged with her hands held up. "What?! She was certainly beautiful, and he is so handsome and fascinating. I think they make a lovely couple."

"Enough!" Bekeh snapped. "It changes nothing. Who cares how this girl came into being? Mer must still make her alliances, and no man will turn down a queen, married or not."

"I will not offer my body up like a boar's carcass to an animal like him." Merneith tightened her jaw. She wouldn't let Bekeh bully her into an affair. That was preposterous.

"I thought he had very nice manners tonight," Penebui muttered, looking down and picking at her dress.

"Stop behaving like a child, Mer. We are all doing our part to gain the guards' favour, but it helps our cause naught if you destroy it all with your impractical emotions and childish behaviour," Bekeh reprimanded Merneith. She opened her mouth to protest but Bekeh cut her off. "Do not think I did not notice your coldness towards him tonight. You may be queen and above the man, but if Wadj's advisors have their way, it will not matter who you are when we *all* lose our heads."

Bekeh sat back, passing a hand over her face and taking a deep breath. After a moment, she continued. "Perhaps you need not take him as a lover. The important thing is to have the guard behind you, and the support of the majority of the *sephats* and their militias. Perhaps if you were more careful in cultivating your friendships with the ladies of the palace and their husbands..." She trailed off, looking pensive. "But this will take too much time." She looked up sharply. "You heard Bey's story of the Eblaiti queen who ruled after her husband's death? Is it possible he knows of your own situation and is," Bekeh paused and her lips twitched upwards, "shall we say, favourably disposed to aiding you?"

"What story?" Penebui sat forward. "I could barely hear anything, except when Atab started that fight. And how rude was *that*?"

"A queen in Ebla may or may not have made a deal with the nobles to rule alone after they may or may not have done away with her husband, the king," Merneith said with a hint of sarcasm. "But you cannot seriously be considering this, Mewet?" Merneith shook her head.

"If it is possible for Wadj to consider doing away with you, should you not be considering doing the same to him?" Bekeh tilted her head and gave Merneith a calm, implacable look.

Merneith scoffed, "But we do not even know that Wadj, or anyone else for that matter, is considering it at all."

"Can you honestly tell me that you trust Wadj to spare your life, and ours, if he thinks you stand in the way of something he wants?" Bekeh gave Merneith another relentless stare.

Just then, a heavy knock came at the door, startling the women. Before they could stop her, Penebui jumped up to run to the door. Merneith's heart pounded as she and Bekeh both stood. *Have we been overheard?*

As Penebui pulled the door open Bey strode past her, nodding his thanks.

"*Hem-etj, Nebet-i,*" he nodded at Merneith and Bekeh. "I am sorry to interrupt you at this hour, but you must prepare yourselves to leave the palace immediately. Your lives are in danger and we have not the men to withstand an attack tonight. I have men preparing the ships with supplies right now and they will be ready to leave within the hour."

Chapter 8 – Flight

Merneith's throat went dry and she wrapped her arms around her chest as a tingle of apprehension spread out from between her breasts. A quick glance around revealed the stunned expressions on Bekeh and Penebui's faces. *Were their lives truly in danger?* Considering that she had just been discussing this same topic with her aunt and cousin, it didn't seem impossible. But could she trust Bey, a man her own devious husband had hired to protect her? Perhaps Bekeh had been right. The story Bey had told her earlier that evening of a queen who had ruled without a king seemed to indicate he was hinting, perhaps even *suggesting*, something to her.

She cleared her throat and dropped her arms to her side, her fists clenching. She steadied her voice to ask in a commanding tone, "What has happened?"

Bey's eyes belied urgency as he said, "I will explain when we are on our way, but you must trust me. I received word just after you left the courtyard that there will be an attack sometime in the next day. We are short of men, with a portion of the guard in the north with the Pharaoh, and half the remaining guard drunk from the dinner. We must go south, where the *sephats* are loyal and will help us protect you."

Bekeh gave a curt nod before saying, "We will need to call the servants to prepare our belongings." Merneith was about to object but Bekeh turned to her with nostrils flaring. Merneith could feel Bekeh's tension despite her ever-calm demeanor. It was clear that Bekeh, at least, did not seem to doubt Bey's intentions.

Bey shook his head and said, "No. You cannot tell anyone. Even the soldiers do not know you will be on board. I have told them it is a drill to test their skills after an evening of leisure. We cannot trust anyone until we are on board the ships and away from here."

Merneith flicked her eyes to the windows that gaped out onto the dark courtyard and the endless mounds of sand beyond. If she chose not to go with Bey tonight and he was right, she could be dead by morning. If she went with him and *he* was the threat, she could also be dead by morning.

"Please, Hem-etj, you *must* trust me." Bey took a step closer to Merneith, looking down at her with his hand resting on the curved blade belted at his hip. "You have to allow me to do my job tonight and protect you. We must leave."

Looking up into his intense eyes and furrowed brow, Merneith felt the same sensation she'd had the first time she'd seen Bey, as if things were swirling away around her, and she was losing her balance. For a second she wondered if she might feel the same way with his arms wrapped around her, or if his muscled, tattooed biceps would steady her and make her feel safe.

She snapped her eyes away from his and acquiesced. If Bey wanted her dead, he would not have forced extra security on her against her wishes. She had to trust him.

Bey agreed to give the women a few minutes to change into their simplest clothing and within moments Merneith was left alone to change and pack only a few small essential items. She took a moment to draw in a shaky breath and collect herself. Bey had told her that Akshaka and Ishara would be on the ship to attend them. The last thing Merneith wanted was to be served by Bey's wife tonight, but even she knew she couldn't afford to be petty at a time like this.

She set about throwing some items into a sack she'd dragged out from under her bed. She pulled her plainest shift over her head, smudged the coal around her eyes, and wrapped her hair up into a scarf, the way she used to as a little girl to copy the Nubian serving women. That is, until her father caught her one day running through the palace with her hair wrapped up and smacked her for behaving like a peasant girl instead of the future queen of Egypt. Tonight she hoped that which her father had abhorred help keep her safe.

Within a few short minutes, Bey knocked on her door again. He opened it a crack and called in, "Hem-etj. We must leave. The other women are here."

Merneith put out the oil wicks in the room and dragged her sack to the doorway. Stepping out into the torch-lit hallway, she could see the surprise on Bey's face.

"Will this do as a disguise, *Sekhrey*?" She narrowed her eyes, daring him to make a comment.

The corner of Bey's lips twitched and he tilted his head. "Nicely done, Hem-etj. You conceal yourself well." He gestured to Batr and Makae to take the women's sacks and gave a quick glance around the empty hallway. "We must not be seen, please take these and wrap them around your faces." Bey pulled out three plain black scarves from a sack and handed them to the women. "We will go quickly to the docks, please follow me."

The women draped the scarves over their heads, winding them around their faces in the fashion of the nomadic desert tribes. The six of them made their way through the dark hallways of the palace and out beyond the darkened garden. Giant sycamore trees offered glimpses of the moon and starlit sky through leafy branches. The women almost had to trot to keep up with the men's quick strides. They passed along dusty trails lined with scrub brush and finally made their way through the reeds down to where the ships were docked. Akshaka and Ishara stood on the dock, while around them men were carrying sacks of food and weapons up planks onto the two large ships.

The ships themselves were typical Egyptian warships. About seventy-five feet long, narrow, and curved sharply upwards at the bow, each ship had a small hut towards the stern for shelter and to house supplies. Along each side of the decks were benches for the rowers. The large linen sails in the centre of the ships were rolled up, waiting for a wind.

"Akshaka and Ishara will assist you to get settled. I must check with the men. Please board immediately and wait inside the shelter. We must leave as soon as possible." Bey strode down the deck, and Makae and Batr herded the women onto one of the warships.

The "shelter" was more of a storage room than any sort of refuge. Wooden crates and sacks were stacked on top of one another from floor to ceiling in the dim space. There was nothing for the women to sit or lie on, so Akshaka and Penebui rummaged for a couple of empty crates and laid down some cloaks.

The women sat in the darkness in pensive silence, listening to the sounds of the soldiers launching the ships and the slapping of oars against the water. After what seemed like hours Ishara's light snores signalled that some of the women, at least, had fallen asleep. Merneith, however, only got angrier with each moment that passed without further explanation for their flight. She carefully drew her scarf over her face and stepped around the slumped women's bodies.

On deck, she walked past the rows of soldiers, rowing as they thrust the boat upstream along the Iteru. The reflection of the moon glowed on the rippling river. She almost lost her balance more than once as the ship rocked. It had been some time since she had been on a ship. She could see Bey's silhouette at the bow of the ship, his back to her as he spoke with Ebrium. As she approached, she overheard the men talking in Eblaite. Ebrium saw her and jerked his chin in her direction. Bey turned and locked eyes with her.

"Hem-etj. What are you doing out here? You must stay out of sight."

Merneith stepped close to the men and cleared her throat, trying to steady herself as the boat lurched. "I demand to know what is going on. You have taken us hostage on this ship and not explained anything."

Bey and Ebrium exchanged a quick glance, and then Bey nodded. "Please, let us move out of the light so you are not a target, Hem-etj." Bey gestured at the side of the ship, where another small structure offered some cover for them to stand near. He stepped in close to her, and Ebrium stood at his side. With the moonlight shining behind the two men they loomed over her.

"Earlier this evening some men in my employ were at an inn in the village. They overheard a conversation between three men discussing a plot to kidnap you in the next day. Right now, it is not clear if it is one of the *sephat* militias or if they are hired mercenaries. But given their accents, my men deemed they were from the north, and that the plot is likely to have come from the northern region of Kemet. We do not know their intent beyond kidnapping you. There may be as many as two hundred and fifty men involved. As soon as the men learned of this they came to me at the palace. We could not be assured of your safety at the palace so we are taking you to Ta-senet, where the *sephat* are loyal to you."

"How do you know they are loyal?" Merneith felt another lurch and grabbed onto the ship's railing. She wasn't sure if it was the rocking of the boat or her own shock and exhaustion causing her to sway.

"I know the militia leaders and the rulers of the *sephats*, Hem-etj. I have trained with them." Bey took another step towards her, "Are you alright?"

Merneith held up a hand to ward him off, but she couldn't seem to get her balance. She gasped and hung on to the rail as she felt acidic bile rising in her throat. "No," she whispered, but it was too late. She ripped the scarf off her face as she leaned over the side of the ship, retching.

Bey was by her side in an instant, his hand on the small of her back. "Best to get it out now." She hung over the side of the boat a few more moments, retching and gagging a couple more times until she felt some of the queasiness pass. She turned and, with her back against the side of the boat, slid down to a sitting position as Bey grabbed her under the armpits and softened her descent. Ebrium disappeared for a moment and returned with a cup of water.

She muttered, "I am fine," and tried to wave them off, but the men ignored her weak protest. Bey and Ebrium crouched on either side of her, and Ebrium gently took her head and tipped some water into her mouth with his bandaged arm.

"Hem-etj, it is good for you to look at something that will not move, like the moon," Ebrium urged. "It helps the sickness pass." Merneith tried to fix her eyes on the sky, but her head kept rolling as the boat rode the waves. Bey reached out and took her wrist. She jerked and tried to snatch it away but he held tight. *Damn him*. But she knew that in that moment she was angrier with herself for once again displaying weakness and being at Bey's mercy.

"I am going to press on spots on your wrist that will help with the sickness." Bey slipped his thumb up under the bandages that were still wrapped around the wrist of her left hand and began to press and massage the inside of her wrist. Merneith felt the nausea in her chest begin to abate somewhat, but her body and jaw clenched at Bey's touch. She could not suppress a slight moan and dropped her head back to rest against the side of the ship.

"Hem-etj, I am going to take you back to the shelter. You need to lie down and try to get some sleep. It has been a long night for you already and you were not prepared for the journey."

Merneith tried to argue, but Bey had already draped her hand around his shoulder and wrapped his arm tightly around her waist, pulling her up to her feet. Holding her up with one arm, he tucked the scarf back around her face. Then, clutching her body to him, he walked her past the rowers to the shelter. Despite her sickness, Merneith was acutely conscious of being pressed against the naked skin of his thickly muscled chest with only her thin linen dress between them. Her head lolled and rested against the hollow beneath his collar bone, and she could smell his scent, comforting and spicy, like cedar wood left out in the sun to dry. She dragged in a deep breath, trying not to admit to herself that she found his smell and his grip steadying.

Ducking his head, Bey stepped carefully into the darkness of the shelter. Finding a corner of the room, he set her down. He arranged some sacks and cloaks for her, then guided her over and helped her lie down.

"I am sorry, Hem-etj, that the quarters are not what you are used to, but we cannot afford to stop to make camp tonight. We must get as far away from Thinis as possible."

Merneith couldn't bring herself to respond, she just wanted to put her head down. As she drifted off to sleep, she was distantly aware of Bey laying a blanket over her, and then she succumbed to the darkness.

Chapter 9 – A History

Merneith was ill most of the next day, becoming alert only when one of the women would urge her to sip something. Mostly the women sat in silence, particularly Ishara, who could barely speak any Egyptian. Bekeh was conspicuously quiet, and Merneith discovered that she, too, was feeling ill. Penebui and Akshaka, however, whispered together as Akshaka timidly questioned Penebui about court matters and proper Egyptian. It was apparent that Penebui was enchanted by her new friend, and thrilled to find someone who would listen in rapture to her tales of court life. She appeared to take the girl's tutelage very seriously as well.

"I have learned only from the soldiers," Merneith opened her eyes at one point to watch Akshaka speak. The girl's smooth white skin blushed as she ducked her head and hunched her shoulders. "And they speak very rough. And also from their daughters, and some girls I have met at market." Then she looked up with a smile, "And Bey helped me practice before the dinner. I think he speaks very good, does he not?"

"Oh he does!" Penebui jumped at the chance to ask about Bey. "I wonder how did he learn to speak so well in such a short time? You are right, Akshaka, he does not speak like any of the servants. He speaks quite proper." Penebui's attempts to garner more information about Bey were thwarted, though, by the entrance of Bey himself into the shelter. He filled the doorway with his presence, casting the entire room into shadow.

"Hem-etj, ladies," he nodded at them. "We will be docking around sunset to prepare a meal. I hope being on solid ground again will help you to feel better."

That was enough to keep the two girls preoccupied as they speculated on where they would stop, what the meal would be, how long they would stop, would they camp, and so on. Merneith fell back asleep and hoped she would feel better on solid ground again.

Several hours later the women sat in a circle in a clearing of reeds by the waterfront. The soldiers sat in their own scattered circles nearby. Clouds had covered the moonlight and the stars, and the only lights were the small bowls of oil with a lit wick that rested in the centre of each circle, casting just enough light for the women to see one another, and the silhouettes of the men's hunched backs.

Merneith had barely eaten any of the simple dinner the men had prepared: charred fish freshly caught after landing, chunks of bread, and dried dates. She had, however, managed to sip a large cup of soupy barley beer which had left her feeling light-headed. There was a lull as the men were resting. They had been rowing the two large ships in shifts, but most had had little sleep. Merneith found herself wondering if Bey and Ebrium had slept at all since before the banquet.

Bekeh cleared her throat. "Now that I am feeling better, Akshaka, please do tell us more about yourself, and how you and Ishara came to be in Kemet." Merneith suppressed a snort. Clearly Bekeh was feeling well enough to interrogate Akshaka. Merneith knew Bekeh was fishing around to find out more about Bey.

Instead, though, Ishara leaned forward. "Ebrium and Bey are sons."

Akshaka whispered to Ishara in Eblaite, then turned to the other women. "I am sorry, what she means is that they are *like brothers*. I am sorry, these words we sometimes get mixed." Ishara said something in Eblaiti to Akshaka and the girl explained to them, "She would like me to tell you about Bey, if you would like to listen. I will translate. She understands some *met rem en kemet*, the language of your people, but only speaks very little." Ishara looked intently at Merneith, her eyes crinkling as she smiled and nodded. "My mother knows you do not know Bey, and maybe you do not trust him well. She… *we* want you to believe that he is a good man and that he will keep you safe."

Penebui jumped in. "Of course we want to hear! We know so very little about him." Merneith wasn't sure she wanted to hear anything else about the man who had, in the span of only a few days, seen her vulnerable so many times. She was sure that as soon as the opportunity presented itself, he would find some way to gloat that he had been correct to increase her security.

"Ishara is my sister. No! My mother, sorry." Akshaka blushed. "She was a servant in the house of Bey's family."

"What family?" Penebui leaned forward, eyes wide. "Was he not born into a pirate family? I assumed he grew up on the seas, raiding and traveling and pirating as a little boy."

Akshaka laughed, an adorable tinkling sound. Again, Merneith thought the girl was just *too* sweet and innocent, but she couldn't bring herself to dislike Akshaka for it. "No," Akshaka began again, periodically pausing to let Ishara speak before she translated it into her broken Egyptian. "Although he and Ebrium both behaved like pirates when they were younger, Bey's father was a merchant. His ships travelled the river near Ebla. He was very wealthy. My mother and father both worked for them in their house from the time Bey's older brother was born. Ebrium was born just after Bey. They grew up playing together all the time. Bey taught Ebrium all that he had learned in his studies when they were children, until Ebrium was old enough to begin work. Bey even taught me some when I was little, before he left Ebla." Akshaka looked down at her hands, which were twisting the fabric of her dress. Then she looked up and smiled. "But Bey was always best with languages. He speaks perfect in the Eblaite of both the noble class and the common people. He also speaks Sumerian, and the language of your people, and even some of the languages of the port cities near Ebla. When Bey was five years old, his father became ruler of Ebla."

"Wait, what?" Penebui cut in.

Merneith surprised herself by answering in a flat voice. "Ebla is different than Kemet. Their rulers are elected, not born into it. They rule for seven years." The old woman, Ishara, was smiling and nodding at her. Merneith found all this surreal. She had not given much thought to Bey's life before his arrival in Egypt, and had never imagined that he could actually have come from a wealthy, royal family. Never mind one that had been chosen to rule by people, not some distant, unknowable gods. She glanced over at Bekeh, who was listening with her chin tilted up, her narrowed eyes glittering in the glow of the oil wick.

"So Bey is a prince?" Penebui's mouth practically hung open, then she clapped her hands and grinned. "I *knew* he must have had some exciting adventures, but I never imagined he could be royalty!"

Akshaka bobbed her head. "But he had *too* much adventure, as you say. Bey was still in school…"

"School?" Penebui's brow furrowed.

"Yes." Akshaka went on to explain that in Ebla the wealthy families sent their sons to school. There, Bey "learned languages, and how to read the land, plants, insects, and about people's bodies." During this time Bey's father had twice been chosen to rule Ebla. Twelve years into his rule, two years before the end of his second term and the completion of Bey's studies, Bey's father grew ill and passed away. When he died, Bey's brother, Shem, received the shipping business and everything the family owned, because he was older and Bey was still in school. Shem also believed that, because his father died in the middle of a ruling term, he should also inherit control of Ebla. This resulted in a power struggle between Shem and the noblemen who disapproved of Shem. According to Akshaka, Shem "drank too much beer, and some even claimed he had dishonoured their daughters, promising them marriage and then, after he had…" Akshaka cast her eyes down, embarrassed. She cleared her throat and continued, "well, he did not marry them."

"The merchants refused to accept Shem as ruler. Then they refused to do business with him. He drank more and more, and spent more time at the uhm… the taverns, and the places where uhm…" Merneith could see the girl's white cheeks turn red, even in the dim light. "Where the women who sell themselves live. Shem refused to pay for Bey's education, or support their mother. My family had to leave Bey's household to find work, and my own father also passed away around this time. I was still very young and it was very hard for us. Bey and his mother were like our family. My mother helped raise Bey and Shem, and Ebrium and I grew up in their house." Akshaka looked over to her mother, whose eyes were shining with tears. The old lady reached out a wizened hand and squeezed Akshaka's forearm. Akshaka smiled and patted her mother's hand. Then she glanced over at the silhouette of the men sitting at a distance.

Akshaka cleared her throat and lowered her voice. "I do not like speak too much of this, Bey does not like to discuss his family, he is shy for others to know about it. I was only a child and hardly remember it myself."

"I understand, dear," Bekeh reached out and patted Akshaka's shoulder. "But you and your mother are correct, this is very helpful. Please continue."

Akshaka drew a deep breath and began again, as shadows from the oil wick flickered across her face. She pushed a strand of hair back behind her ear. "Bey and Ebrium were still just young men, and many, many people turned against his family then because of Shem. Even those very close to them. Nobody would help Bey and his mother. When they were wealthy, everyone loved them. When they were poor, nobody wanted to be near them. My mother says it was even harder for them than it was for us."

Merneith, Penebui, and Bekeh were completely still. Each had experienced loss; each had been left without a mother at a young age. But none of them had experienced total poverty and betrayal on top of loss.

Ishara prompted Akshaka to translate again by continuing the story in Eblaiti. "Then Bey's mother fell ill, also. He could not afford the medicine or the doctors to help her. He begged Shem for help, but Shem had already lost most of their money and their business. There was a big fight, and they almost killed each other one night at the tavern." Ishara passed a hand over face, as if to wipe away the memory, and Akshaka took another deep breath. "Ebrium tried to help, too, but we had no money either. Bey found a little work on the ships, travelling along the river, but by the time he made any money it was too late. His mother had died."

Akshaka had tears in her eyes and, glancing round the circle of women, Merneith could see that Penebui's wide eyes had filled also. Merneith felt a heaviness weigh on her chest, although the evening had begun to take on a dream-like quality, and she could not take her eyes off the flickering shadows dancing across Akshaka's face. The darkness around her swayed and rolled, as if she were still riding the waves of the Iteru.

Akshaka went on to tell them that her mother tried to find work, but it was difficult given that Akshaka was still too young to be left alone. Bey and Ebrium decided they had to leave Ebla in order to find work. The first few years, while the men were sailing the distant seas, were hard on everyone. Every day that went by without news caused the mother and daughter to fear the men might be dead. Sometimes months passed without hearing from them. Bey and Ebrium would try to send some form of currency when they could; little bits of gold, jewelry, metals, anything so the women could buy food or clothing. But sometimes they sent items that never arrived, while other times they had nothing of value to send. The distance was too great, and couriers too unreliable. Things improved, however, when the men finally took control of their own ship.

"And then they were captured here in Kemet by your men, Hem-etj, and were offered the chance to stay. Once they were settled here they arranged for us to make the journey to join them. And finally, my sister... I mean *my mother* was able to see her sons again." Akshaka smiled at Merneith and Ishara nodded and reached out to clasp Merneith's hands in her own gnarled ones. Merneith blushed. *She'd* had nothing to do with it, and felt more than a little embarrassed for having disliked Bey quite so much given the obvious protection, comfort and joy he'd tried to provide these two kind women with.

Penebui wrapped her arms around herself and smiled. "How amazing. And how wonderful it must have been to see them again after so many years."

Akshaka nodded. "It was wonderful! Ten years we had gone without seeing them. We feared we might never see them again. Or that one day," Akshaka's throat caught, "one day we would stop hearing from them and never know…" Then she smiled. "I was just a little girl when they left. To see them again was surely a blessing from the gods."

So there it is, Merneith thought. *He is not a kidnapping rapist. He married his best friend's sister. A girl that he helped support all her life and who grew up into a beautiful, devoted woman.* Although the story of Bey's loss, and efforts to support the peasant servants he'd grown up with, had softened Merneith towards Bey, they had also made her feels worse than before. *So he did marry for love, then.* It hit her that she could never have an affair with Bey. He had married this sweet young girl, and Merneith would be a horrible person to try and take him from her. She also recognized that she was jealous, and that made her want to crawl back into her corner in the dark shelter of the warship. *Ridiculous. What have I to be jealous of? I am queen of Kemet, the most wealthy of lands. I want for nothing in this world. Except maybe a comfortable bed for tonight instead of a sack of grain.* Merneith closed her eyes and felt as if she was falling, and the world swirling. *I am ill, and I have hardly eaten or slept.*

At that moment there was a rustling of the reeds and crackling of dried grass. A breathless voice called out, "Sekhrey? Sekhrey?" Several of the men rose as a scout came running into the shadowy camp.

"Here, Baal." Bey stepped towards the man, who spoke furiously in a low voice. Bey listened for a moment, then turned and snapped out, "Clear out! Take only what we need." Ebrium began calling out orders, and Bey made his way to the women who, unaccustomed to military discipline, were still sitting and looking at each other in surprise.

Bey reached Merneith and, grabbing her upper arm, hauled her to her feet. "What do you think…" She began to scold him, but he cut her off.

"On the ships, now! We have been followed, and there are more of them than us. We cannot fight them on land. All of you, quickly." The other women jumped to their feet and someone kicked over the bowl of oil, extinguishing the flame and leaving them to adjust to the darkness even as Bey pushed them towards the ships.

It was only moments before they launched again, and this time Merneith's nausea was coupled with fear and the furious pounding of her heart. The women huddled in a tense jumble in the shelter, listening to the sounds of swords clanking and the oars hitting the water. Then came an endless silence. Merneith's limbs stiffened, then turned prickly, then numb. A couple of times her head nodded forward as if she were about to fall asleep, but she was too uncomfortable, her adrenaline was running too fast, and her stomach too tumultuous. It felt like days since Bey had ordered them into the dark shelter. *Perhaps the danger has passed?* Impatient to know what was happening and in need of air, Merneith pushed herself up and stumbled towards the door.

"Mer, get back here!" Bekeh called to her.

Merneith stepped out onto the deck and looked around. With no moon to see by, everything was shrouded in such thick blackness that she barely saw the men rowing the boat, the men hunched along the railings with bows and arrows at the ready, or the others tucked between the benches, holding up enormous, man-sized wood-framed shields with leather hide stretched across them. Never in her life had she experienced such an absence of light. The scene had an eerie quality to it, and the murkiness a palpable presence that weighed heavy on the ship. Merneith stretched a hand out over the nearby railing to prove to herself that it was, in fact, only air that surrounded the ship and not some malevolent, pulsating physical force.

"Mer, get in here," Bekeh hissed from the doorway of the shelter. Bey, it turned out, was crouched nearby, and saw her.

"Hem-etj, get down." He ordered, launching himself up from his hunched position to lunge towards her.

All at once, a soughing sounded in the air and Merneith looked up. A volley of arrows streaked through the darkness, their silver points like small insects cutting through the darkness. Blindly, the arrows struck targets at random and Merneith felt a searing pain blaze through her shoulder. Once again she felt the sensation of falling and the world swirling. This time she succumbed to it, and felt wet warmth swallow her.

Chapter 10 - Sickness

Bey saw an arrow skim Merneith's shoulder and her body jerk just as she tipped sideways over the edge of the boat. Bey covered the distance to the ship's railing in two steps and leapt over after her. The river's warm, dark waters washed over his head. He bobbed up and scanned the greeny-black waters around him. *Damn the clouds*, Bey could hardly see a thing. Then he heard a splash to his right and he swam towards it. *Please, Dagon, do not let it be a crocodile or a hippopotamus*. He hoped that the dangerous beasts of the river had not yet been alerted to the potential feast that his and the queen's bodies would offer them.

A wet *thwack* sounded behind him, indicating an arrow had just missed him. The enemies' arrows must be shot at random, as there was no way they could see their targets in the dark. Bey could just make out the ships' black silhouettes against the dark grey sky. Bey, however, was being carried downstream by the current while the enemy ships, and the queen's warships, were stroking upstream to the south. At least the darkness that made it so impossible for him to see the queen at least provided them both cover from the enemy.

Bey heard another splash, closer this time, and he stroked harder. Nearing the noise, he thought he glimpsed an outstretched arm sink under the water's inky surface. Bey took in a deep breath and dipped under the murky waters, arms outstretched. For a moment, he waved his sightless, outstretched arms and then *there!* He felt something soft under his fingers. He grabbed hold of a limb and dragged Merneith upwards. He wrapped an arm around her waist, pulling her to him as he kicked his legs, moving towards the west bank of the great river. Merneith's head rested over his shoulder, and she coughed and sputtered against his back. He couldn't stop. He had to get to the shore before the enemy realized they were nearby, and before they encountered any of the river's murderous beasts.

After a few minutes of hard swimming, Bey felt his feet touch soft ground. Hoisting Merneith up further over his shoulder, Bey stumbled onto the sandy, reedy banks of the river. Looking up along the river, he could just see the shadows of the warring ships shrinking in the distance. He hoped that someone had seen him and Merneith go overboard, for he knew that if Ebrium survived, he at least would be looking for them as soon as he was able.

Merneith wasn't making noise anymore beyond a few soft moans and for now he wanted to get her somewhere safe in order to check her wounds. Bey stumbled along the sandy bank, the sharp reeds jagged against his bare feet. He'd lost his sandals in the river. He didn't want to go too far inland, and make it impossible for the guard to find them later, but he wanted to get far enough that it would be difficult for the enemy to readily see them.

After what felt like some time with nothing in sight but reeds and the odd tree, and nothing of use for shelter, Bey paused to scan the darkness. Suddenly, a break appeared in the clouds overhead, casting a small sliver of moonlight over the treeline and tall reeds. Off a little ways to the west and a bit further south, Bey saw what appeared to be a small shack. He shifted Merneith on his shoulder, switching sides. He had little else in the way of options. He couldn't see well enough in the darkness and had nothing dry or clean to use to administer to the gash on her shoulder. He had to get her to a proper shelter.

Bey approached the hut with caution. He lay Mernieth down in a bed of tall reeds, and went forward to investigate. He tried to devise a story to explain what they were doing out in the middle of the night, half-drowned and arrow-shot. *Lovers out for a late night stroll? She slipped in the water? Sister and brother robbed on their way home from the market? Sleepwalking?* All sounded ridiculous. Nevermind that Bey knew his own appearance, his tattoos, his eyes, his size, all would attract attention. It was unlikely the queen would be recognized by some fishermen or farmers in the middle of nowhere, but her refined beauty could hardly go unnoticed.

Bey rounded the small, mud-brick hut. There was only one small, narrow window by the front door. He peeked his head around the corner to peer into the hut. It was too dark to see anything. Bey growled low in frustration. Left without options, he finally just knocked on the gnarled wooden door. *Nothing.* He knocked again. *Still nothing.* Bey pulled on the handle, and the door swung open. He drew the door open wide to let in the sliver of moonlight and poked his head in. In the gloom he could make out a small, low, empty bed pushed against one wall, and a crudely-fashioned table. *No one home.* Bey breathed a sigh of relief.

He trotted back to the place he'd lain Merneith down and scooped her up into his arms. Her head lolled against his chest, her face coming close to his neck. She mumbled, "Mmmm… shoulder…"

"I know. We are almost there." Bey carried her through the door of the hut and laid her out on the bed, a low wood frame covered with a small pad of linen stuffed with rags. Rummaging around in the darkness, he found a bowl of oil with a wick, and struck a light. Shadows flickered through the tiny, one-room shack. He was able to find a scarf on top of a stack of clothing, and a jug of water in the far corner. These he set on the ground beside the low bed, and he pulled over a stool to sit on. He could feel his adrenaline begin to wane and exhaustion sweeping over him but he ignored it, as he had had to do so many times over the years.

Bey pressed two fingers to Merneith's neck, checking to ensure her pulse was still strong. *At least she is unconscious.* She wouldn't feel any pain as he jostled her around. *Or get herself into more trouble, thanks be to Dagon and Baal.* He couldn't help but notice the irony of how much easier she was to protect when she was unconscious.

By the dim light he could see a spreading blood stain on the shoulder of her light coloured dress. He reached a finger into the arrow hole in the dress and ripped open the collar and sleeve, revealing the soft skin of her collarbone. The wet, now see-through dress clung provocatively to her curves, and even in the low light the dark tips of her breasts were visible through the white fabric, rising and falling with each breath. Bey had to avert his eyes to focus on the task at hand. He knew there was probably already a special place for him in the underworld for all his previous sins. Now he could add getting turned on by an unconscious woman in the midst of a life-threatening situation to the list.

Bey tore the clean scarf he'd found in half. One half he doused with water, dabbing at the deep gash in Merneith's shoulder. Once sufficiently clean, he used the other half to wrap up under her arm and around her shoulder, tying it into a knot. He unpeeled the wet bandages that still covered her skimmed palms from the tiger attack. These scratches seemed to be healing well, and Bey decided it best to leave them uncovered for the night. He hated to leave Merneith sleeping in a wet dress, but to undress her himself would be unforgivable, even if it were in her best interest. *She'd probably try to tear my head off if I got her naked.* He couldn't help but smile at the thought of her naked and fighting like a wildcat.

Bey pulled a blanket up over Merneith. Thoroughly drained and reasonably confident that the enemy ships hadn't seen them go overboard, and that they were therefore safe, he threw himself down on a reed mat and fell unconscious.

Bey woke to the warmth of the sun streaming on his face. Cracking his eyes open in increments, he looked out the narrow window in the wall of the small mud brick hut. He could see the branches of a sycamore tree swaying in the late morning breeze. He turned his head to the left and looked at Merneith on the other side of the room. She was curled up on a low, wood-framed bed covered with a sleeping mat, her kinky black hair spread out behind her like a sensual cape. He caught himself wondering what it would be like to wake up with her head on his chest with that hair draped all around them, down the curves of her naked back, and how it would feel to entwine his fingers in those soft curls, letting the thick coils slide through his hands like ribbons of black velvet as he tugged her head back to press her mouth with his.

She will never let that happen, so do not waste your time thinking about it. But it was too late. He bit back a groan at the aching tightness that spread through his groin and gave a soft snort instead. *Damn the gods and their sick irony. Somewhere Dagon is up there laughing at me and my futile existence.*

He held up his hands, palms facing him, and opened and closed them. His hands were so hardened from years at sea that there were hardly any new callouses from the four hours spent at the oars yesterday. *Well that's something,* he gave himself sarcastic praise. *At least being back at a royal court hasn't made me soft yet.* He raked his hands through his hair, lacing them behind his head and laying back while flexing his biceps to assess the extent of the damage the last couple of days of non-stop activity had done. *Stiff and sore, but not too bad.*

Bey had always made it a point to take his turn rowing whenever he was captaining a ship to prevent any resentment amongst the men. While it had the positive effect of preventing rebellion, something that was always a possibility on a pirate ship full of mercenaries and raiders, it was also Bey's way of proving to himself that he was not like his brother, Shem. Although it had been unintended, he realized that his willingness to labour amongst the men was one of the reasons some of the *sephat* militias supported him. They knew him. He had toiled amongst them as one of their own and now they wanted him to toil for them on the throne.

He took a moment to reflect on last night's events, and to determine the next course of action. Thank the gods, at least, that he had seen Merneith fall overboard as arrows rained down on their warships, and that he'd been able to find her in the inky blackness of the Iteru. Thinking about it evoked anger and frustration that he'd been too busy to acknowledge last night. He was furious with Merneith for being on the deck and putting herself in harm's way, and furious with himself for not having tied the damned woman down in the shelter of the warship in the first place. *I should have known she wouldn't listen for long.*

He was aggravated that the only thing he could do was take Merneith ashore and hope that his men had survived. *And the women, especially Akshaka and Penebui.* He had to fight back a wave of ineffectual rage at the thought of what could happen to the two young girls if they were captured. He knew what mercenaries liked to do with pretty female plunder. Not only that, but with their fair skin and unusual eyes, they'd both fetch quite a sum at the slave markets once their captors had finished with the girls. *If there was anything left to sell...*

But he couldn't do anything about that right now. He had to deal with the situation he was currently in. He rolled to his feet, stretching his sore and tired muscles, and pitching his broad shoulders to work out the snarls from a night of sleeping on the floor. He set about taking stock of their resources. Given the two curved crosiers hanging on the wall, Bey presumed they were in some shepherd's home, and the man must have taken his flock to the markets for shearing, usually a week-long process. Bey wondered how long it would be until the man came back. He intended for them to begin travelling as soon as possible, but he didn't want things to be complicated by the peasant's return.

In a corner of the shack, he discovered a latched wooden grating in the floor and, opening it, found a small storage space dug about two feet down into the dry earth. Rooting around, he was pleased to find a few sacks of lentils and grains, and a couple of jugs of water and wine.

As he was shuffling things around in the hut, Merneith stirred. He poured a small bowl of water for her to sip from and set it beside her then continued to look around. There were two men's full length robes made of coarse linen, and a few scarves, both white and black, folded in a heap. *If I need to disguise the queen, or myself, those could be useful. We cannot sit here waiting for help to come. We will need to start walking south...*

His thoughts were interrupted by a low moan. He turned and saw that Merneith was trying to rise, but was having difficulty. She pulled herself up to a sitting position, looking bleary-eyed at her bare shoulder, and the strip of fabric crudely knotted around it. Merneith fingered the fabric bandage then looked up and around her.

"Good morning," he nodded when her eyes fell upon him. But instead of the caustic response he'd expected, she wore a confused expression.

"So it has happened," she whispered in a voice tinged with awe.

"What has happened?"

"Where is my father, the fishmonger? Did your ship just land?" Merneith seemed to be having a hard time keeping her eyes open. She put her palm up to her forehead, rested it there for a moment, then pushed back her hair, running her hand down the length of it.

"Hem-etj, you must be confused. We were attacked last night. You were shot and fell off the boat." He took a step toward her.

"Hem-etj," she looked out the window, repeating the word as if she were trying it out for the first time. "So it was just another dream. You are not just a sailor." Bey was struck by the sadness in her voice, but couldn't fathom what she was thinking. *Was she dreaming of me?*

"Hem-etj, please drink some water. I will make some food. Did you eat last evening?"

She just looked at him with a blank expression then lay back down on her side.

Concerned, Bey knelt beside her and pulled her upright into a sitting position, but she looked right through him. "Here, drink something." He lifted the bowl to her lips and she sipped some, but then batted it away.

"I am so tired. Please ask them to stop pestering me. I do not wish to speak to anyone today." She waved a hand in dismissal. "Tell Atab perhaps I will receive him tomorrow."

Cradling her in one arm, Bey buried a hand in her thick, dark curls, feeling along her skull for bumps. She muttered vague protests that he ignored. On the back of her head and to the right he felt a small lump. He suspected that she might have hit her head when she'd fallen overboard. Between that and the sickness that she'd experienced the day before on the ship, as well as the arrow wound, it was not surprising that she was not making sense.

Whatever the cause, she'd need rest and nourishment. There was no way they could travel with Merneith like this and no hope of catching up with the warships. They'd have to wait until she'd recovered enough to travel.

He wanted to check the gash on her shoulder. He propped her up in the crook of his arm and the ripped shoulder of her dress flapped open, revealing the hollow of smooth olivine skin below her clavicle. Bey tried not to look down at the top of the soft mound of her breast swelling up as she breathed in, and focused on untying the scrap of fabric from last night. Luckily, the wound did not appear to be worse off, and he was maneuvering the clean scarf up under her arm and around her shoulder when Merneith slumped to the side, against his chest, with her head cradled on his shoulder. He could feel her breath against his neck and the tantalizing scent of her hair wafted up to him. He recalled how good she'd felt pressed against him on the boat the day before when she'd been ill and he'd had to walk her back to the shelter. Just once, he thought, he'd like to know what it would feel like to have her conscious and fully alert when she was in his arms.

She reached out and placed a hand on his bare chest. He froze. *What now?* He looked down at her hand as she began to skim her fingertips along the thick dark lines of the tattoo that wrapped around the battle hardened muscles of his chest, shoulder, and back. She seemed intent on scrutinizing it, and Bey himself was fixated by the sight of her hand tracing along his chest. He felt a stirring below his abdomen.

After years at sea and too much time spent in dirty port cities, he was tired of the types of women who followed the militias, and he certainly wasn't interested in embroiling himself in any scandals, or raising a woman's expectations. He had little to offer, and after what had happened to him in Ebla, he had little faith in a woman's fidelity to a man without means. Since leaving Ebla he hadn't met a woman that held his interest for more than a night or two, and he never led them to believe he could offer more than a brief encounter. But now Merneith's touch sent all his nerve endings jangling into action. He grabbed her hand in his to still her painful caress and drew in a ragged breath.

Not looking up from the lines and creatures embedded in his skin, Merneith said, "I have been wondering where this came from. I have never seen any like it."

Her comment caught Bey by surprise, and he chuckled. "When Ebrium and I left Ebla we were young and stupid. We met a man from the far north, farther north than I have ever been, who was covered in scenes like these. He was an artist, and he told us in his land it was believed that the markings would help people find one another in the afterlife. We had been very far from Ebla for years by this point, and thought never to see Ishara and Akshaka again." Bey pursed his lips in a tight smile. "We hoped that one day, when we had all departed this world, they might find us elsewhere by the markings on our skin."

At the mention of Akshaka, Merneith snatched her hand from his grip as if it had passed through a flame, and sat upright. She turned her back to him, laid down, and pulled the blanket over herself. He was left to try to disentangle her odd behavior and his own conflicting feelings.

Bey set about starting a small fire in the little clay stove in the corner of the room in order to boil up a mash of grains and lentils. Once done, he propped Merneith up again and urged her to eat. Mercifully, she was much more compliant in her present state and only offered weak protests as he fed her scoops of mash and sips of water. When he felt she had eaten a sufficient amount, he laid her back down.

Throughout the day Merneith slipped in and out of consciousness while Bey paced the hut. At times she slept soundly, and at others she muttered to herself. "I wish they would stop following me. Can I not just be alone?" At one point, when he urged her to sip more water, she waved him away and murmured, "Gods take Wadj. He cannot continue like this."

Bey drew in a sharp breath. "Continue like what, Hem-etj? What do you mean?"

"Bekeh is right. He is mad. I do fear…" here she trailed off and although Bey asked her what she was afraid of, he got no answer.

"I will not do it," she said another time. "I will not. I cannot just give myself up to that man." Bey had been standing by the window, musing, and couldn't help but draw closer. *What man?*

"There must be some other way, Mewet," she mumbled. "I cannot just open my legs… even if it means the end of us. Or of Kemet … even if I wanted to… even if he is a prince."

Bey felt as if a wave of ice cold sea water had washed over him. *Was this what the older women were up to the other night with Batr and Makae? Were they plotting something involving Sar Atab? Were they attempting to lure Batr and Makae away from Merneith's room so Atab could slip in?*

He stood in the middle of the hut, besieged by conflicting emotions and thoughts that churned around him like frothing waves. The thought of that filthy Sumerian climbing on top of Merneith caused his gut to twist, and he clenched his fists. He'd kill the bastard before he'd let him touch her. He needed air. Bey stepped outside, shutting the door behind him.

Chapter 11 – Misunderstandings

Merneith awoke shortly before sunset. Alone in the strange hut, she took a moment to get her bearings. The only thing she recalled with any clarity was once again dreaming of being a fishmonger's daughter. She had woken up to discover that, in fact, she had been shot and Bey had once again saved her. Her body seemed to recollect more than her mind did and, unbidden, it summoned up a rapid series of sensations from her sickness-induced haze. Her cheek tingled from the feel of Bey's smooth, hard chest as she had rested her head against it. The spicy, cedar scent of his skin filled her nostrils with its delicious, warm and comforting aroma and she knew at some point her lips, as if possessed of a mind of their own, had almost pressed themselves against the hollow at the base of his neck. Her body ached as the tips of her fingers recalled the feel of the thick black ridges of his tattoos beneath them.

What is wrong with you?! She raged at herself. *Get up, you stupid woman. There are much more important things to do than thinking about something you cannot have.* As if to affirm it to herself, she added, *Not that you wanted it in the first place.*

She pushed herself to a standing position. She was definitely a bit woozy, but at least she was clear-minded. This was the first time she'd ever been inside a peasant home, until now having only seen them from a distance as she traveled along the Iteru, or as she was carried in her litter through the streets from various palaces to temples. She'd always known that she'd lived a sheltered life of luxury, that others couldn't possibly live the same way she did, but hadn't really considered to what extent their modes of living were different. She marveled at the humble hut. *What little people really need to survive, but shouldn't there be more to life than just survival? Shouldn't there be happiness, also?* She couldn't help but feel that, in spite of poverty, some people were more at liberty to find happiness than she. Despite the luxury and comfort she lived in, she felt as if she had spent her life merely surviving, her greatest joy being that there was no war, or that Wadj had *not yet* destroyed Kemet.

Nearby, Bey had left a large bowl of water resting on top of a clean black robe, which she assumed were meant for her. She glanced out the window to make sure Bey wasn't nearby, then took the opportunity to freshen up and change her robe for the clean one. Sipping from a small bowl of water, an image came to mind of Bey holding her upright, and feeding her. *So he had taken care of me when I was ill.* A dull ache settled in to the pit of her stomach, and this time it wasn't of the pleasurable sort. In fact, realizing that Bey had seen her vulnerable *yet again*, the ache turned to anger. *How can this keep happening? He will find a way to use this against me, somehow. I must put a stop to this.* With that thought in mind, Merneith pushed open the door to the hut.

She stepped outside into the gold-tinged streaks of the setting sun. The hut stood in a small clearing, surrounded by tall, lush reeds and date palm trees. Off to the right the empty desert stretched out, a blank sea of beige sand running to meet the setting sun. To the left, a shadowy pathway led down through the reeds to the bank of the Iteru. Out of this gloom Bey emerged, tying up his white shenti. His thick dark hair was wet, hanging around his face in damp waves. Water dripped down over the damp ridges of his molded chest.

As he approached he gave a slight nod. "Hem-etj, I am glad to see you are up."

"Sekhrey, I demand to know what is happening. Where are Penebui and Bekeh?" Merneith realized it sounded childish and demanding as soon as she said it, but she couldn't help herself. She'd been unnerved by the sight of him wet and dripping, the setting sun causing the drops of water to glitter on his brown skin, looking unbearably powerful, erotic, foreign, rough, something totally unfamiliar in her world. It called to mind the first time she'd seen him in the crowd in the palace courtyard, how her skin had prickled and her body had craved things she thought it had long since given up hope of having. *Get a hold of yourself. He is just a man, like any other.*

Bey ran a hand through his hair, causing more water to drip down the thick muscles of his smooth, sun-darkened skin, blowing out a soft snort as he raised his eyebrows slightly and his lips twitched. "I am also glad to see that you are feeling back to your normal self."

"How dare you mock me?" Merneith was making things worse and she knew it.

Bey cupped his palm under his chin, scrubbing the dark stubble that had grown overnight along his jawline. That stubble made him look more rugged, wild, and masculine. He drew his lips in, moistening them, then slowly released them. He pursed them in a small smile that Merneith couldn't help but find carnal. She got the sense he was taking his time, just to frustrate and anger her. It was working.

Finally, he gave a slight bow that Merneith felt was no less mocking than his previous comment. He looked up at her through a lock of dripping hair and his eyes bore into hers as he said, "Hem-etj, let us have something to eat. There is much to discuss."

Bey and Merneith sat on two logs in the clearing outside the hut around a small fire that Bey had built. The fire lit up their faces with a red glow, casting long shadows that stretched out into the reeds and the darkness of the trees behind them. The sky was clear and the moon was almost full, scattering a silvery light on to the endless desert sands to the east. The two had finished eating and Merneith was well into her third bowl full of wine, feeling the need to fortify herself after a hellish couple of days.

While they were eating, Bey had given Merneith an account of what he had seen happen last night. Then he told her his plan for them to begin walking south, to Ta-senet, where the warships had been headed. Ta-senet had a large garrison, one of the few in Egypt. There they could wait while they sent runners out to the *sephat* militias to come and join them, escorting Merneith back to Thinis and serving as a small personal army of sorts. And, he hoped, if all was well the guard would have also escaped whoever it was that had attacked them, and they would be waiting there along with the women.

Based on her reaction to his story at the banquet about the lone queen of Ebla who ruled without a king, and her murmurings while sick, Bey felt confident that she was not unaware of her situation, or the potential harm Wadj could bring to Kemet. Leaning forward with his elbows resting on his knees, he related almost all he had heard from his spies about the anti-Pharaoh sentiments in the south of Egypt, and how he was assured that Merneith had the support of most of the southern *sephats*. He chose to leave out the additional information that some, in fact, had expressed their preference for him as a potential usurper to the throne. Luckily, she listened without argument or snide remarks while he told her that Wadj was causing a division amongst the sephats, and that there were rumours of rebellion and a desire for her to rule instead of Wadj. He even told her of his suspicions that the attack on her was a direct result of Wadj's actions, if not even perpetrated by him. Perhaps the attackers had been a disgruntled *sephat*, angry that Wadj had recently raised their taxes and slighted their priests. Perhaps they had even been mercenaries hired by Wadj.

"Hem-etj, it would be safer for you, and the *sephats* in the south, if Wadj did not know you suspect him, or have cause to blame him for this."

"Of course I know that." She snapped. She stood and began to pace.

Bey had yet to tell her about the concerns of the *sephat* militias regarding Sar Atab, and their fear that Atab intended to manipulate the pharaoh into declaring war on Sumeria. While he believed she was not loyal to the Pharaoh, he was unsure about her feelings towards the Atab, and finding out how she felt about the Sumerian prince was the key to helping her. If she had loyalties to Atab, then there would be little he could do to prevent the *sephats* from turning against her. *Turning to whom, then? Me?* He shook his head.

As she continued to pace, Merneith blew out an exasperated breath. "I know this. I *knew* this all. Wadj *is* mad, and he is driving Kemet to ruin. All the work my great-grandfather did to bring the north and south of Kemet together will be destroyed under him. But what am *I* to do?" She turned abruptly and stumbled.

Bey jumped up and grabbed her arm to steady her. She jerked her wrist from his grasp.

"No!" She blurted out. Bey put his hands up and took a step back, giving her space even as he shook his head in admiration of her stubborn nature. He hoped the shadows covered his smile, lest she accuse him of mocking her again. Then he steeled himself for what he was about to say.

"Hem-etj, you have options."

"Such as?" She whipped her head around to glare at him in the gloom.

"To begin with, you need not give yourself to a man such as Atab to secure your position." The words dropped from him like boulders into the Iteru, and he saw shock and recognition register on her face. Then she reacted.

"*Ebien behau!*" She hissed, calling him a wretched coward as she swung her right hand up to strike him. Bey caught her wrist just before it connected. "Have you been spying on me?!" She brought her other hand up and smacked him hard on the chest. He pinned that hand to his chest with his own palm, preventing her from pulling it away and hitting him again. Their chests were nearly touching as she heaved and wriggled in his gentle, yet unyielding, grip.

"With all due respect, Hem-etj, I am not a slave to be beaten at your whim. And if you keep this up, you will open the wound in your shoulder." He knew it was awful of him, but he was smiling. He could feel the sting of desire bristling the hairs on his arms and a tightness in his groin. *Oh you are a bastard for getting off on this.* But he couldn't help it. She was stunning in her fury, dark eyes blazing, her thick black curls flowing down her back and shoulders.

"Let me go!" She spat the words out, fisting her hand against his chest. She kicked him in the shin with one bare foot, having left her still-damp sandals inside.

Bey barked out a laugh and released her. She gave him a withering look but didn't step away.

He snorted. "I did not spy on you, *Hem-etj.*" Then, unable to keep the bitterness out of his voice, he grimaced and said, "I overhead you in your sleep today talking about opening your legs to a prince."

He watched as her lips parted and her eyes widened. Bey could feel his gut twist. He knew it was completely impractical to feel jealousy, but since he'd overheard Merneith talking about Atab he'd had to struggle to maintain his composure. He knew he could have had this conversation with her in a more tactful fashion, but he'd had a hard time not breaking his knuckles on the mud brick walls whenever he thought of her under Atab, his hips thrusting at her in the same way he'd probably done with multiple women he'd pushed himself on. Some part of him wanted to punish Merneith for putting that image in his head, and for thinking of sleeping with Atab, hell for possibly even *wanting* to. He'd wondered if she was doing it because she thought it would help protect her somehow. He had met plenty of women over the years who sold their bodies to men for money or survival. He knew well enough that some women sold their bodies in marriage for the sake of comfort. He'd never judged, he knew women had a harder lot in life than men. He just didn't like to think that Merneith could have reason to be one of them.

Merneith felt her body sag when Bey told her he'd overheard her talking about a prince, her breath knocked out of her by the revelation that *he knew.* She was overwhelmed with emotion. She was exhausted, injured, weary from wine, arguing, the stress of worrying about Penebui and Bekeh, and whatever Wadj was planning along with the possibility of an uprising. The realization that she had been talking in her sleep scared her, and she feared what else she might have revealed to this man who already knew too much about her. And he knew more than enough to drive her mad with anger, even though she'd only known him a few short days.

She felt tears well up in her eyes and her throat clenched as she dragged in a ragged breath. She didn't have the strength to keep fighting tonight, and she was furious with herself for it.

"I was not speaking of Atab," she whispered, looking past Bey to the fire flickering behind him.

Bey narrowed his eyes as he leaned his head towards her. "What did you say?"

She cleared her throat and turned her glistening eyes up to lock on Bey's penetrating gaze. "I was not speaking of Atab. I was speaking of *you*." She looked away as a tear slid out over her eyelid. She quickly dashed it off her cheek.

Bey reared his head back, as if she really had slapped him this time. "Me?" He rasped. His lotus-green eyes a dark, forest green in the moonlight. "But you were speaking of a prince."

Merneith bit her lip hard to get control of her voice. She couldn't bring herself to look at him. "Akshaka told me about your father."

Bey growled. "I should have known better than to leave you women alone together."

Merneith's anger flared and she snapped her head up, glaring at him. "Why not? Why should I not know the history of the man charged with my life? You cannot blame your wife for wanting me to trust you."

"My what?!" Bey twitched his head to the side, furrowing his brows.

"Your wife!" Merneith clenched her fists. "By the gods, will you make me repeat every single embarrassing thing I say, as if it is not hard enough the first time around?"

Bey threw his head back and laughed, infuriating Merneith and leaving her feeling as if she'd completely missed something.

"What?!" She clenched her fists and stamped her bare foot into the sand. If she wasn't so angry she'd almost cry again in frustration.

With a bitter chuckle, Bey looked down at Merneith. "Hem-etj, the only woman who ever came close to claiming that title made the very choice that you once said you could not understand."

She narrowed her eyes and shook her head. She was still confused.

Bey's mouth quirked upwards. "Ahhh, I see. Akshaka told you *some* of the story, but not all. And let me guess, she mixed up the words *brother, son,* and *husband?*"

Merneith felt her lips part as she sucked in a sharp breath. *Of course. The girl herself had said she got those words confused. I just assumed…*

Bey nodded, raising an eyebrow. "She always mistakes them."

Merneith drew in a deep breath, trying to fight down the tingling lightness that had begun to spread up from the pit of her stomach, and across her chest, hardening her nipples, and running down her arms. She felt a throbbing take up residence in her head, and sensed, as if from a distance, that her body was swaying as it had yesterday when she was ill. *This is all a bit much, now, is it not?* She heard herself mumble, "So there is no wife now…" She looked up into Bey's probing green eyes and perceived the hardness in them soften.

He took a step closer to her, closing the gap between them. "No," his voice was a low rumble, "there has *never been* a wife."

Merneith felt the world reel around her and put out a hand to steady herself. Bey reached out and caught her arms. "Hem-etj, you are still ill. You should go back to sleep." Bey put Merneith's arm over his shoulder as he wrapped a hand around her waist.

"No, no, NO!" Merneith twisted in his arms. With his hand still encircling the soft curve of her waist, she pressed the palms of her hands against his chest, splaying her fingers out. "Cannot a woman for one minute wish her circumstances to be different? Forget for a night that the pharaoh may bring Kemet to ruin tomorrow and there is nothing I can do to stop him? Cannot I wish for one moment that I were not queen, that my life were mine to control, or that I were free to choose what man I wanted?" She pushed against him but he kept her within the circle of his arm.

The flickering fire reflected off her eyes, shimmering with unspilled tears, as she looked up at him with a stubborn frown on her full lips. Her breasts were heaving, so close his skin prickled in anticipation of their touch. She was so perfectly exquisite in her rage, so passionate and wild. Bey clenched the arm that was wrapped around her, pulling her to him, and crushed her lips with his. *Damn the gods,* he groaned inwardly, *how is a man supposed to take that and walk away? Damn Baal and Ishtar and Ra and all the others, and damn this woman for being so impossible to resist. She will be the ruin of both of us.*

Merneith's smooth lips parted as he pressed his tongue roughly against them, pushing through them, wanting to taste every bit of her as the warmth of her mouth opened to him. She tensed and pushed against his chest, but he drew her closer to him, smashing her breasts against him as he sucked in her full bottom lip. He felt her body begin to press against him of her own volition and he wrapped his hands around the soft curves of her waist, running one up her side to her small, perfectly round breasts, so accessible through her thin robe.

Merneith gasped and quivered as Bey's right hand brushed the side of her left breast. *By the gods* the woman made him hard. *You have to stop. Stop now, before it is too late.* But he just couldn't help running his thumb over her nipple through the thin linen as he kissed her and she gasped against his mouth, her trembling reaching near alarming peaks. She moaned as he drew in her lower lip. His left hand ran down her side, over her hip, digging his fingers into that voluptuous curve. He wanted so badly to grab a hold of her firm, rounded behind and grind himself against her, but the small shred of pride he was hanging on to held him back.

Merneith braced her hands on Bey's chiseled chest and thrust herself back a step, breaking away from his grip.

"Bey, I…" shaking her head, she drew in a deep shaky breath before continuing. "I have never been… that is, I have never lain with a man." She breathed out in a rush, turning her head and looking away, her jaw tensing. Tears welled up in her eyes again, iridescent in the moonlight.

Bey's hands and jaw dropped simultaneously. "But the pharaoh? You are married." *As if she didn't know that!* But he was at a loss as to what to say. Then Bey recalled the rumours about the Pharaoh's unusual sexual preferences, and how he and Ebrium had commented on it only a few short days ago. In his travels Bey had met men who preferred the company of other men, and he cared not what their preferences were, but the rumours of the Pharaoh did not involve *men* so much as *young boys*. Bey felt a sudden rush of revulsion towards the pharaoh wash over him that made him feel ugly and violent. He made a note to have his spies investigate further.

Merneith steadfastly stared out in the direction of the Iteru. "Wadj has never once come to me in that way. No man has. I never really wanted one to. Until…" She cleared her throat.

Bey rubbed the back of his neck with his hand, trying to stop his jaw from clenching painfully. *The gods all must be finding this absurdly funny.* Bey had fantasized about tearing this woman's clothes off, throwing her on a bed and driving his raging hard-on into her, only to find that she's never been so much as *touched* by a man? He had never been with a woman who had never been with a man, and was surprised to find himself nervous at the prospect. God forbid he hurt her. *Regardless, it could destroy us both. If she changed her mind… if we were found out… we could both be killed… and even if we were not, what could possibly come of it?*

But still he reached out and caught her around the waist, drawing her to him as he looked down at her. He couldn't help himself. Seeing her vulnerable in the midst of all her wild fierceness made him feel raw and torn inside. "I have thought of you more often than I care to confess, more than I have any right to. I cannot fathom that any man would not want to lay with you…" Bey trailed off as his own breathing became ragged and his voice hoarse with the effort to maintain control. "Nothing good can come of this, you must know this."

Looking up into his eyes through her long, thick lashes as he stood powerless to stop her, Merneith slowly and deliberately ran her hand up the side of his neck, sliding it around to the back of his head and up into his thick, wavy hair where she entwined her fingers.

"Bey," she murmured, "I know this. I live every day with the weight of how my actions affect the lives of those around me. I am aware of what I am doing. For all I know, Ra may stop the sun from rising tomorrow and the world will come to an end, Kemet may lay in ruin in a few short days, my assassins may succeed and I may die. If that happens, at least I will have felt something in my life other than fear, sadness, and loneliness. I want to feel how a woman feels when she is with a man she wants. Let us forget tomorrow, just for tonight."

Bey hesitated for only a second before he scooped her up and carried her into the hut, laying her down on the bed against the wall. He knew there was no way he could bring himself to hurt her by entering her for the first time when she'd been ill, emotional, and drinking. She would come to her senses tomorrow and hate him for taking advantage of her and he'd be no better than men like Wadj or Sar Atab. No, instead he would satisfy her needs, and his own would have to wait. He would do his best to ensure that tomorrow, when she woke, her memories of the evening would be more than pleasant, and obliterate any thought of Atab, or any other man for that matter.

Merneith let her breath out in a long sigh as Bey settled himself over her on his knees and elbows, taking his time to lick, suck and nibble on her lips. He thrilled at the sound of her quickening breath. As he trailed his lips along her jaw he paused to let her feel his breath on her neck, enjoying the sight and feel of her squirming beneath him, rubbing her legs together and trying to arch her back to bring her breasts up to his chest. He pulled back an inch, he didn't want to give her what she wanted yet. He wanted her to feel the exquisite, excruciating pain of desire, of longing that would help to bring her to the height of pleasure he planned to take her to.

When Bey finally flicked his tongue along her neck she let out a gasp and a distressed moan. He brought his lips up near her ear, hovering a hair's breadth from touching her and breathed, "I am sorry, *nebet-i*, my lady," he whispered, "but you must give me control tonight and do as I say." He pulled back and couldn't hold in a wicked smile as she bit her lip and looked at him with a complicated expression of desire and flinty anger.

"Damn you, do not mock me." But she, too, was smiling a little, and she closed her eyes, baring her neck for him as she turned her face to the side.

Bey dipped back down and this time settled a little more of his weight on her so she could rub herself against him. He let his lips and tongue traverse her neck and he took his time around the crevices of her collarbones. He moved to the top of her robe, tugging it down slightly with one finger to bring it closer to her breasts. She gasped and began to pant as his finger traced the collar of the robe, dipping slightly under the trim to caress the skin at the top of her cleavage. She writhed a little, again lifting her breasts up as if trying to meet his finger with them. She was gripping the mat underneath her on both sides when he ran his right hand down the centre of her chest, stopping just below the curve of her breasts. Sliding his hand under and up around the side of her left breast, he reveled in the lusciousness of her curves.

Bey was thoroughly enjoying himself now that he had abandoned himself to his decision to pleasure the stunning woman beneath him. He had never been with a woman that he wanted to know so completely. He wanted to feel every bump and curve and to know what made her writhe in pleasurable anguish. He wanted to know every tongue flick that made her cry out. He relished the opportunity to take his time with her.

She rolled her head from side to side, then opened her eyes and looked into his.

"Please." She whispered.

Bey gave a little curved smile and watched her face as he brushed his thumb over one hardened nipple.

"Gods." She muttered through clenched teeth. Bey chuckled and circled her nipple again.

"I'm sorry, *nebet-i*, but I think you will have to take this robe off in order for me to continue."

She writhed as she pulled the robe over her head and it was Bey's turn to draw in a sharp breath. Her curvature was magnificent. Her smallish, yet perfectly rounded breasts, narrow waist and wide, fleshy hips made him want to bury himself between her legs. His erection was throbbing, and he had to take a deep breath to force himself to focus on the task at hand.

"Gods, you are so beautiful, Hem-etj. Do you know this? More beautiful than any goddess could possibly be."

She took a shaky breath and lifted her chin, "Please, do not call me Hem-etj tonight. Tonight I just want to forget."

She reached up to the back of his head to bury her hands in his hair, pulling him down to kiss her. This time it was her who kissed him with passion and force, and a tinge of desperation. He marveled at the fervent hunger in her kiss, although it had not been entirely unexpected. He'd known all along if he got her in bed it would be nothing short of breathtaking and wild; she was like a feral cat in her passions. Laying her back on the bed, he kissed down between her breasts, working his way over to her small brown peaks. She began to writhe again, rubbing her thighs together as he kissed and licked his way in slow, ever encroaching loops towards her hard nubs. When he finally pressed his warm, moist lips over one swollen nipple she arched her breasts towards him and tightened her grip on his hair.

"Oh gods, Bey."

Bey smiled a little around her nipple, twirling his tongue over it and savouring the feel of her squirming beneath him. He skimmed his hand down her abdomen and over the tops of her thighs. He caressed the side of her hip and thigh, working his way towards the inside of her thighs as he continued to lavish attention on her breasts and nipples. Raising his head, he kissed her lips and slid his hand between her legs, cupping her inner thigh.

Bey looked down at her face through the silvery shadows the moonlight cast into the room.

"You are sure you want me to continue?"

Merneith disentangled a hand from his hair and ran it over his muscular shoulders. She wrapped her hand around his thick triceps and looked up through her long lashes. The mixture of innocence and desire in her big dark eyes nearly sent him over the brink of lust. "This is what I wanted the first time I saw you."

Bey kissed her again as his hand skimmed up her thigh towards the silky, wet lips hidden there. She inhaled sharply and buried her face in his shoulder, moaning into his neck. Bey brushed the rim of her swollen opening with his finger, seeking the tight nub that would hopefully send her over the edge. She bit into his shoulder as he found it and began to draw lazy circles over it with his finger. Merneith's body began to undulate under his, and he couldn't help but press his erection against her thigh, although it afforded him no relief whatsoever and only increased his own discomfort.

Bey switched to manipulating her hard little knot with his thumb and rimming her tender folds with his index finger. He rubbed her slick sex with his finger, slowly working his way between the soft lips to press at her opening. She felt so good, soft as the petals of a dew-moistened lotus flower. He paused, both to give her a final opportunity to stop him, and to torment her.

"Gods, yes. Bey... please...just... I need..."

"Need what?" He knew he was just being cruel now.

"Damn it." She grated out. "Do. Not. Stop."

That's exactly what I wanted to hear. Bey smiled as he began to work his finger into her as she squirmed and panted into his neck. Once in a short ways, he drew it out to rub her juices over her sensitive peak, making it slippery and swollen.

"Oh... just...yesss."

Bey lingered for a moment longer, enjoying the feel of her body vibrating beneath him, then plunged his finger back in. Merneith bit down hard on his shoulder and moaned. He worked his finger in and out, pulling out every few thrusts to rub her nub. When he finally thought she would be ok with it, he began to work a second finger in to her tight, smooth sex. He groaned at just *how tight and smooth* it was, and the thought of *how damned good* it would feel to have her sex clenching around his shaft nearly killed him. Although he knew that tomorrow she could change her mind and that this might be their only night together, he couldn't help but think that *if* there were another night, he would need to make her ready to take all of him in.

Bey was gently able to work a second finger into her hot, slippery sheath and began pumping in and out, curling his fingers upwards as he thrust inside. It wasn't long before Merneith's breathing quickened into sobs and she tightened her grasp on him, digging her nails into his shoulders and mewling into his neck.

He whispered in her ear, "Let go. Just trust me. Let go."

Bey felt her snug cushiony sex grip onto his fingers, then she cried out and her inner walls began to pulse around his fingers.

"Let go. Just trust me. Let go." And in that moment, Merneith did. She gave herself up with wild abandon, letting herself go completely for once, letting go of the restraint she had been taught to practice from an early age. She couldn't control her body as it shuddered and bucked underneath Bey's strong, reassuring weight. She was gasping for breath, overwhelmed by the feeling of the world crashing around her. She had never in her life experienced anything close to the all-obliterating pleasure that wracked her body and lasted for what seemed like eons. Endless tremors, as infinite as the stars that burst in the darkness behind her eyelids, shook her to her core. Bey continued to work his fingers in her, slowing his pace until she was able to gulp in deep, ragged breaths.

"By the gods," she whispered in wonder. Bey withdrew his fingers, but cupped her sex with his hand. She laid her hands on either side of his face and he pressed his lips against hers, his stubble rubbing against her cheeks as he trailed his lips along her jaw. Bey's spicy scent floated over and around her like a warm breeze across the desert, heady and comforting, and an intoxicating yearning coursed through her.

Merneith was shocked to realize that it felt as if she had been missing this moment her whole life. As if she had always known this was meant to happen, but had never realized until now what *this* was. For the first time, she felt as if something in her life was *real*. Her emotions, his emotions, this desire between them, it was raw and alive, like nothing else in her life. She almost laughed at the irony of it. She was queen of the most powerful and wealthy land in the world, and had almost everything she wanted in life at her fingertips, but it was here, in some poor stranger's shack in the middle of nowhere, that she had discovered what she had been missing. For the first time she had truly allowed herself to let go, and instead of feeling like she was falling, she was soaring above the desert.

The lines etched around Bey's mouth were incredibly sexy as the corners of his lips twisted in a cocky smile. He had the air of a cat stretching itself on a sunny bench, languid and confident in its allure.

Merneith felt her own lips twitch in response, and her cheeks ached as she tried not to smile. "Pleased with yourself, are you?"

Bey grinned, his eyes crinkling, and Merneith's gut twisted. *Damn him, he flusters me without even trying.* Bey said in a husky drawl. "Oh, I am pleased. But I am not finished yet."

Merneith's heart quickened and her breath caught.

Bey gave her a wicked smile, and she realized that she was actually a little bit scared. Giving control to Bey in the first place had gone against her nature. Although she had heard other women talk, and she had been told what to anticipate before her wedding night, Merneith's inexperience was vast. She had no idea what to expect.

Bey must have sensed her fear, because he brushed his knuckles along her cheek, lifted one eyebrow and said, "Oh do not worry, Mer," hearing him call her *Beloved* thrilled her, in spite of her nervousness. "I will not take you tonight. But I *do* want to make sure that you will not be thinking of any other man for a long time to come."

She began to sit up to protest, what did he mean he would not take her? But he planted one hand between her breasts and pushed her gently back down on to her elbows, where she braced herself, watching him. He kept his intense gaze and roguish smile on her as he positioned himself between her bent knees and lowered his head down between her legs. *Oh gods, oh Ra, oh no*, her mind babbled in both alarm and desire.

Merneith could feel her legs quiver with anticipation even before he touched her soft inner lips. Bey placed one rough, calloused finger at the entrance of her cushiony sex and she gasped. She was already so sensitive and a little sore from what he had just done. Propped up on one elbow, Bey's free hand clasped her left hand. She gripped him with all her strength, and buried her right hand in his thick, wavy hair, entwining her fingers into the silky strands and clinging to him, steeling herself.

Bey began to press his finger in to the delicate opening and, giving her one last smirk, kept his eyes on hers as he parted his lips and his tongue flicked out to glide across her hooded, swollen peak. Merneith's breath escaped in a whoosh and she immediately dragged it back in a deep gasp. Every single nerve ending in her body had been slammed into action at once. She threw her head back and moaned.

Bey launched an assault on her sensitive nub, alternately flicking, sucking and gently lapping while he worked two fingers in and out of her silky, clenching sheath. Merneith nearly fainted amidst the sensations that wracked her body, the uncontrollable quivering of her limbs, her heavy panting, and the sound of her own whimpering. The sight of Bey's head between her thighs was the most erotic thing she had ever seen. Finally, just when she thought her legs might give out from the quaking and she would go mad, she felt everything inside her pulling tighter and tighter as she gulped for air in uneven gasps. And then came that perfect, shattering moment when a violent current of ecstasy roared over her and she lost control of her limbs. Her upper body crashed back onto the mat with a sob as she shuddered violently.

Bey drew himself up, laying himself out by her side. Merneith curled towards him, her forehead tucked against the nape of his neck, trying to regain control of her heartbeat as she gasped for air. He wrapped an arm around her, drawing her closer and burying his nose in her hair.

"You smell so good, Mer, and you *taste* amazing." She could hear a grittiness in his hoarse whisper.

She lifted her head to scrutinize him.

"What did you mean, that you would not take me tonight? Why?"

He compressed his lips and the moonlight shone on his clenched jaw. "Because." He lifted one shoulder in a shrug. "You have been ill, drinking wine, and under great stress. It would not be right. I do not want you to have any cause to regret this night."

Merneith studied his face. The lines carved along his mouth, his unusual green eyes with their long lashes, his high cheekbones and sensual lips, all drew her in and fascinated her so that it was hard to pull her eyes away from them.

"But what if…" she began, but he cut her off with a guttural noise that came from deep in his chest.

"Please, Mer, it is hard enough as it is for me to stop here. Do not make it harder. And besides," he hitched up an eyebrow and gave her mocking smile, "do you think you could handle more right now anyway?" Merneith drew in a shaky breath. She knew he was right. As good as it had been, she was exhausted.

He chuckled at the look on her face. "No, I did not think so. Let us see how you feel in the morning, shall we?" He ran his hand underneath her hair to cup the back of her head. He planted a soft kiss on her lips and Merneith felt as if she were a bowl full of honey left out in the hot sun, melting into a soft, warm puddle of golden light. She had no idea what was going to happen tomorrow and she didn't want to think about it, but the moment she was more content than she had ever thought she could be. Before she drifted off to sleep she found herself thinking that having to flee a kidnapping and getting shot had been worth it, even if it only lasted for tonight…

Chapter 12 – Ta-Senet

Bey woke just after dawn with his arm wrapped around Merneith, her naked backside cupped against his groin beneath the blanket he'd pulled over them last night. This was not the first time he'd woken up next to a woman, although those women had generally not been the type one was proud to wake up next to. But now, it felt *damned good and right* to hear the soft in and out of her breathing, to be able to watch the particles of golden, early morning sunlight sprinkled across her skin, to run his hand up her side and over the soft flesh of her arm, to bury his nose in her hair, and to feel her stir in her sleep, pressing her rear further against him.

Another sick joke from the gods, Bey thought bitterly as he forced himself to retreat from her. *This could get us both killed if the Pharaoh were to find out.* That soft rear pressing against him was causing another throbbing erection, and the last thing he wanted was for her wake with him pushed up against her, terrified when she realized what they'd done last night and regretting her moment of weakness. *Best to let her wake up alone and give her time to compose herself.* He wanted to let her decide for herself how she felt about last night. Also, and this he was less willing to admit to himself, if she did feel regret he didn't want to see it written on her face.

He carefully disengaged his arm from around her. As he stood and wrapped his shenti around his hips he stepped to the window to check outside and ensure that whoever had attacked their ship had not come looking for them. Thankfully, all was quiet except for the rustle of a slight breeze. *If she is well enough today we can begin our journey south.*

Merneith stirred behind him. He tried to look away from her adorable, kitten-like movements as she stretched, but he couldn't help himself. When she was angry and trading barbs with him he felt positively carnal, wanting to toss her down and tear her clothes off, making her beg him to drive himself into her. But when she was vulnerable, as she was last night and again this morning, she was so endearing he wanted to fold her up in his arms and drink in every tender moment he could get.

Merneith sat up, squinting one bleary eye against the sunlight to look up at him. "Mmmmm." Her soft, red lips curved upward in a slight smile, and Bey's chest rumbled in a chuckle. Despite his conflicting feelings he was pleased that she had not yet thrown anything at him. *If only she wasn't so damnably charming when she's sleepy.* He grinned down at her. "How are you feeling this morning?"

She didn't answer, instead shaking her head and touching her fingertips to her lips, running her tongue along them, as if inspecting them. A look of wonder and confusion spread across her face, and he thought she might be trying to hide a smile. Her kiss-swollen lips were even more crimson than usual. The memory of their bruising kisses caused another stirring in his groin. He had to wonder if she wasn't also swollen and raw *elsewhere* from last night.

Bey couldn't stop himself from teasing her, even as he feared she might rebuff him. "Feeling tender? Perhaps it would be best if you avoided arguing today in order to give your lips time to rest and heal."

"Oh ho ho!" Merneith wrapped the blanket around her naked body, denying him a glimpse of her curves and holding the cover up with one hand as she stood up. "Do you not think it too early in the morning to pick a fight with me?" She took a step towards him, looking up at him with the most inviting glint in her eye.

The corners of his lips twitched, and he reached an arm around her waist, drawing her closer to him. "Not at all. I do not think it could ever be too early to rouse your passions." Bey bent his head towards her face, wanting to taste those soft red lips of hers.

Just then he heard someone clear their throat purposefully, and a knock came at the door. Merneith stepped back, a startled look of panic on her face. Bey put his hand out to indicate that she should get into the corner of the hut and he grabbed one of the shepherd's crooks that was hanging on the wall in case he needed a weapon. He opened the door, blocking the doorway with his bulk.

"Well hello, Sekhrey!" Ebrium grinned as Bey opened the door. Relief washed over Bey at the sight of his old friend. Bey set aside the crook and reached out to clasp Ebrium's forearm, as Ebrium did the same for him.

"Thank Dagon, brother, that you are here," Bey said as he peered out the door, looking around Ebrium. "Are you alone? Where is everyone else?"

"Looking for you, brother. Luckily, I heard your voice before any of them came across you first." Ebrium's eyes flicked meaningfully to the little window in the hut, indicating that he had seen Bey and Merneith and that was why he had cleared his throat and knocked. "It will be about two minutes before someone comes up behind me."

Bey gave a nod to signal he would be right back. He shut the door and turned to Merneith. "Put on that robe from last night and prepare yourself, Hem-etj. We have no time to spare."

Merneith clutched the blanket around her, looking mortified, and Bey stepped close to her and said in a low voice, "Fear not. Ebrium is my oldest and most trusted friend. You are safe with him, he is loyal to me, and to you."

Merneith drew in a ragged breath, tightened her jaw and gave a curt nod. Bey stepped outside while she changed. Ebrium raised his eyebrows and whistled a tune while rocking back and forth on his heels, smiling at Bey. Bey glared at him and then said, "Tell me what has happened. Are we in danger now?"

Ebrium shrugged. "At this *very* moment? I think not, although we should be on our way quickly. We've had no sign of the enemy since the attack, but of course that does not mean they will not try again. We were lucky, there were less of them than we'd expected and we were able to fight them off. We weren't able to take any prisoners, although we did send several of them into the Iteru, and I hope the crocodiles are grateful for the feast." Ebrium grinned. "We tried to pursue them, but they turned and headed back up the Iteru and their lighter crafts were faster than ours."

"And the women?"

"Excellent. And the pretty little blond one is doing just fine." Ebrium winked.

Bey snorted and shook his head, knowing that Ebrium was just baiting him. "Were you able to determine who the men were?"

"Not with any certainty. They dressed like Kemeti men, but some of the guard thought they heard someone shouting in Sumerian."

Bey chewed the inside of his lip, squinting and looking out at the river. "Huh." He grunted.

"That's precisely what I thought." Ebrium nodded gravely, then broke into another grin. "And how have you been, brother?" He clapped Bey on the shoulder with his good arm. "How is our queen?"

Bey slid Ebrium a look through lowered lids, letting Ebrium know that Bey knew what he was getting at and that there was a time and a place to discuss it. This was neither the time nor the place.

"Better today, I believe. She was skimmed by an arrow and was ill yesterday, or else we would have been heading south to Ta-Senet by now. How did you know to look for us?"

Ebrium's eyes were still smiling, but he nodded, indicating that he would let the matter pass for now but that he was well aware that something noteworthy had happened between Bey and the queen. "Bekeh saw the queen go overboard and you go after her, brave hero that you are." Ebrium winked. "Thank the gods we've found you. I must confess I was starting to worry a little, brother. We searched all yesterday, and through the night." Ebrium rocked on his heels again, looking out over the great river. "I feared we might have to send word to the Pharaoh that the queen had disappeared. So far I have not sent any runners to let anyone know she is missing."

Bey nodded. "Good. No one should know of this until we can get the queen safely to the garrison at Ta-Senet. It is enough that she has been gone from the palace two full days. Without a doubt they have already sent word to the Pharaoh."

At that, Bey heard the door of the hut open behind him and Merneith stepped out into the morning sunlight. Bey had to appreciate that, despite wearing a peasant man's plain, loose black robe and her face scrubbed clean of charcoal or blush, she was a striking figure. She drew herself up to her full imperial height, threw her shoulders back, lifted her jaw and leveled her eyes on Ebrium.

"Good morning, *wa'ew,*" she nodded at him, addressing him with the common term for a soldier. "I am happy to hear that everyone has survived the attack." Bey's lip curled a little at her nonchalant manner, as if Ebrium had not just caught the two of them in an intimate situation.

Ebrium bowed and said, "Hem-etj. I am pleased to see you are well. You will be happy to know your mewet and Penebui are both well. The Sekhrey has informed me you were shot, I hope it has not caused you much inconvenience or pain." Ebrium glanced up at Merneith through a lock of his wavy black hair. Bey saw the barest trace of a smile cross Merneith's face as she said boldly, "Only a minor inconvenience, but a fair amount of soreness." With that last word, her eyes landed on Bey, and he could have sworn he saw her eyebrow arch just the slightest, as if challenging him. He had to admire her audaciousness.

Ebrium inclined his head. "If you are ready, Hem-etj, we should make our way back to the ships, Hem-etj. If we hurry, we can make Ta-Senet by sundown."

Bey agreed. "Ebrium is right, Hem-etj. We should be going." Merneith flicked her eyes in his direction and for a second he thought he saw something like regret, or maybe disappointment, cross her face, before her jaw hardened and she wrapped her arms around her chest as if chilled despite the growing heat of the day. She nodded. "Let us make haste, then."

Bey held up a finger. "One moment, I will ensure the hut is put to order." He didn't want the shepherd, or whoever it was that lived in the hovel, to suspect who their visitor had been.

Bey strode inside and swept his eyes around the sparse cabin one last time. *Who knows where things might have gone if Ebrium had not found us...? I am glad they are all safe, but damn him...* Bey knew that he and Merneith might never be alone together again and, despite his desire for her, he wasn't sure if that were a good or bad thing. One night of indiscretion was not impossible to cover up. Two or more could lead them straight to the gallows.

He reached into a leather pouch that he kept tucked into the waist of his shenti and drew out a few nuggets of twisted silver, and placed them on top of the small bed. *That will be more than enough to compensate the shepherd for his lost food and wine, and perhaps buy his silence regarding his unknown house guests as well.*

Bey turned and stepped outside, shutting the door to the hut and, along with it, trying to leave behind the memory of Merneith's body writhing beneath him and the way she'd gasped out his name as she begged him for more.

The large warships cut swiftly south, up the great Iteru. A wind had come from the north and the sailors unfurled the large sails, propelling the ships forward to Ta-Senet. Merneith had was thrilled to find Bekeh, Penebui, Akshaka and Ishara well, and soothed their fears regarding her wound. Bey allowed the women to sit on a bench on deck, where they were able to watch the banks of the Iteru slide by and relate their accounts of the past day. Bey had deemed it safe for them, since their position on the river enabled them to see both upstream and downstream for miles. There was no chance of another sneak attack against the warships in broad daylight.

Although Merneith, of course, excluded any mention of her intimacy with Bey, she got a clear sense that Bekeh suspected something. While the women were arranging themselves, Bekeh leaned in to Merneith and whispered, "So we have determined the Sekhrey is *not* married to the girl."

Merneith, raising her chin and tightening her jaw to prevent any escape of emotion, merely murmured, "I am aware."

Bekeh leaned back, looking at Merneith with narrowed eyes and Merneith knew she was being assessed, even as she kept her own eyes straight ahead. "Ahhh," Bekeh nodded, a satisfied smile playing across her face. "So I see you are."

Merneith chose to ignore this and pursed her lips instead, fighting back her own smile. She had no desire to discuss the matter with Bekeh when she herself was sorting through a myriad of confusing emotions and thoughts. Had Ebrium not arrived when he did, she had no doubt of her readiness to bed Bey right there and then. The thought of what he had done to her still made her squirm and flush with desire. But all her doubts and fears were crowding back in. *If caught, we could be killed. It is bad enough his man Ebrium has suspected us, and now Bekeh. And how can I pretend nothing has occurred? What if it is only a trifling for him? Surely he has bedded many women, what is one more to him?*

Clusters of huts appeared along the banks of the river just as Ra was beginning to push the sun over the Iteru to the west. It wasn't long before the massive walls of the Ta-Senet stronghold loomed in the distance. Set right on the bank of the river, the fortress was built to protect trade vessels heading north from Nubia, as well as to fend off any attacks from the same direction. A garrison town, Ta-Senet was large enough to house around fifteen hundred people. Behind the twelve metre high walls that encased it, the fort housed a market, numerous inhabitants and tradesmen, several temples, and a square mud-brick military building at its forefront.

Along the docks, the guard was met with a small contingent of soldiers, alerted to their arrival by the sight of the warships coming from up the river. Merneith and the other women were escorted off the ship and met by the governor of the city. He was a solemn man who expressed his pleasure and surprise at the blessing Merneith had bestowed upon them with her visit. He assured them of his loyalty and desire to offer the women every possible comfort while in his care.

The women were ushered into litters with Bekeh and Ishara placed together, while Merneith sat with Penebui and Akshaka. Each litter was made of a platform of wooden planks with four poles rising up to create a rectangular frame with a triangular top like a tent, draped with white linen curtains. Inside, cushions allowed the ladies to lounge comfortably. Poles that jutted out lengthwise from the platforms were hoisted up and rested on the shoulders of twelve men who carried the ladies up the bank to the garrison's gate.

Penebui and Akshaka busied themselves peeking out through the fabric.

"How exciting!" Akshaka was clearly overwhelmed. "I have never yet ridden in a litter. How grand it is!"

Penebui glowed with the joy of being able to share this pleasure with her new friend. "It is certainly to be preferred to walking in the sun. And it would not do for the queen to be seen at this time, lest a fuss be made over her. It will generate excitement enough with the ships and the litters to carry us."

"Yes, of course." Akshaka smiled shyly at Merneith. Merneith reached out to pat the girl's hand, and Akshaka's fair skin blushed a pretty shade of pink. Merneith felt much more amiable towards the girl now that she knew Akshaka was not Bey's wife. She was quite willing to even allow herself to like the girl as a companion for Penebui.

Soon they had passed through the first, then the second round of walls, beneath the shadows of the towers that rose above the gates. It was not long before they were deposited within the military fortress itself. They saw Bey only for a moment when they arrived. "I will join you ladies after the evening meal." He bowed to Merneith. "Hem-etj. Senebti." Merneith was disappointed at this curt leave-taking, she had hoped at least to catch his eye. *Perhaps last night was nothing but a trifle after all.*

Rooms were arranged and several local girls were engaged to attend the women. Finally, baths were drawn and the servants helped Merneith wash and arrange her hair, afterwards rubbing her skin with almond oil scented with myrrh. The fort was structured around a courtyard in the midst of the mud-brick barracks. The courtyard served as a meeting space, and here the women sat on benches amongst a cluster of date palm trees. A simple meal of rice, lentils, bread, dates, and beer was provided to them. Since their arrival was unexpected, there had been no time to prepare a feast worthy of royal guests, and Merneith had waived off the governor's profuse apologies and desire to prolong their dinner in order to prepare a grander meal.

At one point though, Penebui sighed. "I am so tired of rice and lentils. While it seemed delightfully rustic at first, I do long for a nice sweet honey cake."

Akshaka looked startled and blushed. Merneith noticed it and addressed Penebui in gentle chastisement, "Now dear cousin, there is nothing wrong with this. Most people eat bread, rice, and lentils at every meal."

Penebui seemed to realize her error. She hadn't thought to consider Akshaka's poorer state, and the fact that meat, fish, fowl, fruit, and sweet cakes were only abundant in the homes of the very wealthy. To cover Akshaka's embarrassment, Penebui gushed, "Of course! There is nothing wrong with these rice and lentils. Perfectly good. Sweet cakes are not so very good anyway." However, she poked rather glumly at her rice and lentil mash with a strip of flatbread before scooping up another mouthful with it. Although she didn't say it, Merneith couldn't help but agree with her. She was getting tired of mash herself.

Dinner was cleared away and bowls of oil were set around the courtyard, casting a ghostly gloom over the hulking garrison. Out of the shadows, two bulky figures emerged. Bey and Ebrium stepped into the light of the courtyard. Merneith was again disappointed that Bey did not meet her eyes as the men both bowed politely and settled themselves on a bench across from the women. Ebrium spread his legs out in front of him, leaning back on his one good arm. Bey sat forward, his forearms resting on his knees.

Merneith watched Bey as he scrubbed his face with his hands, running his palm along the dark stubble on his jaw that, after several days, had almost become a full beard. She recalled how it had chafed against her cheek, her neck, her *inner thighs* just twenty-four hours ago, leaving her raw inside and out. *Damn him to Ammit*, Merneith swore to herself as heat flared through her core. *I will not let him disarm me tonight in front of everyone.*

She composed herself and asked in her coolest voice, "What news, Sekhrey?"

Bey rubbed the back of his neck as he looked off into the distance. Then he turned his face to hers, probing her eyes with his tired-looking green ones. "I have sent runners out to gather the nearby sephat militias together here as soon as possible. We will need all the forces we can muster before returning to Thinis."

Merneith was shocked, and spoke as calmly as possible despite her clenched jaw. "Please forgive me, Sekhrey, I realize I have been ill, but I do not recall being consulted regarding this arrangement. Did I, by chance, sleep through this most important planning meeting?" Merneith cocked her head to the side, arranging her face in a tight smile.

Bey blew out a long breath then glanced around at the other women. "Hem-etj, perhaps we had best discuss this in a private audience. If you will allow me to escort you to your chambers, Ebrium can take the ladies to theirs when they are ready."

Mernieth gave a curt nod and bid the other ladies goodnight, ignoring Bekeh's infuriating upturned eyebrows and knowing smile. Standing, Merneith pulled herself up to full height, adjusting her back into rigid position and lifting her chin in order to draw down upon herself all the imperial composure she had been taught since she was a child. She followed Bey in silence into the building and down a dark hallway, lit strategically by windows that looked out into the quadrangle they had just left. Bey stopped in front of one of the large wooden doors, pushing it open to reveal the sparsely decorated room assigned to Merneith. It had little more than a wide, low bed, a few stools for sitting, a bench, a mirror, and a couple of small, wooden tables. An officer's room, Merneith had been told earlier, rather than a common militia soldier's. The soldiers generally bunked four or six in a room on sleeping mats on the floor, rather than beds.

Merneith stepped inside and Bey followed, shutting the door behind him. She whirled on him, snapping out, "How *dare* you presume to call upon the militias without consulting me?"

He stepped past her into the room, rubbing his neck and rolling a shoulder before lighting the bowls of oil placed around the room. Merneith watched his sculpted muscles ripple as he moved about, the flickering oil wicks deepening the shadows along the ridges of his back, chest and arms. She recalled Atab's words at the banquet as the tigers had paced the courtyard. *He is sexy, no?* The remembrance of how Bey could manipulate her body, coupled with his current lack of acknowledgement of her, made her all the angrier. "Did you hear me?"

Then he turned to face her, his green eyes weary. "It had to be done. Your life has been threatened. It is not yet clear who is responsible for this, and we must draw upon those loyal to you to ensure your safety. With part of the guard with Wadj, we may not have enough men to protect you from another attack." He cocked his head to the side. "Would you have advised me otherwise?"

"That is not the point. I am your queen. I should have been consulted. I *will not* be made a fool of by having the Sekhrey of the Guard knowing more than I and making arrangements behind my back." Pulling herself up to full height and drawing upon all her cold, imperial upbringing, she lifted her chin and narrowed her eyes at him. "Just because you spent one night with me does not grant you the rule of Kement."

Bey snorted. "Trust me, *Hem-etj*, ruling Kemet is the last thing I want to do." He found the way she wore her regal manner irresistible. Some wore royalty like fools, throwing it in peoples' faces the way a selfish, spoilt child knocks a weaker one to the ground. His brother had been one of those types, demanding undeserved admiration based on birth. Others bore it as an imposing force, the way a lion commands respect because it is without question a most powerful, peerless creature. His father had been such a man, and he knew most would see Merneith as that sort of woman. There was no doubt she was peerless. However, he saw her manner in this case for what it truly was, a shield to protect her vulnerable feelings and passionate emotions.

Pinning her against the door with his gaze, Bey ambled towards Merneith. He could see her eyes widen as he neared, and her lips parted, her breasts rising. He placed one hand on the door next to her ear, caging her in on one side. With his other he cupped the side of her neck, running his rough thumb along the soft skin and clenching muscles of her cheek and jaw. He could feel her pulse quicken under his palm.

He had been avoiding looking at her all day, afraid that his desire would be obvious to everyone around. Now, fixating on her full lips as she drew the bottom one in, indenting it with her upper teeth, he groaned inwardly. He didn't have the strength to keep evading what he really wanted, no, what he craved with a visceral need that throbbed through his entire body and crashed about his head like the thunderous waves of a tsunami.

"You are right, Hem-etj," he murmured. "I should have asked you before I called in the sephat militias. I apologize, and I promise you that in the future I will *always* consult you before I take such actions." She had a wary look in her eyes as she raised her chin. Their faces were just inches apart and he could smell the myrrh on her skin and the scented oils of her hair. He watched as her tongue flicked out to moisten her lips, drawing the lower one in and slowly releasing it, a pink, glistening bud.

Bey leaned in to nuzzle at the base of her graceful neck, grazing her skin with his lips. Her subsequent gasp was enough to make him harden. He rasped just beneath her ear,

"But I need to extract a promise in return. I ask that you, in turn, will yield to me in regards to matters of your personal safety. For you see, Hem-etj, you are not *just* my queen. You are far more than that, and the thought of anything happening to you is more than I care to envision. I would rather incur your entire wrath, for you to damn me to Ammit again, than to allow any person to attempt violence against you." Pulling back to see her lips part and her eyes soften, Bey knew he'd been right. Her angry posturing was just armour for her fragile emotions.

Bey pressed his thumb up under her jaw to lift her chin further and she watched as his eyelids lowered, his long thick lashes shading his eyes as he dipped his head down and pressed her moist lips with his firm ones. Merneith gasped against him and her body softened at his touch, as if she were nothing more than desert sand drifting through his hand.

She had prepared herself for a fight, for him to be obstinate and arrogant, to argue with her. Instead, his confession had driven *any* thoughts from her head. She hardly had the presence of mind to be mad at herself for her lack of willpower to stay angry. Heat radiated under her skin from her chest outwards and her nerve endings seemed to have seized control of her body.

She raised a trembling hand under his arm, still pressed against the door, and grasped his bicep. The other hand she ran over the carved muscles of his chest, surprisingly smooth for such battle-hardened skin, as if she were caressing a granite statue warmed by the blazing heat of the midday sun. She pushed against his lips with an urgency that surprised even her, a tumultuous need churning in her belly, setting her nerve-endings prickling up across every inch of her skin. She moaned as he ran a hand up her side to cup one of her breasts through her soft linen dress. He brushed a thumb over her nipples, still sensitive from the previous evening's escapade, and she gasped.

Decorum be damned, she thought, *I have not the patience tonight.* She glanced over at the window to ensure the curtains were drawn tight and then, in one smooth motion, she was out of her shift and naked before him. The cool breeze wafting through from the window made her hypersensitive brown nubs tighten painfully. "By the gods, woman," Bey growled. "You kill me." And in a moment he had her on the bed, kneeling over her as he ran his calloused hands over her supple body.

"Now Hem-etj," Bey pulled his head back and put on a serious face, "I promised I would consult you on all major matters. It seems we have reached one of those times. I am about to declare war on these two mounds here." With this he traced a finger along the underside of one breast. "Do I have your permission to rally the forces and go on the offensive? Now mind you, if you refuse, I will have to argue that perhaps you are not in your right mind and seize control for the good of all involved. I know that I, for one, will be in serious danger of falling upon my own dagger if you say no."

Merneith bit back a laugh, feeling guilty that his teasing helped to dispel some of the tension lingering from the attack and the fear of another attempt on her life. She also knew the dangers involved if they were caught in such an intimate situation. But Bey's words had also eased her doubts about his feelings for her, and the relief of that alone was almost enough to overwhelm her. She pursed her lips, raised her chin, and said in the most imperial voice she could muster given the circumstances, "You have my consent, Sekhrey. What is good for my people is surely good for me." She couldn't help the moan that escaped her thanks to the contrast between the cold air and his warm lips as they trailed over her breasts and belly, setting her squirming and panting beneath him.

Bey brought his lips up and breathed against her ear. "I am afraid that, as much as I love to hear you pant and moan, and there is nothing I hold more dear to my heart than to hear you scream my name, tonight's assault must be silent. I think it best if all of Ta-Senet not know that I will be ravaging you." He rested his weight on his forearm and parted her lips with a finger from that hand. "Bite, suck, kiss, do what you will, but you must be quiet." Merneith glared at him for a moment then wrapped her lips around his finger. "Excellent." He gave her a wicked smile as he ran his right hand down her abdomen, slipping his hand between her thighs and sliding them up the smooth skin, seeking her soft, hidden lips. "Now, Hem-etj, I must ask you to prepare yourself for what may be a rather arduous seige."

She bit down around his finger as he brushed the plush folds of her sex. Pushing aside the luscious pleats, he pressed into her moist, warm opening. Of their own volition, Merneith's hips began to rock against him, and against his large, thick ridge pressed against her thigh, hidden behind his linen shenti. When he pressed a second finger in she choked back a cry from the intense pleasure that lapped over her.

He tsked in her ear. "We must be quiet, Hem-etj, someone out there might hear us. If you must, bite the pillow or my shoulder, but you cannot cry out."

"Please, oh, just…"

"Sshhh," he soothed, although she could hear the smile in his voice.

"Dammit! Let them hear… mmm… just…"

He drove his fingers in to her, pulling them out to rub her inflamed peak before plunging back in, as if he was trying to probe the depths of her insides. Her legs quivered, her breath became sobs, and she dug her nails into his shoulders. "That's right, Mer, just relax." Bey whispered. A violent wash of ecstasy pulsed through her and she bit into the warm flesh of his shoulder, muffling her cries.

Her body slackened and Bey rolled off of her to lay himself out beside her, resting on a forearm and gazing down at her with a questioning look in his eyes. She entwined her fingers through the soft curls of his hair, pulling his face down to hers to press her lips against his. She thrust her tongue into his mouth, tasting his warmth. She wanted more of him. Not just his fingers, not just his tongue, *more than that*. She would not be content to just lie back now as she had the previous night. Inexperienced though she was, she knew that she would not be satisfied with half-measures tonight, however deft and pleasurable they may be.

When he finally pulled his head back, she raised an eyebrow and asked, "Now Sekhrey, suppose you were to encounter a counter-assault? What course of action should you take?" She slid a hand down the hard muscles of his chest, tracing along the soft dark hairs that trailed below his belly button and into the folds of his shenti. Nervous but determined, she wanted to see the hard bulge that was pressed against her thigh. Even more than that, she wanted to feel it deep inside her.

Bey's eyes widened as they scrutinized her. In a gritty voice, he muttered, "That is no joke, Hem-etj."

"No. It is not." The corner of her lip curled up as she slipped a hand under the belt of his skirt, running her fingers through the thick curls there. "I believe, Sekhrey, that I should like to surrender my fortress to, uhm," she licked her lips, keeping her eyes locked on his, "your imposing forces."

Bey forced out a shaky breath, running a hand through his hair as he stared down at her. "By the gods, are you serious?" He had wanted this moment almost since he'd first laid eyes on her, but now that it was here he found himself hesitating. He didn't want to hurt her, didn't want her to do something she might regret. *And she will, most likely, regret this late. Especially if we are found out.*

But she shook her head with a silky, irresistible look of mischief hovering in the corner of her upturned lips. "You have approximately one minute to accept my capitulation, and then the drawbridge will be forever closed and we shall always be at war."

"Then I would be a fool to wait one more second to accept." He said as he lept to his feet, tearing off the last shred of fabric that kept him from her. He stood before her in the flickering light. He saw her take in all of him, and he couldn't help but congratulate himself for all the hours he'd spent rowing alongside the soldiers and training for combat, with their benefit of keeping him as well-muscled as any man could be. That and the one natural endowment in particular that he knew to be larger than most.

Merneith trailed her eyes over him, biting the soft cushion of her lower lip as she brought her wide eyes up to his. She had drawn her knees up, pressing them together. As he approached the bed, her knees fell open and he was rewarded with the most delicious vision of her pink, glistening folds. She was *so damned gorgeous, amazing, wild, powerful, fearless, fragile*, unlike anything and anyone he'd ever known. A groan escaped him, and he wrapped a hand around his shaft to momentarily ease the painful throbbing that coursed through him.

He knelt between her legs, nestling himself up against her lush opening as he propped himself up on his forearms on either side of her head. He pushed a strand of hair back off her damp forehead and looked deep into her beautiful dark eyes.

"You are sure of this?" He asked in a husky voice, holding his breath and steeling himself in case she might say *no,* wanting with every fiber of his being for her to say *yes.*

She ran her hands up his sides and over the muscles of his back. "Strange, that you are so decisive when it comes to defying me, yet so cautious when you have my full consent." She murmured through a smile. "Surely your one minute is almost up, Sekhrey."

With that, Bey pushed the tip of his hardness through the lush folds of her sex. A deep curse escaped him as Merneith arched her back and gasped. "I am sorry, Mer, are you okay?" She nodded, her eyes glazed. With pain or pleasure he did not know, but he held still just in case. "Just breathe and relax," he murmured. "We have all the time in the world." *By Dagon* she felt *so good* wrapped around the head of his thick shaft. *Tight, wet, soft, clenching.* It was everything he had expected and more. He wanted to drive himself into her as deep as possible, hard and strong, wearing the both of them down until they were breathless, sweaty, and senseless, until she no longer had the energy to cry out his name. But at the same time he wanted to be tender, to show her with each slow thrust just how precious she was and how good this could be.

She looked up at him, her eyes clearing. "Now," she whispered and he pushed himself in another inch. He saw her jaw clench and he waited. The slow pace was killing him, she was so damned small inside it felt like his shaft was being strangled in the most insanely pleasurable way, but he didn't dare go faster. Then she nodded, "More." They continued in this way until finally, *thank the gods finally,* his length was almost entirely sheathed within her hot, slick walls. Bey almost sobbed with relief, and feared that he might lose himself right then and there. *Like an eager boy, his first time inside a woman. By the gods what this woman does to me.*

Merneith gripped the muscles along the sides of his back, lifting a knee to rub her inner thigh against his flank before wrapping it over his back, then whispered through clenched teeth, "Now *move.*" Bey pulled back, then slowly sank down into her. Her nails dug into his flesh and he covered her mouth with his as she moaned into his lips. He had been holding his breath for so long, had been so worried about her discomfort, that the sensation of finally moving inside her made him light-headed. *Oh the gods would just love it if I passed out now, wouldn't they?*

Merneith locked a leg around his, and he began to thrust in rhythm, pushing through the searing heat of her sex. She ran her hands over him, throwing her head back and panting as he picked up speed. "Oh," she suddenly gasped, shuddering violently, and the sleek muscles of her inner walls gripped and pulsated around him. *For the love of Dagon, she is tight enough inside to choke the life out of me.* He slowed long enough to let her ride out her pleasure. He didn't think he'd be able to last much longer, but wanted to make sure that she was more than satiated. He needed her to climax one more time. He rocked his hips, hoping to reach the spot that he knew might drive her over the edge. Reaching beneath her, he cupped her soft bottom and drew her hips up to meet his thrust, driving in to the very base of his length. And then she was thrashing, throbbing, mewling into his neck and clutching at his arms.

He couldn't hold himself back any longer as everything in him drew tighter and tighter until, in one explosive moment, a crashing wave of ecstasy roared over him. His shaft pulsed and jerked and finally went still. He collapsed over to the side and wrapped Merneith in his arms as she trembled against him. Both of them were shiny with sweat, and he picked a curl of hair off her cheek. "Mer, are you okay?" He whispered as he curled a finger under her chin, tilting her face up to look into her eyes.

"Mmmm," she nodded, her eyes hooded and a light smile playing across her lips. She asked with a voice full of awe, "Why in the name of Bes did I wait so long to do that?"

Bey chuckled, and stamped her lips with his. "I am hoping the answer to that is that you were waiting for me to come along."

"Mmmmm. It seems you are just the pirate-prince I was looking for." She smiled, nuzzling closer against him, like a kitten seeking warmth. *By Dagon she is adorable.* Her breath slowed, her body slackened, her lips parted slightly, she twitched, her hand curling into a light fist against his chest. Bey was struck by how perfectly content he was to watch this woman fall asleep in his arms. He'd never wanted a woman so badly, no, *needed* a woman, the way he did Merneith. Even after making love, he still wanted to press her tightly to him, as if by doing so he could somehow absorb her into himself. Having such a woman in his arms now was more than he could have ever dared to hope or expect, given his past. Nothing in his life had ever been constant, the gods always saw to that. He reminded himself not to get too comfortable in Merneith's bed. They would have to be constantly vigilant now lest they somehow give their secret away. Bey resisted the temptation to fall asleep by Merneith's side and forced himself to get up, dress, and slip quietly out the door.

Chapter 13 – The Return

Four weeks later Merneith leaned against a mud brick column in the shade of the covered walkway that lined one half of the garrison's quadrangle. Midway along the length of the courtyard a row of archers nocked their arrows. The bows were of simple design, curved wood with sinew strings. Their arrows were made of reeds, tipped with sharp flint heads and balanced with feathers at the end, and their targets were coarse linen shifts stuffed with dried papyri leaves and reeds. As their leader called out, the men let their arrows fly in unison. Another line of men stepped up to take their place. Since most battles in Kemet occurred along the great river, archers and those proficient with projectiles, such as slings, throwing sticks, and spears, were of particular importance to the military. Behind the archers, groups of men practiced hand to hand combat with daggers and small hand axes.

Bekeh came up beside Merneith and spoke in a low voice into her ear. "He is certainly much respected by the soldiers." She nodded in the direction of Bey, who stalked amongst the men, making adjustments or suggestions here and there. "I believe without a doubt he is a better choice for a lover than Atab. He is a favorite amongst the militias and leaders. Though if Atab were indeed an enemy it might be wise to be as close to him as possible. It is, perhaps, not too late still to acquire the both of them."

Merneith gave a soft snort. She had no interest in *acquiring* Atab now. It had been almost four weeks since they had arrived in Ta-Senet, and Bey had spent several evenings in Merneith's room. Despite their attempts at discretion, Merneith was finding it difficult enough to keep one affair secret, never mind if she were to begin a second one. Never mind that she feared she was developing real feelings for Bey, and that was dangerous and foolish considering their precarious circumstances.

"How do you know the men prefer Bey?" Merneith asked, even though it was obvious watching them that the soldiers had respect for him. He worked alongside them, was not ungenerous, and treated them with respect. But Merneith secretly enjoyed the opportunity to hear Bey praised, and she felt a swell of pride at the loyalty he seemed to inspire in those around him. Then she chastised herself for her impractical feelings, it wasn't as if she had any hand in his behavior, or the feelings he evoked in others. *It has nothing to do with me.*

Bekeh gave her a sly smile. "Well I have heard from *some* of the men that he is much admired."

Merneith raised an eyebrow but her lips twitched upwards as she cocked her head to the side. "*Some* of the men? How many have you spoken to about this?"

Bekeh gave a languid shrug as she kept her eyes on the soldiers. "Oh I know not. Three or four, perhaps." Merneith snorted again. She was quite sure that Bekeh had done more than *speak* with the men. Bekeh had far less need for secrecy in her affairs than Merneith did, and she had certainly seemed to enjoy her time amongst the admiring militia men and visiting governors. *If only I had no one to be accountable to.*

In the few weeks they'd been in Ta-Senet there had been a flurry of letters and messengers between Merneith and the court of Thinis, and with Wadj in the far north. She had sent word of her safe arrival in Ta-Senet and her wish to remain there for a time in the safety of the garrison. Wadj, for his part, expressed less concern for her well-being and more anger at her willingness to leave Thinis in the hands of Amka, the advisor. He refused to cut short his trip through the north, and demanded that she return to the capital herself. She knew that there would be an argument when they both returned to Thinis, but the several days distance between letters as the messengers traveled up and down the great river bought her extra time, and enabled her to defy Wadj's orders of a swift return.

"And what of the governors and priests?" Merneith turned to Bekeh, taking her arm and walking with her in the shade of the covered walkway that lined the quadrangle. She didn't want to be overheard. "Have you *spoken* with many of them recently?"

Merneith had spent much of her time in Ta-Senet meeting with some of the nearby high priests and priestesses, as well as the governors of the various regions, the *sephats*, of Upper Kemet. As soon as word of the assault on their queen reached them, most were quick to pledge their fealty to her and her protection. Many traveled to her in person, heading their militias to prove their loyalty.

Bekeh widened her eyes in an innocent expression and placed a hand to her chest, feigning surprise. "I would be remiss if I spent all my time in discussion with the soldiers and ignored the governors and priests, would I not?"

Merneith threw Bekeh a sidelong glance through slanted eyes, and Bekeh smiled, then continued. "Well of course they have many grievances against Wadj, many of which I believe you already know. They fear Wadj wants to go to war with Sumeria for Atab's sake, to place him back on the throne. Especially now that Atab's uncle has recovered from his illness. They fear that Atab will be especially impatient to lay siege to Sumer." Merneith nodded. In the course of receiving news from Thinis regularly, and frequent letters from Atab himself, Merneith had heard that Atab's uncle had recovered from his illness and had not recalled Atab to Sumeria. Atab was less than pleased.

"Also," Bekeh continued, "the priests are upset about this year's harvest. They expect a small harvest and some of the people are blaming Wadj because he failed to organize the reinforcement of the embankments."

Merneith made a noise of surprise. "He did not reinforce the embankments? This is the first I have heard of it!" At the beginning of the current season of *Akhet*, or the Flooding, it was always necessary to ensure that the Iteru would be directed over the agricultural fields. The flooding of the Iteru during the Akhet season was integral to a good harvest, and the pharaoh was expected to oversee the maintenance of the irrigation system that helped spread the fertile silt of the river over the farm lands.

Bekeh nodded. "Apparently he put off the priests and governors, telling them he would send in overseers, but he never did. Now the waters are flooding too much in some places and not flooding at all in others. And of course the waters are lower this year, so even if he had organized in time, the Akhet would still not be enough to ensure a good harvest. The priests are interpreting this as a sign of the gods' disfavour with the pharaoh."

"No!" Merneith stopped, looking at Bekeh in shock. If the Iteru wasn't flooding high enough, and the flow was not properly directed, the next year would be a lean one for everyone. Some might even starve. Merneith shook her head. "That will not help the unrest in the least."

Bekeh nodded, her mouth a tight, grim line. "Of course the priests are not pleased. They are already upset that Wadj is taking more than the usual share of the taxes. If the harvest is not good, there will be little enough left to collect the taxes and feed the gods, the temples, and the people altogether."

The temple priests controlled much of the farm land, and collected taxes, stored food, and accepted the offerings to the gods. Each temple employed hundreds, if not thousands, of people. Workers were paid in daily allowances of bread, sacks of grain, and jugs of beer, which could then be traded as currency if needed. If the harvests were to be bad, as predicted, thousands stood to go unpaid and face starvation.

The temples not only held power over the economic lives of the people, they also held spiritual power over them. In order to maintain support for his divine rulership, Wadj was expected to supply the temples with a portion of the collected taxes, as well as gifts and offerings. In his desire to drive people in the direction of his recently established cult of Wadj, in worship of himself as a living god, he had been neglecting the temples. And now they had even more reasons for dissatisfaction.

"The good news, my dear," Bekeh took Merneith's hand and tucked it into her arm, resuming their walk around the quadrangle, "is that you are still very popular with the priests. They see your arrival in Ta-Senet during the season of Akhet as a sign from the gods, and from the goddess Neith herself, that they favour you during this time of need." Ta-Senet was home to the largest temple of Neith in Kemet and Neith, Merneith's namesake, was considered the goddess of war and water. "They believe that Neith has expressed her will that you be the one to save Kemet from ruin. The flooding, your arrival in the home of Neith, the failed attempt on your life, they believe that all have aligned to prove your divinity and closeness to the gods."

Merneith took a moment to process this new information. It was more important than ever that she find a way to control Wadj. Hunger made people desperate, and that made them dangerous, particularly if they believed Wadj was the cause of their desperation.

"Yet," Merneith countered, "not all of the priests and governors of the south have come to Ta-Senet. Their allegiance may still be in question. And then there are the nobles. Wadj has many supporters among them." Merneith felt her mouth twist in scorn. "They love his hunting parties, and the gifts of land and titles."

Bekeh nodded. "And there is still no way of knowing for sure what is happening with all the sephats in the north. If Wadj is traveling there perhaps he has made a better impression." Bekeh gave Merneith a sidelong look, one eyebrow raised in skepticism. "Then again, perhaps he is making a worse one."

Merneith sucked her lips in derisively. "The latter is the most likely. Except amongst his entourage, who are currently enjoying his food and drink and entertainment."

Bekeh and Merneith turned into a hallway in the garrison, passing through to the other side of the building and out into a vegetable garden. Root vegetables, lettuce, and celery were arranged in orderly rows. Date palm and sycamore trees clustered around the walls that enclosed the garden. The two women walked along a path in the shade of the trees, where they were completely alone.

Bekeh cleared her throat and turned to Merneith. Her eyes had that hard, analytical look that Merneith was accustomed to. "And what will you do now that the militias have almost all gathered and are preparing to return to Thinis? Wadj is due back from the north shortly."

Merneith shook her head and looked off over the rows of vegetables, chewing her inner lip. "I know not how to proceed from here."

She felt as if things were moving towards something. As if a sandstorm were building off in the distance, evident only by the hazy gray outline of the horizon rather than the crystalline break between beige desert and blue sky. Like a sandstorm, though, she had no idea when it would hit or what the resulting damage would be.

Bekeh nodded. "I see. I realize this is difficult. But Mer, there are many who favour you over Wadj, and would support you."

Merneith compressed her lips, pulling them in. Determined, she said, "I am not yet prepared for a coup, Mewet. It is only fair I speak with Wadj before acting, or else I may lose the people's support."

Bekeh gripped her forearm tightly and hissed close to her ear. "If you wait to speak with Wadj it will be too late. You will lose the element of surprise. You *know* he might have been the one who ordered the attack against you. Was it not convenient that the assault came mere days after he left for the north?"

"I cannot in good conscience wage war against him without just cause." Merneith insisted. "There is no proof of anything."

Of course there are suspicions, but if being under suspicion of wrong doing was cause enough for warfare there would be few people left in the world...

Bekeh licked her lips and gave Merneith a scornful look. "You need not wage war against him, silly girl. There are other ways to *eliminate* a problem."

Merneith narrowed her eyes. "No. Not like that. I will not just 'eliminate' Wadj."

Bekeh shook her head. "Then what are you doing with this army you have brought together, my dear? Why not just throw yourself in the Iteru now and let Wadj do as he pleases? He will not listen to reason any longer."

Merneith clenched her fists. "I must try. He is still my brother, and my husband."

"And what do you intend to do with the Sekhrey?"

That question caught Merneith off guard and she looked back out over the garden, watching as the sharp needle-point fronds of the date palms rustled in the breeze. She had no idea what would happen between her and Bey when they returned to Thinis, and she had been trying to avoid thinking too hard on it. She feared that her affair with Bey was obvious to others, despite their attempts to keep it hidden. Although they were careful to not be seen standing too close to one another, or caught alone, she worried that there had been clues, secret smiles and glances that others may have noticed. Once they returned to Thinis, things would have to change drastically. They could not afford to be discovered, especially by one of Wadj's adversarial advisors.

There was something else that Merneith was beginning to fear as well, a nagging suspicion that had begun to take seed in her mind but that she kept putting aside in the hopes that it could not be true. She was over two weeks late for her time of the month. She had not had a flow since before leaving Thinis. *Since before Bey and I...* She prayed that it was only the stress of traveling and everything else that had interrupted her monthly cycle.

She kept her eyes on the trees, wishing she could see beyond the walls of the garden to the world outside. On the one hand, the walls of Ta-Senet, and the presence of so many people who supported her, had afforded her a sense of security that had carried over to her evenings with Bey. She had felt safe and secure sleeping with Bey by her side, no matter how impractical it was for the future. On the other hand, the walls of Ta-Senet now seemed to be closing in on her, and she felt their heavy, impenetrable weight crushing against her, rendering her immobile.

She sighed. "I do not know what to do about Bey, Mewet. If Wadj found us out he would doubtless suspect us of conspiring against him. He would have Bey executed, and possibly myself. And you, and Penebui, simply for being close to me." She added with sarcasm, "If we were lucky, he might *only* exile us, or just imprison us for life."

Bekeh quipped at her in a low voice, but it was obvious from the frustrated tone of her voice that she knew Merneith wouldn't listen to her, "All the more reason to prevent Wadj from getting the chance to catch you."

Merneith sighed. "Not yet, mewet. I cannot yet." Merneith knew she wouldn't be able to explain to Bekeh that if she were to have Wadj murdered, Merneith would be no better than the monster Wadj had become.

Later that night Mernieth lay with her head on Bey's chest, tracing a lazy finger over the lines of his tattoo. It was late, and Merneith knew these moments were precious. Her earlier conversation with Bekeh was replaying in her mind.

"Mer," Bey cupped a hand around her shoulder.

"Mmmm?" She stayed focused on his chest.

Bey cleared his throat. "I do not think you should return to Thinis with us."

She lifted her head to look at him, startled. "What?"

His intense eyes bore in to her. His mouth was a grim line. "You should stay here and send an ambassador and some of the militias to Thinis instead. It is not safe for you there. We still do not have proof of who is responsible for the attack against you. Wadj and Atab and any number of dangerous enemies will be waiting for your return. It would be best not to give them another opportunity to threaten your safety."

"I also cannot hide in a military camp in Ta-Senet forever." She kept her face neutral although her eyes narrowed. *Why is he saying this now?*

"Mer, that is not what I am proposing." Bey blew out a deep breath, and Merneith felt his chest rise and fall beneath her palm. She snatched her hand away and pushed herself back across the bed, putting a couple of inches of space between them as she propped herself up on one elbow and drew the sheet up over her breasts.

"Then what *are* you proposing?"

He put up a hand as if to calm her. "Mer, please do not get defensive. I am trying to discuss your safety."

"Fine. Then who do you propose I send in my stead? *You?*"

"I did not say that, although I do think I should be there in case something happens. You could send Bekeh or write to Amka to act on your behalf. Just until we know more."

"Yes, I think that would be a wonderful plan. I do not foresee any problems arising from sending *my lover* to speak with *my husband* about him possibly trying to kill me. And what do you propose that my *ambassador* relate to the pharaoh on my behalf?" She was in a foul mood now, being forced twice in one day to think of departing Ta-Senet, and the sense of comfortable security that had enveloped her since she'd first fallen asleep in Bey's arms. She dreaded the return to the scandal-ridden, treacherous world of responsibility, and Thinis. It felt good to release some of her tension in venom-laced verbosity.

Bey ran a hand through his hair and swore under his breath, then said through clenched teeth, "I did not *say* that *I* should be the one to speak with him."

But Merneith didn't appreciate being ambushed with this notion while naked, in bed, post-coital, even though she knew that they were never otherwise alone. If he had brought this up during a meeting with the governors and priests she would have been even more incensed, but she refused to acknowledge that he had acted with tact. "What shall you tell him? That he is widely disliked, and that he should step down and let me rule?" Her eyes narrowed even further. "Or would you prefer to tell him that he should just hand Kemet over to you instead?"

"Mer, what are you doing? You are not listening to me."

"What is there to hear? You do not want me to return to Thinis. You would prefer to leave me here in seclusion, to exclude me from the operations of my own land."

"What? No! That is ridiculous, Mer, and you know it. By the gods, will you listen to me? I am trying to arrange it so that you are in a better position to take control of Kemet. I care nothing for my own role in it. If I thought for a moment you would acquiesce I would tell you to come away with me and flee to the south, to Nubia, or to the other side of the great ocean. Forget Kemet and Wadj and all these problems." Bey pinched a thumb and forefinger over the bridge of his nose, then scrubbed the palm of his hand across his jaw. Over the past month he had allowed the stubble to grow into a closely trimmed beard that only served to enhance his rugged handsomeness and make his unusual green eyes stand out all the more. It was his handsomeness, and the effect it had on her, that now that incensed her all the more. She could not allow her feelings for him to make her weak.

"Flee? That is an option? And do what? Live in poverty? Or will you return to pirating?" Bey looked stung, and Merneith felt a small bit of remorse for her harsh comments. Although she herself had fantasized about what it would be like to live a different life somewhere, without the constraints of her responsibilities as queen, hearing Bey say it out loud made her realize how absurd it would be to just run away.

"That is not fair." Bey clenched his jaw.

"*Life* is not fair. I cannot just abandon my duty, and run away. *I* have people who depend on me. Perhaps we have taken things too far. Perhaps it is time to end this now before it gets out of control." She couldn't believe that she had said that. *This is not what I want. But what else can I do? I cannot run, I cannot abandon Kemet. We cannot get caught, I cannot let my emotions take control of my reason.*

"*Duty.*" Bey's face twisted in an angry grimace. "No, I suppose you cannot possibly fathom happiness without the comforts of the court and your *duty* as an excuse to continue on as before."

It was Merneith's turn to be stung. "What does *that* mean?"

Bey stood, snatching up his shenti and tying it roughly. "Oh do not think I did not know about all your letters from that Sumerian bastard. I know that he writes you regularly, and that you promptly write back."

Merneith started. She hadn't known Bey had been monitoring her correspondence. *Not that I have done anything wrong.* From the moment they had arrived in Ta-Senet, Sar Atab had sent several letters expressing his concern for her safety and his desire for her to either return to Thinis or to allow him to join her in the garrison with his own guard. He'd also shared the news that his uncle, King Alalngar of Sumeria, had recovered.

Merneith had politely declined Atab's requests, especially after she learned that some of the men who had attacked their warships were said to have spoken Sumerian. She wasn't ready to implicate Atab yet, as she well knew that mercenaries could come from anywhere and if someone were to attempt to kidnap or kill her, it would make sense to hire from outside Kemet. But the possibility remained that Atab was involved somehow, and she had decided it best to keep him at arm's length. Furthermore, Atab was perceptive, and he would have quickly realized the nature of her relationship with Bey if he'd seen them together. She hadn't told Bey about the letters simply because she hadn't thought much of them. Now, though, she was angered that Bey had been watching her, and evidently didn't trust her.

She glared at Bey down the length of her nose. "And so what if I write Sar Atab? I assume that if you are spying on me you also know the nature of the letters."

Bey growled, "I do not need to know the particulars. Your desire to return to Thinis says it all."

Merneith's cheeks flushed at the accusation. "Well then, *Sekhrey,*" she placed a bitter emphasis on the title, "if I have already been convicted of an affair with Sar Atab then there is nothing more to say, is there?" She saw him flinch and felt both remorse and triumph for the wound she'd inflicted. Merneith didn't want this. She wanted him to call her bluff, to stop her from saying the things she was saying, but she couldn't help herself.

"I suppose not," Bey turned to her with narrowed eyes, his hands clasped into fists by his side and his thick muscles clenched, "since *I* have already been convicted of attempting to steal the throne of Kemet."

Merneith couldn't bring herself to answer him. She only lifted her chin and hugged her knees tighter to her chest.

Bey gave her a hard look, "Good night, Hem-etj. *Senebti.*" Bey bowed stiffly, spun on his heel, threw open the door and slammed it behind him.

Merneith drew in a shaky breath which turned into a sob. She keeled over on her side, her face pressed into the pillow, and let the painful, wracking contractions of her chest take over.

The next few days the preparation for the return to Thinis kept Bey busy, and he avoided Merneith. Their argument had upset him more than he cared to acknowledge. *It's not as if you did not see this coming. It could not last.* He told himself. *This was bound to happen.* Regardless, he'd been angry. Angry that after the nights they'd spent together, and all he'd done to prove himself to her, she still didn't trust him. He was angry that she'd accused him of trying to take the throne, and angry that she hadn't told him about the letters from Atab. He felt betrayed and wrongfully censured.

He also felt like an ass. He should have kept his cool. He was fairly sure that there was nothing between Atab and Merneith, despite the Sumerian's attempts to woo her. He'd let his own past get in the way, and he'd spoken out of resentment at her accusations and the things she'd said. *Life is not fair. I cannot just abandon my duty, and run away. We have taken things too far.* She'd said. *Perhaps it is time to end this now before it gets out of control…* He'd heard it before. Still, he wished he could take back what he'd said to Merneith. In the end though, he doubted it would make much difference. *She* was the one who had started it. He had tried to placate her, and *she* had been unreasonable.

Then again, he always suspected she would not sacrifice anything for a man of little means. *It is no surprise that a woman should choose comfort and power over an unsteady life. It is just like the gods to put such a woman in my path then snatch her away to watch me squirm. I will not give them, or her, that satisfaction this time.* Experience had taught him that emotion and attraction and perhaps, maybe, even love, were not enough to appeal to a woman.

A week later, when they were set to sail back to Thinis, Bey made sure that Merneith and the women were placed on another warship with Ebrium at its helm. He felt it best to keep as much distance between them as possible. After all, it was what *she* had said she wanted.

Bey was also irritated by the lack of planning. He knew that Merneith didn't want to launch any sort of offensive against Wadj. They had discussed that already. But he wished that there was some set course of action. They were to return to Thinis with an army, and *then what*? He was no longer privy to her plans, and he had no idea what she would say or do when Wadj returned from the north. He was frustrated and there was nothing he could do about it, except harden his heart and do his best to watch over her from a distance.

Chapter 14 – Wadj

Merneith paced the length of one of Wadj's meeting rooms, twisting the ends of the white scarf draped around her shoulders. The room was spacious and bright, with a south facing row of windows along one wall, veiled by sheets of billowing white linen. Beneath one window was a large, ornately carved desk made of yew imported from the far north of the great sea and inlaid with ivory, behind which Wadj was known to sit and bark out his commands. Several stools were clustered near the desk. An arrangement of carved wooden chairs rested in one corner and a large cupboard stood against one wall.

Wadj had arrived in Thinis last night and had sent word that he expected her presence in his chambers after the morning meal. She had been walking up and down his meeting room for some time and with each moment her heart beat harder, her hands twisted tighter in her scarf, and her gut grew heavier.

Merneith herself had returned to Thinis just five days ago. The trip home along the Iteru was uneventful, although there had been much anticipation of a repeat attack. This time, however, they were traveling with a few dozen ships full of militia soldiers from the southern *sephats*, along with various governors and priests. Anyone would be a fool to attempt an attack against such a force without months of preparation to gather enough forces to prepare an effective assault.

Merneith had now spent two weeks in agony. Two weeks since she and Bey had argued and it had been near impossible to push him from her mind. He hadn't spoken to her directly since their argument and she could tell he was avoiding her. Merneith knew she was mostly to blame for the fight. She'd taken her frustrations out on him, lashing out at him and unjustly accusing him of trying to seize power for himself, something that, deep down, she didn't really believe he wanted. But then he'd accused her of wanting to return for Atab's sake, and she believed he'd done it just to hurt her. And it had worked.

Since their argument she'd immersed herself in the affairs of Kemet, but her body betrayed her with its memories of his smell, his touch, *the taste of him*. She would catch a glimpse of a servant rubbing a hand over his chin and, in her mind's eye, would see Bey scrubbing his stubble the way he did when he was tired, or agitated. Her body ached to wrap her arms around him and press her face against his chest, to draw in a deep breath of his warm, comforting scent. She hated how her body's weakness divulged the secrets of her heart that her mind was trying to hide. *But in the end, this is for the best, no matter how it ended. We cannot be together.* And then there was that nagging anxiety that had been growing stronger each day… her time of the month had still not come.

None of these thoughts eased her anxiety about seeing Wadj for the first time in two months. Batr had accompanied her and was outside the closed doors as, upon leaving Ta-Senet, Bey had placed her back under guard. Makae, Batr had told her this morning, had been assigned to safeguard Wadj. Merneith marveled at that as she doubted Wadj would appreciate being trailed any more than she did.

Finally, the great doors to the room swung inwards and in strode Wadj. Merneith drew herself up to her full height, standing rigid while trying to assess her husband's mood. He wore a plain white shenti, but around his shoulders was draped a large leopard skin, its great head and front paws hung over one breast, while the hind quarters dangled over the other. Around his neck he wore a wide beaded collar of gold and blue beads. The striped linen *nemes* headdress of the pharaoh flared up and around his shaved head. He certainly *dressed* like a pharaoh, and had an imperious air to him, Merneith thought, but compared to Bey, Wadj was like a boy playing dress-up. Bey, unadorned in nothing but a plain shenti, had a far more regal air to him. And it was not just because Bey was larger than Wadj in both height and width. Wadj was not ill-conditioned. He was, after all, a sporting man

174

who excelled in hunting and fishing and fighting. Compared to many men, Wadj was in fine physical condition. No, it was something else that made Bey the superior of the two. *Not that it matters now*, Merneith reminded herself.

There was no time to think of Bey, though, as Wadj stalked towards her. His dark, long-lashed eyes were narrowed, full lips tightened in an angry slash. His chin thrust out as he glared at her. There was an energy surrounding him that push at her with an oppressive force, and she took an involuntary step back. Panic rose up into her throat as she realized something about Wadj had changed, something inexplicable, something that *frightened* her.

"*Sister*," Wadj hissed as he came to stand mere inches in front of her, assessing her with his cold, dark eyes.

Merneith drew in a shaky breath to calm herself. "Brother," she gave a slight bow of her head. "Pharaoh, Hemek." She called him *Your Majesty*, in the hopes that a show of respect would soften him enough to speak calmly with her.

"Do not feign deference, *sister*," Wadj tossed out the last word with bitterness, not even bothering to call her by her rightful titles. "You have flagrantly disobeyed my orders on several occasions and defied my authority. Let us not *pretend* that you respect me."

Merneith was shocked by his venomous attack. It was true they had argued before he left Thinis, but even then there had been some modicum of decorum. Never before had there been such a verbal assault against her. Merneith took a step back from him and bumped into the corner of his desk. She placed her right hand on it for support.

"Brother, that is simply not true. *My life* was threatened. I had no choice." Merneith reached her left hand up to her throat, pulling the edges of her scarf together as if to protect herself.

"No choice?" He mocked, raising his voice an octave to imitate her. "No choice but to disobey me and leave Thinis when I explicitly told you before I left that you were to *stay here?!*" Wadj said the last two words as if they were a command, and he thrust his pointed finger towards the ground to emphasize his point. "No choice but to flee to Ta-

Senet with the royal guard and stay there for almost *five weeks* when I very clearly told you to *return immediately to Thinis*?!" Wadj thrust his finger down again and took a step towards her. "No choice but to stay there in order to raise an army *to bring against me here*?" Spittle flew from his lips as he took another step towards her.

"What? No! Of course not." Merneith took another step backwards, looking around for she knew not what, but perhaps to find something to shield herself with. "No, the militias were to protect me, to protect *us*, in case something else happened." She would not tell Wadj that it was Bey who had originally summoned the militias without her consent. If Wadj found out he would have Bey executed for treason.

Wadj barked out a laugh. "Protect us," he sneered. "Protect us *from what*, exactly, dear sister?"

"Fr-from another attack. *I was attacked,* Wadj. There have been rumours that the Hor-sekhenti-dju domain may rise up against you. Against *us*."

Wajdet's full lips twisted in a sneer, and Merneith thought that she had never seen him look so positively *maniacal*. His voice was low but clear as he scoffed, "Oh you need not fear an attack from *them* anymore. In a few days' time there will be no one left in Hor-sekhenti-dju to so much as squash a sand flea." Wadj gave a terrible grin and Merneith went cold all over.

"No," she breathed, taking a step towards him in her shock. "What are you doing?"

He ignored her question. "To prove my righteousness and power, tomorrow I leave to hunt the hippopotamus. I *will* show all in Kemet that *I am* the conqueror of evil and greater than the gods themselves." Wadj was referring to the custom of a pharaoh staging a hippopotamus hunt to prove his supremacy and might, as the animals were both revered and feared as powerful creatures, protective of their young and territory. They were extremely dangerous, and killed even more people and livestock along the great river than the vicious crocodiles. "Once I have returned victorious, and the Hor-sekhenti-dju domain has been vanquished, my power will be absolute and unquestioned." Wadj balled a hand into a fist and smirked.

"Wadj, you *cannot* do this. You cannot *kill* the people of Hor-sekhenti-dju. They are your subjects." Merneith stepped closer and grasped his left wrist, hoping to supplicate and calm him.

Wadj reacted as soon as her skin touched his. Faster than the jaws of a crocodile, the palm of his right hand cracked against her cheek. Merneith's head snapped back, she twisted, her abdomen slammed into the corner of the desk and the breath was knocked out of her. Pain stabbed through her side but she pushed herself upright and raised her own hand as if to strike back. "How dare…" but she was cut off by another rapid blow. This time she folded over the desk, her splayed arms sending papers and trinkets clattering to the floor, even as she herself bounced off the desk and fell crashing into the nearby stools. She cried out in shock and her hands flew to her belly even as she curled around herself. *Oh gods, if I truly am carrying Bey's child please protect it.*

Wadj moved to stand over her, spittle spraying again as he jabbed a finger at her huddled figure tangled in the broken stools. "It is time you and everyone else in Kemet remembered that *I* am Pharaoh. *I* am god-chosen. *I deserve* to be worshipped, and for those that question *my divine right to rule* there *will* be consequences."

At that moment Batr and Makae wrenched open the doors to the room and rushed in. Merneith realized they must have heard her cry out. She tried to shift and pull herself from the wreckage of the crushed stools.

"By the gods, Hem-etj, are you alright?" Batr was reaching down to pull her up, and Merneith was grateful for the strong, comforting arm he wrapped around her. They were risking their own positions by entering the Pharaoh's quarters without permission. In that instant Merneith knew Bey must have ordered them to protect her at all costs, and she felt a rush of gratitude and longing for him.

Wadj stepped behind his desk and said coolly, "The queen tripped and fell. You may remove her from my presence and see that she is safely deposited in her rooms. I think it best if she not leave them for a day or two." Wadj glared at Batr and continued. "And in the future, *wa'ew*, you would do well to remember your place and never enter my rooms without sanction." He turned to Makae and said, "You are not needed today. You may tell the Sekhrey I have dismissed you." Makae nodded, and accompanied Batr out the door. As Batr helped Merneith limp out of the room, her hand pressed to her abdomen, she could have sworn she saw Atab lurking in the shadows at the end of the hall.

A short time later, Merneith was laid out in her bed with Bekeh at her side. Bekeh had been in Merneith's rooms, waiting her return from her audience with Wadj, when Batr had carried Merneith in. Bekeh had been stricken by the sight of Merneith so disarrayed, by the trickle of blood seeping from the corner of her lip, and the bruise blossoming on her right cheek. She had immediately sent Batr to fetch the healer, a woman who lived in the palace complex. While they waited for the woman, Merneith related what had happened while Bekeh held her hand. At the end of her story Merneith closed her eyes, laying the back of her hand over her forehead and resting her head against her pillow.

Merneith whispered, "I am such a fool, Mewet. I thought I could help my brother to see reason. But he is beyond reason. He is no longer *even human*. He is a monster." She shook her head and opened her eyes, looking at her aunt. "I must find a way to stop him from harming our people. But I drove Bey away. I am all alone now. Alone with *that monster* of a man." She turned her head away into her pillow as tears began to ooze from her lids as she squeezed them shut.

"Nonsense." Bekeh patted her hand. "You are not alone. You have me, and we will find a way through this."

On Bekeh's insistence, the healer gave Merneith a careful, full body inspection. There was a small gash on Merneith's forehead, a deep splinter in her wrist, and a dark bruise forming on her belly from where she'd hit the desk. Running her tongue gingerly over her lips, Merneith could feel the right corner was cracked and she tasted blood. Her cheek was swollen and throbbing, and she worried that the flesh around her right eye was also beginning to swell. Finally, the healer smiled and nodded and said, "Aside from a few cuts and bruises, all is well." Bekeh let out a sigh of relief. The woman continued, "And you need not fear, Hem-etj, nothing has been harmed." Bekeh started, and Merneith's heartbeat froze.

Bekeh tilted her head. "What do you mean, *nothing* has been harmed?"

The woman proceeded to confirm what Merneith had been trying to deny, that which would incontrovertibly reveal the nature of her relationship with Bey. Merneith was pregnant.

Bey sat on the roof of his small hut. The sun was just beginning to set over the desert, and normally he would enjoy the vision of the mounds of bright sand turning pink under the dying rays of Ra's light. But tonight he was furious, and just barely able to contain his rage. And now, Batr and Makae had just related to him what had happened in the palace earlier that day, as far as they were able to determine. Bey had sworn deeply and ferociously when he'd heard how the men had burst into Wadj's room after hearing Merneith cry out, only to find her battered on the floor. To add to his fury Makae related what he had overheard when he'd snuck outside to listen to the pharaoh's conversation with Sar Atab after the trio had left Wadj's rooms.

"Batr took the queen to her rooms. I saw Atab in the hallway, and I was suspicious since the pharaoh had dismissed me, so I thought to try to listen to their conversation." Makae gave Bey an imploring look, as if seeking his approval. Bey nodded. "Good. And were you able to overhear them?"

Makae nodded. "I stood near his windows, and was not seen by any." Makae hesitated, looking uncomfortable. Bey held his breath. "Sekhrey, Wadj planned it. He *planned* the attempt on the queen's life, along with the Sumerian. He berated the prince for not accomplishing what they had agreed upon, even though he had been given not just one, but *two* opportunities."

Bey was not surprised by the revelation that the duo were involved in the attack on the warships. *But what was the second opportunity?* Then it hit him.

"Do you mean they planned the tiger attack, also?"

Makae nodded. "From what I gathered, I believe they paid one of the handlers to release the animal when they were near the queen. Atab was to maneuver the lady towards it. The plan was that if the tigers did not take her, they would move forward with the kidnapping and make it appear as if the Hor-sekhenti-dju had risen up and taken her. It would have given Wadj a perfect excuse to wipe out the domain and get rid of the queen at the same time."

"That bastard," Bey growled. Bey had hoped that time apart would make him forget his desire for Merneith. It had worked once before. When he had been rejected back in Ebla, it had not taken long before his pride and anger had helped him to overcome his sense of loss, although the feeling of bitter betrayal remained even now. But Merneith was not the same as *that* woman. Time apart had only enhanced his desire to see her, and with it, his profound loneliness at having lost her. *Not that you ever really had her to begin with.* He was continually reminded of the taste of her body, the smell of her hair, the feel of her legs wrapped around his, the look in her eyes as he entered her, the way she curled up against him after. Perhaps if he had only been truthful with her about how he felt… but it didn't matter now. Once again someone he cared for had been snatched from him and been badly hurt.

And the pharaoh was to blame. How sick Wadj must be, and how desperate was Atab, to devise such a plot to do away with the queen. Never before had Bey taken much pleasure in killing, it was simply something that had to be done. But now he relished the thought of it. He wanted to feel his hands wrapped around both their throats. A dozen possible deaths ran through his mind, each one too good for these men.

His murderous thoughts were interrupted by Makae clearing his throat. "Sekhrey, we must return to the palace. But there is one last thing you should know. The pharaoh is angry that you saved the queen. He had not expected you to be so efficient in your new position. I do not know what he intends to do about it, but I believe you should be on your guard."

"Of course. Thank you." Bey clipped. "Well done, men. You did well to protect Her Majesty today, and come to me when you could."

Bey led the brothers down the stairs along the side of his house and said his goodbyes as they made off through the back alley. As he turned to go back inside, a loud rapping noise echoed out and Bey strode around to the front of his house. There he was surprised to find Bekeh standing at his door, fist raised to knock again.

"*Nebet-i*, are you well?" Bekeh's face was ashen. She looked tired and drawn.

She shook her head. "I need to speak with you."

"Of course." Bey took her arm and tucked it into his, leading her up the stairs to the roof.

Bey poured Bekeh a mug of wine from a jug. She accepted the mug with a grateful nod and settled herself awkwardly, clearly unfamiliar with sitting on the ground in such a setting.

"I apologize for this, *nebet-i*," Bey waved around at the plain reed mats laid out on the roof and the lack of furniture. "I have little need for, well, *things*."

Bekeh waved her hand in dismissal although he saw her give a curious glance around the roof. Then she gave him a thin smile. "I had to ask one of the guards to lead me here. I have not been into the village in over a decade." Bey was surprised to hear that she had ever been in it at all, since the women of the palace almost never left the confines of one another's family houses except to be carried in a litter to the temple. "Sekhrey," Bekeh leaned forward, her face pinched. "There is something you must know."

Bey clenched his jaw and spoke in a gritty voice, "Batr and Makae have just informed me of what has happened today. *Nebet-i*, how is our queen now? The men tell me she is doing well, in spite of…" he cleared his throat, "*her husband.*" He couldn't stop the bitterness from lacing his words. He didn't know how much Bekeh knew about him and Merneith although he suspected that, given her perceptiveness, she knew more than enough.

Bekeh clenched a hand in the folds of her dress and stared off in the distance at the sun setting over the desert dunes. She said in a low voice, "Wadj is an animal, Sekhrey. You know what Batr and Makae *saw*, but not what Wadj *said.*" Bekeh told him of Wadj's plans to slaughter the unruly domain in the north. "I have spoken with Amka, their governor and advisor to the queen, and he will send word to prepare the people for battle, but we must find a way to stop it from happening."

Bey could hardly be shocked by Wadj's flagrant admission of his plans. Clearly the man thought he was unstoppable, or else he would not be so forthright. He shook his head, drawing breath in through flared nostrils. He wanted Wadj dead more than he had ever wanted any man to die. Instead, he said, "*Nebet-i*, I do not know what you would like for me to do. Wadj and Atab have conspired to harm the queen and yet she has bound my hands. I repeatedly warned her. I *asked her* not to return to Thinis and to let me come in her place, for you to speak on her behalf. She refused. She has," he paused, looking for words, "*dismissed me* from her presence." He drew in his lower lip and bit down on it hard to stop himself from growling his frustration. Even as he said it, though, he knew that regardless of whatever Merneith had said, he would find a way to rid the world of Wadj. Better that he incur Merneith's wrath and never see her face again, or even be executed for murdering the pharaoh, than live with the knowledge that he could have stopped her from getting hurt again and didn't.

Bekeh rested her eyes on his, searching his face. "I am aware there has been some sort of… disagreement. But this is nothing," Bekeh waved her hand dismissively again. "Mer can be *difficult* sometimes, but if you care for her you will not let this stop you." Bey opened his mouth to protest and she cut him off. "Unless, that is, you prefer sitting on your roof alone at night to the warm bed of a woman." Bey's eyebrows rose slightly. It had been a long time since anyone had deigned to chastise him, as his own mother used to.

Nonetheless, he knew that she was right. Before he did something to Wadj that might result in one or both of their deaths, he needed to see Merneith.

Bey waited outside Merneith's door for no more than a moment for Bekeh to warn Merneith of his arrival before he strode in to her room. Bekeh had seated herself a little distance from Merneith, who was sitting in a chair near the window, bathed in moonlight and the wavering glow of oil wicks. Seeing her left side in shadowy profile looking out the window, Bey was suddenly hit with the immense weight of his feelings for her. It wasn't just because she was beautiful, and the queen of Kemet, the land that had adopted him when his own had essentially exiled him. He admired her strength, respected her conviction, appreciated her sharp wit, and desired her in a way that he had never before wanted a woman. She drove him mad with her obstinacy, made him desperate and furious when she refused to listen, and yet inspired a vengeful, protective instinct in him that he never imagined feeling for a woman. But she had turned him away and, despite what Bekeh had said, he felt there was nothing he could do except to harden himself to her.

He hadn't needed the knowledge that Wadj intended to murder a whole town to inspire him to kill the pharaoh. It only made him burn to end the man's existence all the more. He just had to find a method that wouldn't cast suspicion on Merneith.

"Hem-etj," Bey stopped a few feet from Merneith's chair and gave a courteous bow. His face felt tight and his breath shallow.

She turned to him and it was then that he saw how puffy the right side of her face was. Bey swore under his breath, he took a step closer and his fists clenched. *He was going to kill Wadj.* The thought looped through his head, over and over. His hands could almost feel the pharaoh's throat under their grasp.

Merneith lifted her chin in a way that he had come to recognize as her steeling herself, preparing for a fight. Whether that fight would be with him or her own self he didn't always know. Tears glistened in her eyes and she turned her face away from him.

"Hem-etj," he continued in a strangled voice, only the last scraps of his ragged pride enabled him to keep his voice from breaking, from running straight to the pharaoh's rooms and strangling the bastard in his bed. "I promised you once that I would consult you before acting on anything of consequence. I have come to inform you that I have learned that your husband and the Sumerian prince have conspired against you, planning both the tiger attack and the assault that ended with you being shot. Makae overheard the pharaoh and Atab speaking after..." he clenched his fists tight and cleared his throat. "After your meeting this morning." He paused. Still gazing out at the desert, she gave a slight nod, as if this were expected.

"And to tell you," he paused and licked his lips. "I received a summons this afternoon. I am expected to accompany his majesty on the hippopotamus hunt tomorrow. Ebrium will remain here to assist you with governing the militias. Makae will also remain, and there will be guards with you *at all times.*"

Merneith still did not turn, but gave another nod of her head. He thought he saw her jaw clenching, but it was difficult to tell with the shadows dancing around the room.

He steeled himself for what he was about to tell her, in case she tried to fight against it. "Hem-etj, *Mer*," he allowed himself the liberty of using the term of endearment, in case he never had another opportunity. At the same time he tried to soften his voice, knowing how likely she was to get angry if she thought he was pushing her too much, but the intensity of his rage at seeing her so silent and bereft left his voice a hoarse growl. "While we are away I intend to ensure that Wadj will *never* touch you again, nor will he be capable of engaging

184

anyone   else   to   do   so."

He waited. He hadn't asked her a question, and he intended to act regardless of her response. But still he wanted, no *needed* to know that she would not condemn him for it. He didn't want to leave thinking she would hate him if he returned alive and Wadj did not. He could see her draw in a breath, the silhouette of her breasts, those beautiful breasts that he had once cradled in his hands and nuzzled with his lips, rising and stilling as she hesitated. Then she released her breath and gave an almost imperceptible nod of assent.

"Then *senebti, nebet-i*." *Be well, my lady.* They were not the last words he would have liked to say to her, but since she had chosen not to speak with him, there seemed little more for him to do but take his leave and find a means to end the pharaoh's life. *And quite possibly lose his own in the process.*

Bey was just turning to leave when Merneith cleared her throat. "Sekhrey." She spoke in a throaty rasp. Bey looked back at her. She inclined her face in his direction, her large eyes studying him with a look of trepidation. Bey gave in to his inclination, crossed the room to her in two strides, cupped her dark face in his hands and tilted her lips up to his. *The gods be damned, if killing Wadj is the last thing I do at least I can take this to my grave.* Bey pressed those soft lips with his own for what would likely be the last time. He had no words to express his feelings, but in that moment he hoped that his kiss had said enough.

When he drew back he thought he saw the ghost of a sad smile cross her features and then she lifted her chin just a half an inch and said, "Do come back alive."

Chapter 15 – The Thrill of the Hunt

Early the next morning, while the stars were still twinkling in the sky and the sun was just beginning to emerge over the great river to the east, Bey and Ebrium sat atop Bey's roof. Ebrium, his arm finally healed enough to be of some use, was resting on his side, his elbow propped up on a cushion. Bey paced the roof.

"You will need to help the queen to keep the peace between the militias, and the governors." Bey reminded Ebrium in Eblaiti, although they had already gone over this as soon as Bey had received the messenger yesterday letting him know that he was expected on the hunt. "And no one is to go *near* her. Amka will take care of any minor disputes." Bey didn't stop to look at Ebrium as he paced back and forth. Bey had told him of Wadj's assault on Merneith, but so far the news had been contained within the small circle of those directly involved. Bekeh had made it clear that no one else was to know, and Bey had wholeheartedly agreed. If the servants got wind of Wadj's assault, it wouldn't be long before all of Thinis was talking of it. And if Bey should succeed in doing away with Wadj, he didn't want a shadow of suspicion to be cast over Merneith as a result. Wadj still had some loyal supporters, and it wouldn't do for there to be any stain of guilt on Merneith for them to accuse her of.

Bey didn't yet have a specific plan for killing the pharaoh. Around fifty men were to make up the hunting party, including some of the royal guard, the Sumerian's own royal guard, hunters, fowlers, some noblemen, and Wadj's attendants. It would be difficult to get Wadj alone and murdering the pharaoh out in the open would likely result in either Bey's own immediate death, or one that Merneith would have to command. For all he knew, someone might oppose him if he were to kill Wadj, and if he were to kill the pharaoh in front of witnesses Merneith would have no choice but to sentence Bey to death. There was no way she could let the pharaoh's murderer go free. But that in itself could cause dissent amongst those loyal to Bey. He had to act carefully.

However, hunting trips could sometimes present opportunities for "accidents" to happen. A mad hyena or wild cat could attack and take multiple lives, a wrong step could result in being sucked into the muddy marshes along the banks of the river, an arrow or a knife slash could go awry in the heat of the moment. He just had to maintain his composure long enough for such a chance to present itself.

Ebrium applied to Bey. "Brother, let me go with you." Ebrium gave a grim smile, wrapping his hands into fists and cracking his knuckles. "Lest you rob me of the satisfaction of watching the Sumerian's heart bleed out. I would like nothing better than to take care of that smug bastard for you, while you deal with the pharaoh. And should you encounter any opposition, I will at least be there to assist you."

Bey shook his head. "No. I need you here to watch over Merneith. I do not trust that Wadj will not try something else against her. She will need someone loyal by her side while we are gone."

Ebrium leaned towards a bowl of fresh dates. Plucking a handful out and popping one in his mouth, he mumbled. "But if you take me with you, you are more likely to return."

"No. There is also Akshaka and Ishara to think of. They will need you alive more than they need me." Bey had reached the length of the roof. He turned and made his way back towards Ebrium. Ebrium was about to speak, likely to refute this last statement, when Bey cut him off and gave him a hard look. "And brother, you must promise me that whatever happens, if Wadj should come back instead of me, you will find a way to protect the queen."

Ebrium cocked his head and studied Bey. He didn't answer for a moment and Bey knew what he was thinking. In his agitation and insistence he had revealed the depth of feelings towards Merneith, the feelings that he himself had only finally acknowledged to himself last night.

Ebrium was the first to speak. "So. It is like that." Was all he said.

Bey clenched his jaw and gave a low grunt. "So it is." He squinted off in the distance, towards the rising sun. He rubbed his jaw with the palm of his hand, then ran it up through his hair.

The skin around Ebrium's blue orbs crinkled as he narrowed his eyes and nodded. "Well then, brother. All the more reason to kill the pharaoh and come back alive." *Come back alive*, rang in Bey's ears as Merneith's last words echoed back at him. He hoped he would be able to do just that.

That day the palace was busy with preparations for the pharaoh's hippopotamus hunt. The ships were due to leave late in the afternoon and there was much work to be done to prepare the large hunting party. Through the windows of her private rooms, Merneith watched the servants scurrying back and forth across the courtyard and gardens, carrying supplies and messages. Bekeh had put out the word that the queen was ill and not to be disturbed under any circumstances. The exotic and imposing Makae, posted as always outside her door, ensured that no one even tried.

Merneith could not help but find it ironic that the one time she did not want to be alone with her thoughts she had no choice but solitude. The mere thought of the women of the palace fussing over her bruises and gossiping and questioning her about Wadj and his rapid departure was enough to make her cringe. The truth of the situation must be kept a complete secret, something not easily done in the palace.

Bekeh and Penebui sat with her periodically, but Merneith couldn't bring herself to talk, though she longed for distraction. The other two women tried, but Merneith knew that they, too, were too much focused on the troubles they would all face if Wadj were not stopped.

Merneith was agitated and wretched beyond imagining. The moment Bey had walked out her door last night and Bekeh retired for bed, she had succumbed to the painful, wracking sobs she had been fighting back since Bey had arrived. She had unleashed such cries that made her bruised abdomen ache, her throat raw, and her eyes hot and swollen. *What a mess I have made of things. Me and my insufferable pride and stupidity.* Bey was leaving tomorrow with Wadj, and it was almost certain that only one of them would be returning alive, if either of them did at all. While she couldn't quite wish Wadj or Atab dead, she feared for her own safety, and that of her child. *Bey's child.* If Wadj learned of her condition, he would most assuredly have her killed. Merneith scoffed to herself. *There is no doubt of that. He has tried to kill me twice already, and I was still faithful then. Imagine what he would do if he discovered I have been with Bey.*

She was desperate for Bey's safety, but she'd been unable to say more than she had last night. A mix of pride, fear of rejection, and shame had kept her silent. She could only hope that she had conveyed at least something of her feelings in the little she *had* said.

When the preparations for the hunt were complete, the pharaoh, the hunters, and a group of soldiers packed off and the ships were launched. An eerie silence fell over the palace and the courtyard. Merneith was left to wait for news of death, either of her husband or her lover she knew not which.

The ships traveled slowly up the great river the first afternoon, heading towards a marshy location north of Thinis where hippos tended to congregate. The hunting party consisted of about fifty in all; the pharaoh, Sar Atab and his guard, noblemen of the pharaoh's entourage, about twenty skilled hunters and fowlers, servants, and a small contingent of the Royal Guard. Bey was stationed on a different ship than Wadj and Atab, although he kept an eye on the men as best he could from a distance. The two had begun drinking almost as soon as the ships had left Thinis. Although he knew it was too much to hope for, Bey found himself wishing Wadj would be stupid enough to just stagger overboard and disappear beneath the ripples of the Iteru.

That night, after the ships docked and the party had pitched their tents, Wadj and Atab sat around a fire along with their entourage of degenerate noblemen, getting drunk and obnoxious. Their raucous noise made it impossible for Bey to sleep and instead he prowled the edges of the camp late into the night, attempting to devise a plan to do away with Wadj. If he could find an opportunity to be alone with the man, perhaps in the swampy reeds along the river, he could slit his throat and toss him into the water. With any luck, the fish or the crocodiles would make short work of any evidence. If it came down to it, if he had no other option and could find no way to make the death look like an accident, Bey would kill the pharaoh out in the open, even if it meant his own death would shortly follow.

A contingent of guards ringed the camp and kept watch. Most of the guards were men who had traveled north with Wadj recently, and although Bey had met all of them when he became captain, they were men who had been a part of the guard before he'd joined. Wadj had chosen them to accompany the party, while Bey had only been instructed to choose three of his own men. He'd brought Batr and two soldiers he'd worked with for years. Not knowing for sure where the rest of the mens' loyalties lay put Bey's nerve on edge.

Eventually, the noise around the pharaoh's fire quieted. Noblemen nodded off in the sand, slumped with their heads on their chests. Some, like the pharaoh and Atab, staggered back to their tents with the assistance of servants. Bey laid down on a blanket stretched out on the hard ground inside his own small tent, lacing his hands behind his head. He watched the shadows of the nearby trees become elongated and grotesque; dancing in the remnants of the fire's dying light against the leather hide of the tent's surface. Sometime before dawn he nodded off into a fitful, unsatisfactory sleep.

Later that morning Bey stood near the edge of a clearing as the twenty hunters, along with some of the noblemen, gathered in a semi-circle to prepare the rites for Sobek, the crocodile-headed god of the river and hunting. It was customary to make offerings to the god to safeguard a hunting trip along the river. Like a crocodile, Sobek was believed to be vicious and cruel, and hunters feared incurring his displeasure. A priest of Sobek had been brought along by the hunting attendants to lead the rites.

The priest, a small, thin man with a shaved head and humble expression, was about to begin his supplications when Wadj stepped into the semi-circle of kneeling men. He wore the striped nemes headdress of a pharaoh that flared up and around his pate and, despite the growing heat of the day, a leopard skin draped over his naked shoulders. In his right hand he carried an elaborately decorated curved crook, the symbol of pharaonic power.

Wadj stabbed the end of the crook into the soft, sandy earth. His lip was curled up in a sneer and his shoulders thrown back, thrusting his chest out. "Fools," he hissed. "Who is this god you pray to? Have any of you seen him?"

The men looked at one another in confusion. Wadj continued to ridicule the men on their knees around him. "If you are to pay anyone tribute for a hunt, better you petition me, for *I* am the one who provides your weapons, your food, your drink. It is *I* who command you, and *I* to whom all the land and creatures of Kemet belong, yourselves included. Do not waste your time with gods you cannot see. I am a god of flesh and blood. Bow to me for your protection."

The priest, still standing in front of a small dark statue of the crocodile-headed god, cleared his throat. "Hem-ek," *Your majesty,* he began in a small voice. "Sobek is the god of the river, and without his blessing the hunt could go badly."

"The *god of the river?*" Wadj snorted, narrowing his eyes at the small priest, who seemed to grow even smaller under Wadj's stare. "*I* am the god of *everything* in this land. What use is one puny river god in the face of my greatness?"

Bey watched as the priest appeared to struggle with himself then, bravely, the man said with a gentle, yet quizzical expression on his face, "There is no denying your greatness, Hem-ek. But with all due respect, Hem-ek, no one man can be god of everything."

Wadj's eyes narrowed even further and Bey saw the hunters, still kneeling, appear to collectively hold their breath in fear. *Would the pharaoh actually kill a priest in front of them? What fresh madness is this?* Bey was about to step forward to do something, anything, to stop it when Wadj himself seemed to change his mind.

The pharaoh bared his teeth in a grin more wolfish than benign. He opened his arms wide, holding up his crook with its curved end, and said, "Lucky for you, priest, I am a benevolent god. Rather than strike your head from your shoulders for your insolence, I will teach you the correct path. This Sobek of yours is nothing to me. From now on, when you hunt you may pray *to me*," he emphasized this by pounding on his chest with his fists, the crook still clutched in his hand, "and *only* me."

The priest opened his mouth to protest, but appeared to think better of it and hung his head instead, wagging it gently. The men kneeling around the pharaoh did as they were told, but Bey could see their eyes narrow, their lips tighten, muscles tense. Even the pharaoh's entourage of noblemen shifted their feet and threw one another flitting glances of unrest.

Wadj then ordered the fowlers to prepare for a day of birding. Since they had yet to spot a hippopotamus, Wadj seemed eager to hunt and kill *something*, even if it were small prey. While the hunters prepared, Wadj sent a messenger to find Bey and bring him to the pharaoh's tent. Bey had been expecting they would have to meet at some point to discuss the events of the last two months. Nevertheless, he could feel his heart rate accelerate and adrenaline, rather than fear, coursed through him.

The pharaoh was seated inside a large tent set separately from his sleeping tent. Although the tent was sparsely decorated, Wadj sat on a large carved throne that had been brought on the ships specially for him. Two guards, men who had been in the north with Wadj, stood towards the back of the tent, on either side of Wadj's throne. A young servant boy, nude except for a flap of linen hanging in front and in back from a belt around his waist, placed a mug of wine on a stand next to the throne. Bey stepped in through a rolled up tent flap and kneeled. "Hem-ek." He ground out his respects through a tightened jaw.

"Sekhrey Bey," the pharaoh gave Bey the same wolfish grin he'd given the priest of Sobek earlier that morning. "Please accept my apologies that we have not had the opportunity to meet before now to discuss the *situation* with my sister." Wadj steepled his fingers and paused, watching Bey, obviously waiting for a reaction. Bey kept his face impassive. "I believe you are to be commended for your valour in saving her not once, but twice. You have done an admirable job of keeping the queen safe. I understand your actions have elevated you even further in the estimation of the people of Kemet. I would say you should be honoured, but I believe my sister has already," here the pharaoh's eyes narrowed and he paused as if searching for the right word. His lip curled upwards, "Shall we say she has already rewarded you with her favour?" He raised an eyebrow and studied Bey.

Bey kept his eyes on the pharaoh. His hands almost shook with the desire to wrap themselves around the sick bastard's throat. It was clear the man knew something had happened between him and Merneith, or at least he thought he did. But Bey couldn't kill him. Not here. Not yet. Not in front of the guards and the servant boy and with the tent flap open and exposed for all to see.

Bey arranged his face in a pleasant smile. He pretended to misread the pharaoh's insinuation and said in a calm voice, "The banquet the queen threw after the tiger attack was a generous affair, Hem-ek. I know the guardsmen enjoyed themselves as did I. Unfortunately, we have yet to catch the men who attacked our ships when we were traveling to Thinis. But rest assured, we are close and will find them and when we do, we will be sure they are harshly punished and put to death."

A smirk grew across the pharaoh's features. "I would expect no less, Sekhrey. *All* wrongdoers must receive their punishment, mustn't they?" He cocked his head to the side, never once taking his eyes off Bey's.

Like two lions circling, Bey thought. *Who will expose their weakness first?*

"Sekhrey," the pharaoh stroked a finger along the arm of his chair. "Tomorrow you and the priest will accompany me in the hunt when we search for the hippopotamus. I believe it will be good luck for me to have the both of you by my side."

Bey bowed his head, but kept his eyes on the pharaoh's. "As you wish, Hem-ek."

The pharaoh waved his hand in dismissal. "Good luck in the hunt today, Sekhrey."

"And you." Bey ducked out of the tent, knowing that he had better find an opportunity to kill the pharaoh soon, lest he be the one sacrificed to the crocodiles.

The papyrus reeds, towering twice as high as Bey's scarf-wrapped head, rustled while the tops of the papyrus' umbrella-shaped tufts billowed back and forth in the warm breeze. Hidden somewhere in the marsh, a mongoose mewled a series of growls and hisses, while a striped hoopoe bird perched on the spikey leaves of a doum tree called out a low "whup whup" amongst the buzzing of insects. It was an unusually hot day for so late in the flood season, and the sweat was rolling down Bey's sun-bronzed chest as he wove through the dappled shade, wary of the soft earth of the marsh. Crocodiles favoured these spots during the day for naps, and hunting of prey that might not detect their scaly, mottled flesh in the shade.

Bey paused for a moment to shift the strip of white linen wrapped across his face and around his head to block out the sun and prevent the flies that hovered over the marshy soil from flying at his nose and mouth. He knew Wadj was somewhere nearby, he had watched the pharaoh enter the thicket with a couple of fowlers about twenty minutes ago, short spears and nets in hand. Bey had waited a few minutes while the rest of the party had organized themselves and spread out along the river's west bank, then had plunged in after Wadj. Curved blade at the ready, Bey had been tracking the pharaoh for about ten minutes now, following the path of bent and matted reeds.

He knew it was a small chance, but he was hoping to catch the pharaoh separated from his attendants. If he could slit his throat and toss him into the watery depths of the marsh, it might be some time before he was found and hopefully, if and when he was, either the fish or the crocodiles would have wiped out any trace of Bey's crime. After what had happened this morning with Sobek's priest, Bey believed that many of the hunting party would, in fact, see such a death as evidence of the gods' displeasure. The pharaoh's arrogance could, in fact, work in Bey's favour and help shift blame for the pharaoh's death to the gods themselves. If Bey could just kill the man.

Some twigs snapped to Bey's right. He hunched and whirled. Not far off, he was able to make out the shape of a man's profile, facing away from the river. *Wadj*. Despite the linen that swathed his head, Bey recognized the elaborate beaded collar the pharaoh wore even while hunting. Bey began a cautious arc around the man, intending to come up behind him and catch him unaware. The pharaoh stood perfectly still, a short spear raised at shoulder height. He appeared to be watching something.

As Bey neared, he was able to see what the pharaoh was looking at, and what he saw caused him to freeze. Several meters in front of Wadj a large spotted leopard, at least the height of a man's hip, paced back and forth, watching the pharaoh with its yellow eyes. The cat's maw hung open as it made a low chuffing noise that came from deep within its belly, causing its whole underside to contract and expand with each resonating grunt. The beast's sleek, speckled coat shimmered as its thick muscles rippled and the dappled sunlight filtered through the reeds onto its lustrous golden and black speckled fur.

For several moments, the air hung still and heavy. It was as if all the creatures of the marsh, of one mind, had stopped their buzzing, whooping, crawing, and chattering, holding their breaths as this predator stalked amongst them.

If I could startle the beast into attacking the pharaoh... but Bey had no chance. A twig cracking off to the right side caused the beast to bare its vicious teeth, let out a snarl, and leap towards the sound. A man shrieked and there was a sickening, wet, tearing noise. Wadj lobbed his spear in the direction of the leopard and the cat screeched. Then the beast came crashing into view, the body of one of the fowlers gripped in its jaws and Wadj's spear protruding from its shoulder. It continued on its course, loping through the reeds until it was no longer in view. Behind it raced several men, and Wadj joined them, calling out orders to catch or kill the beast. Bey slipped back into the shadows of the reeds, having gone unseen throughout the whole ordeal.

That evening the pharaoh's entourage was more subdued as they sat around the fire. Throughout the day there had been uneasy glances shared between the noblemen as the pharaoh had ordered the hunters about. Bey could tell that the hunters, servants, and noblemen alike were concerned about Wadj's behaviour towards the priest of Sobek earlier that day. There had been a palpable tension and strain in the way that they interacted with the pharaoh.

Bey had overheard some servants discussing their fear that the pharaoh's disrespect towards Sobek's priest would anger the god and bring misfortune down on the lot of them. From Batr, he had learned that a group of hunters had even risked the pharaoh's displeasure and gone to Sobek's priest in private, when the pharaoh was resting before the evening meal, and asked the little man to perform the rites for Sobek away from the camp. Bey could only hazard a guess as to what the pharaoh's reaction might be when he found out about their betrayal.

The fact that the rest of the party was uneasy didn't stop Wadj from boasting loudly of his kill that day. Bey sat at another circle of fire a ways away. Next to him sat Batr and another guard, and the little priest was nearby. Bey could see the pharaoh stand up with the flickering flames at his back and announce, "Tomorrow *I* will show you all that I can command the creatures of Kemet to do my bidding. Today you saw that I was face to face with a leopard and yet he did not attack me. He bowed to me, and offered me his life." Some of the men cheered. Bey scoffed to himself. A dozen men with bows and spears had, in fact, taken the life of the leopard, and that animal could have torn Wadj's limbs from his body if it had not chosen to do so to another man first.

"Bay Irsu here," Wadj gestured to one of the noblemen at the front of the ring of men around the fire, a man whose face looked pale and drawn even in the darkness, "fears that we might incur Sobek's wrath, and has expressed his doubt that we will find a hippopotamus to hunt. Lucky for Bay Irsu," Wadj spread his arms out wide, repeated his refrain from that morning, "I am a benevolent god. Rather than striking Bay Irsu's head from his shoulders for his insolence, as I should have done, when we find a hippopotamus I will instead prove that I can submit a river monster with nothing but my bare hands and my spear." Some of the men gave their drunken, noisy approval while others shifted their weight, throwing one another sidelong looks.

"As I have already proved my greatness in the hunt, I have another great announcement tonight." Silence fell over the entire camp as the men waited, trepidation descending like a thick black cloud around them. "In two months time, the militias of Kemet will be called upon to gather and march upon Sumeria. We will join with the followers of Sar Atab, rightful heir to the crown of Sumer, and take our neighbours to the north!"

Bey almost laughed at the reaction of the noblemen, so unlike what Wadj must have been expecting. Instead of cheers, an uncomfortable silence fell as the men gave one another uneasy glances. Wadj's words revealed to all present that their fears had been confirmed. Atab's uncle had recovered from his illness, and he and Wadj were planning to go to war against the Sumerian king to seize the throne of

Sumeria. While most of the noblemen there were content to fawn over the pharaoh in exchange for his lavish parties and gifts of land and wealth, none were enthused at the prospect of dying in a foreign land away from the comfort of their extravagant, luxurious homes, servants, and multiple wives.

Furthermore, in two months time, when the march to Sumer was planned, they would be in the middle of farming season. This was the time when the common men who served in the militias would begin planting, and in some cases, harvesting crops. The season was already set to be a slim year, what with the pharaoh's inadequate guiding of the river's flooding. If there were no men left to harvest what little crops could be grown, all of Kemet could starve, noblemen included.

Bey glanced over at the priest, whose face was pinched with concern. When Bey caught the man's eye, Bey gave a small shake of his head and the man seemed to understand. Bey was warning him to stay silent. When Wadj had settled back down and the circle of noblemen began to talk amongst themselves, the thin little priest moved to sit near Bey. Although Bey didn't know the man, it was clear the priest knew something of him.

The man whispered to Bey, "You are Sekhrey Bey, the man who has twice saved the queen?" Bey grunted his assent and the man continued. "So you are loyal to Her Majesty?" Bey narrowed his eyes at the little priest, who held up his hands as if to proclaim innocence. "I love the queen with all my heart, sir. She has been good to the temple. I have spoken with some of the other priests, and know of her trials."

Bey cocked his head and growled, "What do you want, then?"

The man tightened his lips and leaned in towards Bey. Bey felt a little sorry for him as he realized the man was in a similar situation to himself. The priest knew his own life was in danger. "You are accompanying the pharaoh tomorrow on the hunt?" The priest whispered. Bey nodded and the man continued. "I do not understand all this. What does the pharaoh want from us? What are we to do tomorrow?"

"Just try to stay alive, priest, and stay out of my way."

The man sat back and looked Bey over. Bey ignored him and leaned forward to grab a stick and poke at the fire. One way or another, the pharaoh had to die.

Bey, Wadj, the priest, and two attendants had been circling in the reeds along the Iteru for hours. Earlier that morning the hunting party had split off into small groups and Bey had spent a tense day in anticipation of an attack that had yet to come. At any moment he expected the pharaoh to turn on him. For his part, though, the pharaoh had been in high spirits. The man had bared his teeth in a predatory grin when his first arrow had flown true and brought down a duck. As he swung the bird up by its legs he'd said, "A good omen for a triumphant hunt," while his cold eyes had rested on Bey. There had been no sightings of the hippos the pharaoh was so keen to kill.

Bey had hoped for an opportunity to separate the pharaoh from the other attendants, but so far none had presented itself. Wadj had kept the group close together, never more than a few steps from the two other men who accompanied them. Bey knew that, one on one, he would stand a good chance against he pharaoh, but not if he had to fight off two men first. The night before Bey had asked Batr to follow them in case something went awry. However, Bey had been unable to determine if Batr had manged to keep track of them throughout the day.

Now one of the attendants led them through the reeds, using a stick to beat a path towards the river, while the other brought up the rear of the party, right behind Bey. The rear attendant was carrying a large, curved blade similar to the one Bey was holding. Bey cast wary looks around him.

The men made their way through the tall reeds until the ground began to soften and squish beneath their feet. They were approaching the type of marshy area where crocodiles liked to nap during the day. The group broke through into a small clearing where the reeds gave way to moist earth. The attendant who had been behind Bey shifted until he was standing behind the priest, while the other one stopped beside Bey.

Wadj turned and gave a leer. Bey tensed and in the same moment he felt the heat of a sun-warmed blade press against his throat.

Chapter 16 – Sobek's Revenge

A man stepped out from the concealment of the reeds behind Bey to hook an arm around his, while the attendant beside him held his knife to Bey's jugular. *He must have planned this and arranged to have men laying in wait.* The two attendants hooked their arms through Bey's to prevent his escape.

At the same time as Bey was seized, the attendant behind the priest pressed his beating stick up to the little man's throat, grasping both sides of the stick from behind the priest and causing the little bald man to cough at the strain against his gullet. The priest's eyes bulged in fear and shock as his glance shifted from Bey to Wadj and back.

Bey still held his own blade in his hand and clenched his fist around it. Wadj, however, pulled out a six inch long double-sided knife and stepped forward. He used the butt of the knife to crack down hard on Bey's wrist, causing his hand to jerk and drop the blade.

Bey tried to swear at him, but the attendant put more pressure on the knife against his throat. Wadj sneered as he circled around Bey. "Now, *Sekhrey*, we can have the conversation I really wanted to have with you yesterday. But, of course, propriety constrained me then and I did not feel it was the appropriate setting. You see," Wadj tossed his blade handle from hand to hand, clearly hopped up on adrenaline and his own inflated sense of ego, "I am, actually disappointed with your performance in my absence."

Bey snorted and his throat bobbed painfully against the knife. Wadj grinned at his discomfort and continued. "You have caused me quite a bit of trouble, Sekhrey. I had some rather well-laid plans to do away with both you *and* my sister, and you have both proved to be rather more difficult to kill than I had anticipated."

Bey was surprised to hear that the pharaoh had wanted him dead before his return from the north, and the pharaoh must have seen it register on his face because he raised his eyebrows and nodded before he spoke. "Ahhh, I see. I will admit that I may have underestimated your skills. I had not expected you to do quite such a good job of protecting my sister. But just as I have underestimated your skills, you have misjudged mine, have you not? You did not think I knew that you had the favour of the sephat militias of the south? You did not stop to think that I might want to do away with one of my greatest rivals? No, Sekhrey. I can assure you that I was aware that many of the soldiers favoured you over me. I do have a spy or two of my own. I knew that some might want to replace me with you."

Bey could see that the pharaoh's ego was driving him to explain his plotting to Bey. He wanted Bey to know how cunning he really was, and to gloat. Instead of the awe Wadj seemed to expect, Bey could only feel disgust. Wadj continued his account. "By elevating you to sekhrey, I intended to discredit you when the queen died under your watch. You see, if you had failed to protect her, there would be no way the militias could continue to hold you in high regard. Then, nobody could fault me for executing you for ineptitude. Perhaps I might even have framed you for her murder." The pharaoh gave a casual, one-shouldered shrug and tilted his head to the side, watching Bey's face. Bey realized he *had* underestimated the man. Wadj was even crazier than he'd thought.

One corner of Wadj's lip curled and he began to pace again, even as he kept his eyes on Bey. "But things have become more complicated. Now that my sister is pregnant I no longer have the luxury of time." Bey's heart dropped into the pit of his stomach like a stone. He realized he had grunted only after the sound escaped him. Until now he had held himself rigid in the grasp of his two captors, but now his body went slack. When had Merneith found out, and how did the pharaoh know? Why hadn't she told him? *Because I was an ass, and accused her of being with Atab.*

"Ahhh," a cruel smile twisted the pharaoh's lips. "She has not told you." It wasn't a question, but a statement. "No. I can see that. Well let me be the first to tell you then, Sekhrey. My sister, *my wife*, is carrying what I can only assume is your bastard. That is unless, of course, she is sleeping with someone other than you as well? For all we know," he raised an eyebrow and leaned forward with a mock conspiratory look, "she has been with half the guard!"

Bey glared at the man, but Wadj only shrugged again. "The woman who attended her the other day after her "fall" and discovered her secret happens to be the same woman who nursed me as a small boy. She has always loved me as her own. She came to me as soon as she discovered the queen was pregnant. I knew it could not be mine, I have never had any interest in my shrew of a sister." Bey tensed as his mind raced for a means to escape the grasp of the two men holding him. If the knife was not at his throat, he was fairly confident he could disentangle himself.

The pharaoh bared his teeth in a grin. "So you see, Sekhrey, I have had to devise a new plan." Bey's arms strained against his captors. They had wrapped their arms around his to lock them out and back from his sides. "But the good news is that I like this new plan much better."

Wadj stepped closer to Bey and drove his right fist into Bey's right side, hitting the tender spot above his liver. Pain exploded in his side and Bey grunted, but couldn't double forward without putting pressure on the blade against his jugular. Wadj grinned and punched Bey in the side again. The priest made a noise of protest but ended up coughing and choking against the stick held at his own throat.

Wadj stepped back, assessing the look on Bey's face. Bey did his best not to give the man any satisfaction and tightened his lips against the pain. Wadj nodded at the men behind Bey and the knife was removed from Bey's throat. It was only a momentary reprieve, however, as Wadj swung his fist at Bey and hit him once, twice, three times in the face. Bey's head snapped to the side. Wadj was even stronger than he looked, and Bey found himself wondering if the man practiced his punches on those who incurred his displeasure.

Bey felt a burning sensation on his eyebrow and blood oozed into his eye and dripped on to his cheekbone. He blinked to clear the sticky substance and remove the stars that had begun to dance behind his eyes.

Wadj hopped from foot to foot. He wrung his right hand out to loosen it after the punches he'd doled out. Bey kept an eye on the blade still clutched in Wadj's left hand. Wadj swung up with his fist again and this time Bey felt his teeth rattle and he tasted blood. He spat red and snarled at the pharaoh, "Come on, you coward. Are you afraid to fight me fairly?"

Wadj swung at his side, again punishing his liver. He hissed, "I am enjoying this so much more than a fair fight, Sekhrey. But I will do you the favour of telling you exactly what I plan to do, so that I can enjoy the look on your face before I finish you off."

Wadj stepped back, wiping his mouth with the back of his left hand. The blade of his knife flashed in the sunlight. "You see, I intend to do away with this insolent little priest here. Then I will do away with you. I will tell everyone that you and the priest conspired to kill me, and in turn I crushed the both of you.

"Then," Wadj bared his teeth in a terrible smile, "when we return to Thinis, I will cut your bastard child from my sister's belly while she watches. I will make sure she suffers dearly, and then I will kill her. Very slowly and very painfully." Wadj's words had numbed Bey's body to any pain, and he curled his biceps and pulled against the attendants. He could feel the men straining to contain him as he thrashed and flexed against them.

The pharaoh laughed. "I will tell everyone that my poor wife died carrying our child, and that it was a great sadness to me to lose my heir. I will have all of Kemet's sympathy, and there will be no one to oppose me when Atab and I march on Sumeria." Wadj turned and stepped towards the priest. He switched the knife to his right hand.

Just then Bey managed to break free from one of the attendants. He backhanded the man on his right and sent him reeling backwards. The attendant grunted and fell into the reeds with a crash. Wadj whirled around, his eyes wide in surprise as they flicked beyond Bey.

It was Batr hurtling through the reeds that had caught the pharaoh's eye. Batr knocked the remaining attendant off Bey and down to the ground. The man cried out, but his voice was cut off into a bloody gurgle as Batr's knife slashed through his throat.

Bey lept forward and grabbed Wadj's wrist, preventing the pharaoh from stabbing him. Bey swung out and his fist connected with Wadj's solid abdomen. Wadj grunted and stepped back, twisting his wrist in an attempt to dislodge Bey's iron grip.

Bey had the advantage of height, weight, and plenty of fighting experience. But Wadj Wadj was lighter, faster, and uninjured. His punches had left Bey favouring his left side and half-blinded by the free-flowing blood dripping in to his eye. The two men circled one another. Bey wrenched Wadj's wrist back and punched him in the face, hoping to make him drop the knife. Wadj countered with a hard kick to Bey's left side, his shin connecting with Bey's ribs with a sickening crunch. The wind left Bey in a whoosh, and Wadj managed to get his wrist free. He slashed out at Bey with the knife, catching him across the chest and opening a deep gash over one pectoral.

Bey back-stepped and almost tripped over something hard in the mud. *His knife.* He tried to bend down to snatch it up, but Wadj rushed at him and forced him to step to the side to avoid the slash of the knife. Wadj's momentum was such that he couldn't stop in time. He passed Bey and as he did, Bey reached out, grabbed one of Wadj's wrists, and swung the man's arm out straight. Bey brought his other arm down on Wadj's tricep and there was a loud *crack* as Wadj's bone snapped.

The pharaoh cried out in shock and pain. "You bastard!" He shrieked at Bey. "I *will* see you dead." He lunged at Bey with his knife straight out towards Bey's abdomen. Bey saw him coming too late, thanks to the blood in his eye. But the pharaoh stumbled in the soft, marshy ground and the knife glanced off Bey's side, just nicking him. Bey caught the wrist of the pharaoh's knife hand and managed to twist the arm up behind the pharaoh's back. Wadj groaned and the knife slipped from his grasp into the moist earth.

Bey wrapped his free arm around the pharaoah's throat, pressing the man's jugular into the crook of his elbow. The pharaoh burbled into Bey's arm. "I will kill you. I will kill your bastard baby." Bey tightened his grip, gritting his teeth against the pain in his side as the pharaoh struggled and writhed.

Wadj choked against Bey's arm. "I will make her watch when I kill your bastard."

"No." Bey ground out through clenched teeth. "You will not." Bey released the pharaoh's arm, wrapped one large hand over the pharaoh's forehead and twisted it. There was a *snap* and Wadj went limp in Bey's arms. Panting, not knowing which side to clutch first, the bruised liver or the possibly broken ribs, Bey let Wadj's body slip down in a heap onto the spongy earth.

For the first time in several minutes, he thought to look around at how Batr and the priest fared. The two attendants who had held Bey lay dead in the mud side by side, their throats slit. The priest stood over the body of the attendant who had held him captive. The priest's dark skin looked ashen, and his hand shook even as it held the stick, now covered in blood, that the attendant had once held against his throat. Batr caught Bey's eye and grinned. "My apologies for the late arrival, Sekhrey. I lost you for a while there."

Bey nodded. He was having a hard time breathing. The pain in his sides was crushing. He sank down to his knees in the mud. Batr rushed over to him and knelt by his side. Bey blinked and used the back of his hand to swipe blood and sweat from his eyes. From the corner of his eye, he caught movement behind the priest, near the edge of the river.

"Get back," he gasped.

"What's that, Sekhrey?" Batr leaned his ear to Bey's lips.

"Get back. Crocodiles." Bey waved his hand in the direction of the priest.

Batr started up. "Get back, man! There are crocodiles!" The priest turned, wide-eyed, to glance over his shoulder. There was rustling in the reeds, and dark shadows were wavering in the rosy light of the setting sun. "By the gods," the priest breathed, then looked down at the man laying in the mud at his feet.

"Help me," he whispered to Batr. "Move the bodies there."

Batr stared at the man for a minute, comprehension dawning on his face. Bey nodded. "Yes. Do it."

Batr grabbed the pharaoh's body under the armpits and dragged him through the mud towards the edge of the clearing. The rustling and shadows moved closer. He and the priest pulled the three attendants close to Wadj's body. Then Batr came over to Bey, draped Bey's arm over his shoulders, wrapped a hand around his waist, and hauled him up.

A shiny, scaly snout with glistening, deadly white teeth pushed through the reeds near the pile of bodies. The priest gestured with his hand for Batr and Bey to get back, even as he stepped forward. The little man bowed his head and began to mutter a prayer to Sobek, the crocodile god.

"Sobek, greatest of the gods of the Iteru, hear my prayer. Take these malefactors unto you and protect the life of your most devout of followers. These men defied your greatness and trespassed on your sacred ground without your blessing. Punish them as you see fit, and let your wrath be known."

Bey snorted at the irony of praying for harm to come to others at the same time as he dearly wished the priest's plan to work. He watched as three more scaly snouts pushed through the reeds and then the monstrous heads of several primeval creatures emerged into the deepening gloom of the late afternoon. One of them stepped forward on its impossibly small legs, hauling its thick knobby body through the muck. It reared its head up, exposing the pale skin under its enormous maw, opened its ferocious fang-lined jaw, and gave a low, rumbling growl that sounded deep in its belly and echoed through the clearing.

"Thank you, Sobek." The little priest stepped back from the bodies, and the crocodiles. Faster than he could ever imagine such great, awkward looking beasts could move, the crocodiles were upon the bodies. Their great jaws snapped as they tore, wrenched, and dragged at the pharaoh and his attendants.

"Move. Now. To the camp." Bey wheezed.

Batr and the priest half-dragged, half-carried Bey through the reeds, back towards the camp. When they were within sight of the campfires the priest stopped them. "Let me go first," he said. Bey could do little more than nod his head. He watched as the bald man left Batr and Bey at the edge of the clearing, still shielded by the reeds.

The priest ran towards the camp, calling out. "Help! Please come! The pharaoh has been attacked by crocodiles. He has been killed. Sekhrey Bey and some other men tried to save him and the Sekhrey is half-dead himself. Please come help him, he is still back there somewhere, he may not make it." The priest gestured back towards the reeds.

Batr dragged Bey a few steps forward so that they could be seen. A few men jumped up and rushed to them. Bey ordered some of the men to leave him and go find the pharaoh's body first. He knew by this point the crocodiles would have done enough damage to mask any injuries he might have inflicted on the pharaoh. *If the pharaoh's body is still even to be found.* He only hoped that the shadows cast by the setting sun would be enough to mask his own injuries long enough to cover them and avoid suspicion.

As they neared the camp and news spread, Atab emerged from his tent. His eyes widened as he watched them drag Bey's body towards the fire. "No." Atab breathed. "No! NO NO NO NO!" His voice rose to a screech. "You did this!" He pointed to Bey. "You killed him!"

The priest shook his head. "No, Sar. The Sekhrey tried to save the pharaoh, even as the other dead men did. His own body barely escaped the beasts' jaws. But Sekhrey Bey cried out for Sobek's mercy at the last minute, while the pharaoh would only repudiate the gods." Bey bit back a snort, it hurt too much to laugh and laughter would be untimely given Atab's accusation.

It seemed the priest couldn't help throwing another jab at the dead pharaoh. "The pharaoh brought the gods' displeasure down on himself and Sobek displayed his wrath. I am saddened that Kemet has had to lose such a great man as the pharaoh as a result." The little man shook his head with a solemn, sorrowful look on his face. Bey marveled at the priest's ability to lie, and made a note to himself to find a way to thank the man later.

Atab edged around Bey and the priest. "No," he was shaking his head. "No. It cannot be." The Sumerian began to mutter to himself as he stumbled backwards away from them and towards the edge of the river, where the ships were docked. He kept his wary gaze on Bey, but didn't seem to realize that everyone could hear him speaking. "I am ruined if it is true. *Ruined.*"

Everyone, including Atab's own guard, watched in wonder as the Sumerian prince whirled around, ran towards the dock, and jumped on a reed skiff. The small fishing vessel was made of papyrus stalks lashed together and was about fifteen feet long, three feet wide, and just one foot deep. Atab unlashed the boat and grabbed the long pole that was used to guide the boat. He stabbed into the river bed and pushed the boat away from the shore.

Bey gestured to Batr to help him and the two men made their way to the river bank along with most of the men from the camp. They watched as the current pushed the boat up the river. It was impossible to follow Atab's progress too far, as in this area the reeds grew up too thick to venture through and still see the small boat.

But they didn't need to wait long to see what would happen to Prince Atab.

A murmur rose up amongst the crowd, and some pointed to the far bank. Slightly behind and to the right of the boat, and therefore unseen by the floating passenger, the rays of the setting sun shimmered off a moving figure.

As the apparition neared the boat and reached shallower waters the leathery pate of a hippo began to emerge.

The great beast brushed near the boat and its shoulder struck the underside of the shallow vessel, causing it to rock. Atab, unarmed except for a small blade belted at his side, dropped his centre of gravity for balance and hunched low. The hippo reared its great maw up, spreading open toothy jaws wide enough to engulf a man's head, and let out a series of angry, echoing grunts.

Then the beast disappeared beneath the smooth surface of the Iteru.

There was a tense silence on the shore, and Atab dropped down to his knees in the boat, gripping the edge as he leaned forward, searching the smooth surface. A collective buzz rose up amongst the onlookers as the hippo's leathery head bobbed up above the water.

"No! No!" Atab yelled in a panicked voice. He looked back towards the crowd on the shoreline. "Help me! You filthy cowards! Someone help me."

But there was no help to be had. Atab's guardsmen shifted uncomfortably. One or two took steps towards the dock, as if they thought they might reach the prince in time to help him, but then thought better of it. A couple rested their hands on their own belted knives, but seemed to realize the impossibility of helping the prince. Bey looked around at Batr and the two guards he'd selected to come with him. He saw that the other guards were looking to him for direction. Now that Wadj was gone, there was no doubt who was in charge of the hunting party. Bey nodded at his men and they immediately understood, while the other guards followed their lead. Bey's men seized Atab's royal guard and took their weapons. Atab's men offered little resistance and seemed resigned to their fate. Bey would question them later and determine just who had been involved in the attacks on Merneith.

For now, though, all eyes turned back to Atab. The hippo circled the unsteady little skiff, closing in. In the gloom Bey could see another, smaller hippo near the boat. It seemed that Atab had come between a mother bull and her baby, and the mother was clearly not happy.

She bumped the boat, and this time the skiff flipped over and Atab was tossed into the water. He emerged in a moment, scrabbling at the underside of the reed boat that now bobbed belly-up. "Nonononono!" Atab gibbered. He tried to climb up onto the upturned boat, but only succeeding in rolling over it completely, as the boat flipped round once more. This brought him closer to the vicious beast.

Atab's arm emerged above the water, clutching his knife. He lashed out at the hippo, managing to lodge his knife in the beast's shoulder. But this angered it all the more. The monster opened its enormous maw, let out another bellow, and in an instant it had snapped its jagged-toothed chops around Atab's arm. Atab shrieked, but the hippo gave a great heave and sucked the Sumerian prince beneath the surface of the great river.

The men on the shoreline were left staring at the underside of the skiff as it bobbed and floated upstream along the serene current of the Iteru. Atab and the hippo were nowhere to be seen.

Chapter 17 – The Proclamation

Merneith sipped her morning tea in one of the rooms overlooking the palace gardens. She was thankful for the soothing breeze that fluttered the leaves of the sycamore trees. She had been feeling ill in the mornings and couldn't imagine how much worse it would be suffering through the hot, dry season of Kemet. It was the fourth day since the hunting party had left and Merneith had received no word since the day before yesterday. She had also remained mostly confined to her rooms. Although Bekeh had put the word around that the queen had suffered a fall and some bruising, Merneith was unwilling to answer the questions that would inevitably follow. As such, she had been left mostly to her fears and anxiety, although Bekeh, Penebui, Akshaka, and Ishara often sat with her, and Amka came regularly to update her on the happenings of the court.

Ebrium had also come each day to report on the state of the militias, and Merneith found that she enjoyed Ebrium's company. He was, after all, Bey's trusted man. By spending time with him she felt that she was somehow closer to Bey. Furthermore, she had always taken pleasure in watching the comfortable, easy banter between the two men. There was something in it that set those around them at ease, herself included. Ebrium had an open, casual manner that by court standards would be shocking in its lack of pretense and decorum, but Merneith found it refreshing. He spoke the language of Kemet like a commoner, without the formality of court diction, and she liked to hear his lilt and foreign accent.

Her musings were interrupted by a knock at her door and she called out for Makae to enter. He opened the door and slipped in. Discreetly, he asked in a low tone, "Hem-etj, Ebrium is here to see you. Are you well, or would you like me to turn him away?" Despite her assurances, Makae had continued to treat her as if she were an invalid. She appreciated the man's gentle concern, and could understand why Bey had chosen him and his brother to guard her.

"I am well, thank you. Do let him in."

Ebrium entered, stopping nearby to bow. "Hem-etj." He glanced up at her with his sea-blue eyes through a few locks of thick black hair.

Merneith smiled at the handsome, good-natured man. "*Wa'ew*. Please, draw up a chair." She gestured towards one of the nearby chairs. "If you are not in a hurry you may assist me by keeping me company for a time. I am sorely in need of a diversion today."

"Of course." He bowed his head in deference, placing a hand over his heart. "A man would be a fool not to willingly give up every moment of every day to sit by your side and listen to each word that passed your lips as if they were nourishment from the gods." Ebrium arranged himself so that the two were almost facing one another.

Merneith chuckled in spite of her dark mood, knowing his outrageous flattery was designed to make her laugh. "Dear me, if you were to subsist off the harvest of my words alone I fear you would suffer from malnourishment and die, *wa'ew*. And then what would your dear mother and sister say?"

Ebrium grinned, a dimple materializing in one cheek. "They would say I died a happy man."

Merneith smiled, appreciating the levity the big man brought into the room with him. She couldn't stop herself, though, from adding, "And what would your friend Sekhrey Bey say?"

Ebrium gave her an intense, searching look, his merry blue eyes softening. He gave a slight smile and said, "He would say that I'd passed to the underworld in the noblest of pursuits, for I know that he believes there is nothing finer than to be at your side."

Merneith jerked and looked away. "You tease me, *wa'ew*."

"No, Hem-etj, not in the least."

Merneith kept her gaze on the garden outside. She knew there was no point in attempting to hide her relationship with Bey from Ebrium. It had been he who had discovered them in the shepherd's hut, after all, and he was Bey's closest friend. If he didn't already know about them he must at least suspect. "Perhaps there was a time when that were true, but I believe that time has passed."

She could see Ebrium shake his head out of the corner of her eye. "Hardly, Hem-etj. There has only ever been one other woman that he felt anything close to what he feels for you."

Merneith frowned. "I recall that Bey once said something about almost marrying."

Ebrium's eyes widened. "You didn't know? But you know about Bey's family, my sister and mother told you?" She nodded, wanting him to continue. He leaned back, resting his elbows on the carved arms of the chair and steepling his fingers against each other. "Well there was a girl back in Ebla." Ebrium snorted and Merneith caught the hint of disdain in his voice, "Daughter of a wealthy nobleman. She and Bey had been engaged since Bey was about fourteen. The girl's father was a groveling fool who had always wanted to make ties with Bey's father." Merneith listened, not daring to interrupt. "The girl *was* very pretty, and better educated than most women. You know in Ebla, most of the nobles' daughters don't know anything outside their own homes." Merneith murmured that this was not so different from Kemet, and urged him to go on.

"The girl's temper was sometimes uneven, but Bey, well…" Ebrium gave her a sly smile and said, "He likes a woman with a bit of fire in her, such as yourself, Hem-etj." Merneith raised an eyebrow and he laughed, continuing. "The poor fool couldn't wait to marry her when he finished his schooling. But then everything happened with his family. His father died," Ebrium paused, shifting in his seat. He dragged a hand through his dark locks, glancing out the window away from her.

Merneith leaned forward and touched his hand with hers. "I am sorry; you lost your father around the same time, did you not?"

Ebrium nodded, then shrugged one shoulder. "Such is life. And Bey's brother Shems was such a bastard, I mean, sorry, forgive me, Hem-etj."

Merneith smiled. "It is fine, I have used the word myself on occasion. And once, even in regards to your dear friend."

Ebrium chuckled, "Did you now? Well I'm on your side, whatever your reason he probably deserved it. And so did Shems, I suppose, given the way he lost the family's money and respect. The girl's father broke things off with Bey. Within a few days he had engaged her to a fat nobleman old enough to be her grandfather. Bey pursued the silly girl, even though I tried to convince him otherwise. I'd always suspected she was only feigning her feelings for him because he came from a wealthy and powerful family. When his mother passed and we decided to leave Ebla, he went to her and asked her to run away with us. She chose the fat, wealthy old man over Bey." Ebrium snorted in disgust. "The girl claimed it was her duty to her father to stay, but in truth, it was obvious she preferred a life of comfort and luxury." Ebrium raised his eyebrows in a sympathetic expression, although he lightened the story by adding with a smile, "There are few things more damaging to a man's ego, Hem-etj, than to be rejected for such a man as that one."

Merneith recalled Bey's words to her during their argument in Ta-Senet. He had accused her of being unwilling to give up the comforts of the court, and using her duty as an excuse for pushing him away. It was unjust of him to accuse her of being the same as this girl who had refused him for another man, but at least it made sense. He'd been hurt before. Merneith's heart ached knowing that they'd fought so needlessly, taking out their own frustrations over past and current wrongs on one another, when instead they should have been seeking comfort and shelter in one another's arms. If there was a chance to make things right, Merneith knew she had to take it.

Just then a knock came at the door and Merneith looked up. Makae had left the door open when Ebrium had arrived for propriety's sake - it wouldn't do for Merneith to be alone in the room with a man behind a closed door. Makae stood in the doorway and announced Amka, the advisor. The tall, thin man strode into the room. Merneith and Ebrium both rose to greet him.

"Amka, I believe you know Ebrium, the Sekhrey's man." Merneith gestured as Ebrium rose to greet Amka. The men nodded at one another.

Amka turned to her. "Hem-etj, please sit down. I have news."

Merneith's heart raced and she slid down into her chair. *Oh gods, please don't let it be Bey.* Amka flicked his gaze to Ebrium, a questioning look in his eyes. Merneith waved her hand as if to let him know Ebrium was in her confidence. "Amka, just tell me."

Amka cleared his throat and kept his voice neutral as he said, "There has been an accident. The pharaoh is dead. The hunting party is due back this evening with his remains."

"And the rest of the party?" She gripped the arms of the chair.

Amka shook his head. "Sar Atab has been lost, and three attendants were taken."

"No one else?" Merneith managed to squeeze out, although she'd been holding her breath almost since Amka had entered.

"None. Only those five." Merneith breathed out and dragged her breath back in, almost sobbing with relief.

Ebrium clenched his jaw and their eyes met as he slid a glance down at her. He compressed his lips and gave her a slight nod, as if to say he understood her feelings. She turned back to Amka, whose placid expression was only betrayed by the light in his eyes. The two men didn't know one another well enough to express their relief openly, but in front of these men who she believed knew enough to understand and sympathize with her she felt no need to feign distress over the deaths of evil men such as the pharaoh and prince.

She managed to recover herself enough to say, "Well then, I suppose we must prepare for their arrival. Amka, will you be so good as to warn the servants, and call for the priests. They must begin the preparations for the pharaoh's passing into the next realm. Tomorrow we must call for an assembly of the court to announce the news."

Amka nodded and took his leave. Ebrium asked if he could summon anyone for her, but she thanked him and said that she only needed a few minutes to compose herself and arrange her thoughts. "The time is come," she told him, "for me to take control of the situation myself. Until now I have allowed circumstances to push me in one direction or another. The gods have placed me in this position and now I must act accordingly."

Once alone, the magnitude of the situation hit her. *Bey is safe. I am safe. Our child is safe. Amka's domain is now safe. The people of Kemet are safe. But now who will rule Kemet?*

Wadj had named no heir, and there had never yet been a queen who ruled Kemet alone. Unlike in Bey's story of the Eblaiti queen, there had been no tacit agreement between Merneith and the governors of Egypt. Even though some of the governors and priesthood from the south had professed their loyalty to her, there were still those in the north to be consulted, and then there were the nobles to consider. Without an heir the nobles would be in an uproar. Those who had been loyal to Wadj might yet contest her claims to the throne, hoping to replace her with a man more favorable to them.

Or worse, the governors and nobles might press her to re-marry one of the next in line for the throne. The man with the strongest claim was a young uncle, a sickly fool of a man too inbred to tie his own sandals. But any power struggles amidst the heirs or the nobles now could result in civil war, the very thing she'd been trying to avoid.

In the past two months she'd endured a great deal because she'd been hesitant to act, afraid of disrupting the order and peace, the *ma'at*, in Kemet. As a result, she'd been knocked to the ground and almost torn apart by tigers, almost kidnapped, shot at, beaten by her husband, and she'd given up the man she wanted more than anything else she'd ever desired. She could no longer sit idly by and wait for some resolution to her problems. Wadj's death was the best thing she could have hoped for. She stroked her belly and stared out the window, contemplating her next move.

It was midday on the next day when Merneith approached the dais in the courtyard of the palace of Thinis. Makae and Batr flanked her, while a contingent of guards surrounded her, cutting through the crowd and preventing anyone from approaching. The sephat militias that had first gathered in Thinis, and then traveled north with her, now lined the courtyard in rows. Their presence was an irrefutable display of power; there was no doubting that Merneith had control of a sizeable army, and that this was only a small sampling of her influence. She hoped it would serve as a warning to any who might want to contest her announcement.

Nobles thronged the courtyard, murmuring to one another with an air of anticipation and confusion floating around them. Merneith was well aware that the palace had been buzzing with the news of the pharaoh's death since the hunting party had arrived last night. But her duties in dealing with Wadj's and Atab's remains, along with the three other deaths, had kept her busy all day and well into the evening. As a result, she had yet to officially announce the pharaoh's death, or see Bey.

She had dressed herself accordingly for the occasion. Her finest striped shift dress was wrapped around her waist, then crossed over her breasts and tied in the back. A large beaded collar of gold and turquoise beads hung round her neck. Her hair was elaborately braided and looped around her ears. The coal around her eyes was drawn in two long lines over her upper and lower lids on each side, in what she hoped gave her an intense, fierce look. It was imperative that she look as imposing as possible.

As Merneith took to the dais a hush fell over the crowd. When she turned to face the gathering of nobles she could tell that people were trying not to stare at the ugly bruises that coloured her face. The area around her right eye and cheek were still swollen, the bruises fading to a sickly purple-green. The corner of her lip was still slightly puffy, but barely noticeable now. She couldn't let that cause her to falter. It was absolutely essential now that she keep this short and commanding, and to avoid any questions.

Merneith drew herself up to her full height, drawing down upon her all the grandeur of four generations of pharaohs. *I am the great-granddaughter of Narmer, who united the two lands of Kemet. I cannot allow his work to be undone. I must be strong now.*

"People of Kemet," her voice rang out across the courtyard, clear and steady. "Two days ago your pharaoh died in the most noble of pursuits, fighting the great beasts that plague the waters of the Iteru, stealing livestock and killing our farmers. For his efforts, he will surely be well-received by Ammit and pass on to spend eternity amongst the gods. Even now, we begin to prepare him for his journey through the afterlife."

Merneith paused to lick her lips and steel herself. She drew in a deep breath and lifted her chin. "My husband did not publicly name his heir before his passing, but I am pleased to announce that the succession to the throne of Kemet will remain unbroken. Before he left on his expedition to the north of Kemet two months ago, he planted his seed in me. I am carrying the pharaoh's child." Here a murmur of surprise broke out, as happy congratulations mingled with restrained sounds of distress. Not everyone was enthused by the news.

Merneith continued, "I will remain as the regent ruler until our heir is of age. I am confident the child will be a strong, healthy boy who will rule Kemet for many years with the same might that my ancestors have displayed for over a century, since Kemet was united as the most powerful and prosperous land on earth." A cheer rose up from the crowd. Merneith's reference to her lineage was a deliberate reminder to all that any break in the stability of Kemet was a break in the wealth and prosperity the nobles enjoyed. As Merneith looked out over the crowd she relaxed her shoulders a little, beginning to sense that her plan was working. At least no one was openly questioning the lineage of the child. Whether or not they did in the privacy of their own homes was another matter. She could only pray that her words would be a prophesy, that she would be able to carry this baby to full term, and that it really would be a boy.

Then she caught sight of Bey, standing off in a corner at the far edge of the crowd. His sculpted arms were crossed over his massive, tattooed chest, his face impassive as he watched her with his stunning green eyes. She could see bruises mottling the dark skin along his torso, and the white bandage that stood out starkly over one muscled pectoral. She jerked her gaze away as her heart began hammering. She had to get off the dais, or risk losing her composure.

She addressed the crowd again, "Thank you all for your kindness in this time of great sadness. It is the great people of Kemet that make it the most blessed of lands. And now I must begin the process of mourning my husband, your pharaoh, and preparing for his great journey." Then she turned and signalled to the guards to lead her back to the palace.

Late that evening Batr announced Bey at the entrance to Merneith's rooms. Merneith composed herself, resting a hand on the back of a chair for support. Bowls of oil flickered around the room, casting long shadows, and the gaping maw of the doorway was pitched in darkness. As Bey materialized out of the gloom, his white shenti glowing in the lambent light, Merneith's grip on the chair back tightened.

"Hem-etj, you summoned me?" he bowed his head, but did not go down to one knee as was customary. She noticed it, but let it go. He had a right to be angry.

She cleared her throat and addressed Batr, "Thank you, *wa'ew*. You may take the rest of the evening off." Batr glanced at Bey, who jerked his head in acquiescence. Batr barely raised an eyebrow as he pulled the door shut, leaving

Merneith and Bey alone together for the first time in several weeks.

Merneith took a moment to arrange her thoughts. She had called for Bey, and now she must say what she had to say, regardless of the outcome. She wanted to just throw herself into his arms and sob with relief that he was alive, but the hard look on his face indicated that things wouldn't be that easy. She hated that he alone had the effect of humbling her. Apologizing was not something she was familiar with, but she knew that it was only fair. She was the one who had begun their argument weeks ago in Ta-Senet, and she had compounded the problem by her announcement today.

"Bey," she started, but faltered. She drew in a deep breath then pushed on. "I am sorry. This was the only way. I had to do it." By this she meant her announcement that the baby was Wadj's, and next in line for the throne. Bey's lips compressed and he crossed his arms over his chest. She let go of the chair back and stepped to him, laying a hand on his forearm. She thought she saw the wary expression in his eyes soften as he watched her, but then she had to avert her eyes from his. If she looked up at his closed countenance she would lose her resolve.

"Bey, I had to do it for Kemet, to keep peace in my homeland, and *your* homeland too, now. But this child *is* yours. There has been no other, and I would not wish for one. I am sorry I broke with you in Ta-Senet, I was scared and could not see my way through the danger that hung around us." She paused and looked up at him. Although he hadn't moved, his green eyes searched hers, and once again she had that feeling that they were delving deep inside her, drawing her out and probing at her spirit and her heart.

Painful as it was, she kept her eyes on his as she licked her lips and pushed herself to continue, although she felt tears welling up again and a constriction between her breasts. "Being apart from you has only showed me how much I need you. I was terrified when you left with Wadj and the entire time you were gone I felt my chest aching. The fear of losing you has showed me just how much I love you."

"I love you." Bey heard Merneith utter those words and felt his anger at her earlier announcement melting into a confused jumble of emotions. He understood the need for her to claim the baby as Wadj's. If there was doubt about the lineage of the child both her life, and that of the child, could be in danger. Kemet would fall into civil war as heirs and noblemen battled for the throne. He just wished she'd talked to him first. And what did she want from him now? She had once accused him of wanting the throne of Kemet; he would not give her the opportunity to do so again.

Merneith continued, stepping closer and pressing a palm against his chest. Her warm touch caused him to flinch, but she persevered. "Bey, please," there was a pleading look in her eyes. "There was no time to consult you. When you left you were angry with me, and I could not bear to distract you when your life was in danger while you were with Wadj. I want, no I *need* you to help me, to be by my side while I rule Kemet, and to help me raise our child. And when the time is right, I need you to help me tell him who his true father is."

Bey searched her face and her wide, dark eyes. They were like oasis pools turned black in the moonlight, overflowing with emotion. No woman had ever looked at him like that; he had never thought it could be possible. A fountain of warmth flowed up through his chest and he unfolded his arms, cupping her face with his palms. For a moment they both held still while he reveled in awe at the look in her eyes. Then he leaned forward to taste her soft pink lips.

Her body went soft against him, and he shifted his hands from her face to her waist, drawing her to him tightly as their kiss deepened, his need for her intensifying as he felt himself stiffen against her thigh. But he pulled back, and she gave a sound of protest.

"Mer," he rubbed his jaw with the palm of one hand. "I am sorry for what I said to you in Ta-Senet. You did not deserve it." She moved to dismiss his apology, but he shook his head. "No, I have not told you before, but there was a woman once. We were to be married."

Merneith brushed her fingertips over the bandage that covered the gash Wadj had opened on his chest. She kept her eyes on him as she said, "I know all about you have done, and I know about this other woman. Ebrium told me." She raised an eyebrow and a mischievous little smile played on the corners of her lips. "I think that, seeing as how I am queen of Kemet, and currently the *only* ruler of the most powerful land in all the lands under Ra, you need not fear that I shall have need to seek another lover, or a fat old husband, to increase my fortune."

Bey chuckled, running his hands up the sides of her back. "Hmmm, are you sure you do not want to trade me in for a rich, flabby, older man?" His sides and abdomen ached from the brutal beating Wadj had given him, but pain be damned, he wanted this woman in his arms and under him. With his hands on her upper hips, he walked her backwards towards her bed. When the back of her knees bumped the bed he lowered her onto the soft sheets, the thick coils of her raven-black hair spread out around her in stark contrast to the white bedding. He laid over her, pressing his elbows down by her ears, his lips playing on her neck. Her scent was intoxicating; her pulse under his lips enthralled him.

"Mmmm," she murmured, shifting under his weight so that her mound rubbed against his hardness. She began to grind against him. "Perhaps. Perhaps it is not too late to find myself some wealthy old grandfather. There is a distant cousin as well who is about seventy-five, but quite well-off. Although they say that he is so feeble he often drools and does not know it. And then there is that uncle who cannot tie his own sandals…"

Bey snorted against her neck then reared back, giving her a stern look. "Let us make an agreement then." She sat upright, and he raised her dress up and over her head, tossing it over his shoulder and delighting in the sight of her lush curves. "I will accept your apologies, and vow to stand always by your side," here he laid a hand on her belly. He could hardly wait for the day when he could feel his child pressing against the soft, warm flesh of her abdomen. "If you promise not to bed any old cousins, grandfathers, uncles, foreign princes, or any other man that takes your fancy."

One corner of her full lips curved up in a half-moon smile. She reached out to undo the tie of his shenti, letting it drop to the floor to pool at his feet. "Agreed. You shall be my only foreign prince." She pushed him down on to the bed on his back, and threw a leg over his thighs, straddling him. He reached up to grip her hips, to settle her on to his pulsing shaft, but she held up a waggling finger. "Uh uh. You must also promise that there will be no more daughters of wealthy old men, none of the women that you pirating and soldiering types meet in your travels, no more queens, or any other woman that takes *your* fancy."

He squirmed under her, focusing on the place where their bodies met, trying to position her to his advantage, to rub against the slick opening of her sex. "Mmmm hmm. Indeed. No more pirating women and no more queens. Nasty things anyway, those queens. Always getting themselves into trouble." She cleared her throat and he looked up at her. She had narrowed her eyes, compressed her lips, and crossed her arms over her breasts. He chuckled and ran a hand up to tangle into the hair at the back of her head, drawing her to him and thrusting his tongue between her lips, taking her mouth in a ravaging kiss. When he finally released her she gazed down on him with soft eyes. He smiled and rumbled in a low voice, "Without a doubt, you are the only queen I will ever need. I love you, Mer."

With that she shifted herself so that his shaft pressed at her hot, slippery opening. In one smooth motion, she pushed down and he slid part-way into her, her tight walls wrapping around him in a rapture of sensations that drove all thoughts from him.

Merneith gasped as Bey entered her. "By the gods how I have missed this," she groaned. Bey gave a grunt of assent as his fingers dug into her flesh, pulling her down onto him as he thrust his hips up. Merneith gave a soft cry, pleasure and pain mingled as her body adjusted to his length. "Yesss." Then she arched her back, sitting upright, propping herself up with her hands wrapped around his thick biceps as she began to move against him with urgency. Before long they were pitching against one another with the rough rhythm of a ship at sea, riding along turbulent waters towards the peak of pleasure. Sweat trickled down between Merneith's breasts as she rode the man beneath her, the man that was now *hers* for as long as he would keep her. She ground herself against him as he thrust upwards, and she felt a surging warmth and tightness spreading through her until finally an explosive flash crashed through her body and she cried out, convulsing. Wave after wave shook her and every pore throbbed with intense sensations. It was so overwhelming that tears stung her eyes and one or two escaped down her cheek.

She dropped, panting, against his chest and Bey wrapped his arms around her back as he continued to surge up within her. It was only a brief moment later when he moaned and she could feel him jerk and buck under her, then go still. He lay silent for a moment, crushing her to him as he hauled in breath, and she continued to tremble.

She disentangled herself gingerly, sliding off his hips to roll on to her back, head resting on his chest. She heaved a great sigh. "Oh I feel so much better now. Like an enormous weight has been lifted." He chuckled, and she loved the sound of his chest rumbling. She rolled on to her side, running her fingers along the damp ridges of his chest. "But I do believe that we may have to do that one more time. Just to make sure you drive out any last thoughts of drooling cousins and flabby old men."

Bey raised an eyebrow, looking down at her without lifting his head. She grinned back at him and he rolled over her, gently pushing her into the bed. He growled "You kill me, woman. And if you want to do this again you are going to have to stop talking about other men, unless you want me to run out this door and toss every man I see into the Iteru for the crocodiles." She opened her mouth to protest and he cut her off. "No. If you want there to be a next time I expect to hear all those sweet words you were uttering when I first arrived here, to remind me why I put up with your caustic tongue."

"Mmmm," she smiled. "What if I just showed you what else I can do with my tongue?" She raised herself up onto her elbows and kissed the hollow of his collarbone, licking at his salty skin.

He groaned. "That will do, too."

Epilogue

One month later Merneith sat in the garden in a circle of friends and family, her hands resting on her growing belly as she leaned back in the shade. Bey was seated to her right, and Ebrium sprawled in a chair to her left, with Penebui and Akshaka chattering nearby. Bekeh and Nenofer, Merneith's distant divorced relation who had once flirted with Batr and Makae in this same spot, gossiped over Ishara's head, and Ishara practiced her language skills by listening to stories of scheming women and cheating husbands. Merneith was reminded of that time, now three months passed, when she had sat here with prince Atab the day after he had pushed her down the steps in the midst of a tiger attack. Then, she had been forced to suffer under the constraints of decorum, watching her every word in fear of being misconstrued. Or worse, being *understood* and having it used against her.

What a contrast to today! Today she felt safe and content. A warmth had been growing in her chest that made her feel like a wild cat curled up on a soft bed of grass in a puddle of warm sunlight. In the past she'd felt exhausted after being in the presence of others, as if they had greedily sucked up her energy to feed their own needs and desires, and the exertion of choosing every word with care was numbing. But being around these people whom she loved, and whom she was confident loved her back, she felt tranquil, safe, and free to speak her mind unguarded without fear of consequences. This, she truly believed, was the answer to the question she had asked herself so long ago in that shepherd's hut. She had wondered then if there shouldn't be more to life than mere survival, if there shouldn't be happiness as well. She knew that as long as she had the love of these people whom she cared for so deeply she could give up all the power and wealth of Kemet, and she would still find happiness.

Her desire to keep those she loved close to her was one of the reasons why, once things had settled after Wadj's death, she had asked Akshaka and Ishara to move into the women's quarters of the palace. She knew how well Penebui and Akshaka got along, and at the palace the young girl would learn the ways of the court, and have a better chance of marrying well. Merneith also knew the girl would not leave her mother, and Merneith had been happy to have the kind and gentle older woman move into the palace as well. As a result, Ishara's language skills were also improving. Ebrium's reaction had been to thank her profusely for taking his "ill-behaved sister" off his hands, although it was obvious to all that he was glowing with pride for her.

Ishara cut into Merneith's reverie by saying something to Akshaka in Eblaite, and then repeated herself for all to understand. "I am beyond happy to see that Bey, who is like son to me, has settled himself. And he could not find a better woman to match with." Ishara nodded and smiled. Merneith and Bey had announced to their family circle earlier that, once the mourning period for Wadj had passed and the child growing in Merneith's belly was born, they intended to marry. Merneith, as queen, was expected to marry within the royal family only. Their marriage would have to be a quiet affair. They would announce it after the fact, when it was too late for anyone to dispute it.

Ishara ventured to continue. "Now I wait for other son," she gestured towards Ebrium, "to make babies."

Ebrium shook his head, grinning. "Well now, Mother, I don't think I'll be able to find another woman quite like the queen. Bey is a lucky man indeed."

Ishara narrowed her eyes and wagged a finger at him. "I do not need another queen. Just *nice girl* that will take care of you and keep you... what is the word?" She whispered to Akshaka in Eblaiti and Akshaka answered with a mischevious look in her eyes, "*Civilized.*" Ishara smiled. "Yes, girl to help keep you civilized, now that we live away from you."

Ebrium feigned a look of shock, tenting his fingers on his chest. "I, not civilized? I am truly hurt, Mother. And I am more than capable of taking care of myself, I'll have you know."

Bey raised an eyebrow and interjected, "Tell you what, brother. While I agree with our little mother that you could use some civilizing, let me do you a favour and help keep her off your back for a while." Here Bey threw Ishara an apologetic smile. "There is still much unrest amongst the noblemen and some of the governors. Those who were loyal to the pharaoh have been grumbling about their reduction in favours and tax revenue, especially since the harvest season will be small and we will need to make sure the people do not starve."

Merneith nodded. "Although you men have rounded up those involved in my kidnapping attempt, and Atab's guard has been sent back to Sumeria in disgrace, there is still much work to be done to root out Wadj's corrupt nobles. Several people have come forward already since Wadj's death to report cases of bribery and dishonesty in the temples and the sephats. Perhaps we can keep you busy for a time investigating them. And then," Merneith felt her lips curl upwards, "when you are ready, I will do my best to find you a girl who will keep you happy *and* civilized." There was nothing she'd like better than to see the big, blue-eyed Eblaiti man go head to head with a girl who had the same impish spirit that he did.

Ebrium jumped to his feet and, with a mock flourish, gave a deep bow. "Hem-etj, I will forever be at your service. But when it comes to women I am more than capable of finding one. Or two even if needed." He gave her wide grin, looking up through a lock of thick black hair. His eyes twinkled.

Merneith pursed her lips and tried not to laugh. She gestured for him to rise. "And this is precisely why you need help, as I doubt such women as you seek out are the type to keep you civilized." She clapped her hands. "But please, we will talk about all this later. Today, let us enjoy ourselves." Bey reached out and placed a hand over hers and they exchanged a smile. Then Merneith settled herself back in to her chair and let the happy chatter of her loved ones wash over her.

FINIS

Fact and Fiction
For
In the Court of Kemet

In the process of sharing this novel with my writing critique group, I was asked several questions about the accuracy of various details in the story. I thought that since my group was curious about things, other readers might be as well. I've shared their questions, as well as trying to anticipate some others in case people were wondering just how historically accurate this novel might be.

This novel is set in the Early Dynastic Period of Egypt (3100-2686 BCE). We have less archaeological evidence for this period than later times such as the New Kingdom (1550–1069 BCE). Since we're lacking details for the Early Dynastic Period, I've taken some liberties and extrapolated some information from later periods, such as common foods, or styles of dress. However, we cannot assume that over the course of 3,000 years (the Pharaonic period) that Egyptian society did not change. It did.

In 2975 BCE (when this novel is set), Egypt had yet to become the land of opulence and grand structures that most of us are familiar with. Although it was still wealthy and powerful, much of what we associated with Ancient Egypt had yet to come into being. Upper and Lower Egypt had only recently been united as one land by Narmer, Merneith and Wadj's great grandfather. The first pyramid had not yet been built. Camels, horses, and chariots did not exist in Egypt until much later and the only means of travel was likely along the Nile, in litters (as described when Merneith arrives in Ta-Senet), and possibly by a few people on donkeys. The military was unstructured, and was mostly made up of common men that were called into militias as needed, unlike the more organized armies of a thousand years later.

I've put the questions into a Q and A format in order to simplify things.

Q: Did the characters in the story really exist?

A: Merneith – Merneith was one of the first queens of Ancient Egypt that we have evidence for. She may also have been the first female pharaoh, and ruled as regent for her son, Den, after the death of the Pharaoh Wadj (a.k.a. Djet). There is not much information about her, but her tomb in Abydos is of the same size and scale of other pharaohs/kings of her time, as well as in the same area associated with the tombs of the pharaohs. She's listed in her son Den's tomb on a list of kings of the time period (she is the *only* woman listed amongst the pharaohs). In Den's tomb she is referred to as "King's Mother Merneith," a royal title that indicates that at the very least she was the Pharaoh Den's mother.

It is likely that Merneith and Wadj were indeed brother and sister as well as husband and wife. I was intrigued by a woman who might well have been the very first female ruler of Egypt, and she was the inspiration for this entire novel. There is no evidence that she and Wadj were really in a power struggle, that Wadj was killed under suspicious circumstances, that she had an affair with a foreigner, or that Den was an illegitimate child. But that doesn't mean it *couldn't* have happened…

Wadj – As mentioned above, Wadj, or Djet, was one of the first pharaohs of Egypt, and likely ruled around 10 years. His name meant "Serpent of Horus." He was married to Merneith, who was probably his sister, and possibly a woman named Ahaneith. Wadj had a son called Den. Wadj's tomb, like Merneith's, is located in Abydos.

Amka – Evidence shows that Amka was a manager of Hor-sekhenti-dju under Djer, Merneith's father. Amka became an advisor and royal steward under Wadj and Merneith, and later became a mortuary priest under their son Den. Amka's name is listed on the tombs of Djer, Wadj, Merneith, *and* Den.

Bey – Bey's character is fictitious. However, his character was inspired by a much later story in Egyptian history. 1,500 years after Merneith, Pharaoh Ramses II defeated a group of raiding sea peoples from the north known as *The Sherden*. Ramses then incorporated many of these Sherden warriors into his own personal guard. This served as the basis for Bey's story. In all likelihood, it wasn't common practice to incorporate foreigners into the royal guard. That said, Ancient Egypt probably did have a fair amount of foreigners traveling through the region, as slaves were brought in from neighbouring regions, and trade was strong with the Mesopotamian Levant to the north and what is now Sudan to the south.

Ebrium – like Bey, Ebrium's character is inspired by Ramses II's co-opting of the Sherden pirates that raided the northern coast of Egypt.

Batr and Makae – The brothers who are assigned to guard Merneith, while fictitious, are based around ancient Libyan tribes such as the Libu and Meshwesh. There isn't much evidence for them from Libyan sources, but there are some from Ancient Egyptian ones. They describe the Libu, and other Libyan tribes, as having long braided hair decorated with feathers, and their faces and legs were tattooed. Sources for these tribes are for much later than the period the novel is set in, they may or may not have been in existence during the First Dynasty.

Q: Did brothers and sisters really marry in Ancient Egypt?

A: Yes, but it is seems sibling marriages were only common amongst royalty. Some famous Ancient Egyptian rulers who married their siblings include King Tutankhamen, who married his half-sister. King Tut himself was the son of King Akhenaten and Akhenaten's sister-wife. The famous Cleopatra also married two of her own brothers, and was probably the daughter of a sibling marriage. Ramses II married several of his own daughters, some of whom became pregnant with his children.

Q: Did Ebla exist?

A: Yes. Ebla was located in what is now Tell Mardikh, Syria, a place southwest of Aleppo. Ebla was a prominent city at the same time as the First Dynasty in Egypt. They did have rulers that were elected for seven year terms, as well as schools of the type that Bey attended in the novel. The story Bey told Merneith of the queen who ruled Ebla without her husband is fictitious.

Q: Did they have beer and wine in Ancient Egypt?

A: Yes. There are numerous shards from beer and wine caskets in archaeological sites that indicate there was a strong trade at the time of the novel with regions as far north as what is now Palestine and Israel. The beer was typically made of barley, and was nutritious and soupy.

Q: Could women get divorced in Ancient Egypt?

A: Yes. The character of Nenofer, Merneith's distant cousin, was based off an Ancient Egyptian tablet that described the legal case of a woman that divorced her husband. Because she was wealthier than he when they married, she ended up paying him an alimony of sorts which included a portion of her landholdings.

Q: Are the Sumerian insults that Ebrium and Atab exchange during the banquet scene authentic?

A: Yes. They are taken directly from Ancient Sumerian tablets that listed some common insults at the time.

Q: Did people really hunt hippopotamuses along the Nile?

A: Yes. There are many tomb paintings of Pharaohs hunting hippopotamuses. In the ancient period, there were numerous hippos along the Nile and they were very dangerous, often killing people who got between them and their babies or infringed on their territory. Although hippos no longer exist in Egypt (they have been hunted out), even today in Africa dozens of people are killed every year by hippos. In Ancient Egypt they inspired both respect and fear, and some Egyptian gods are depicted in the form of a hippo. An Egyptian named

Menes (who may or may not have also been one of Merneith's grandfathers, Narmer or Hor-Aha) is said to have been mauled to death by a hippo, and at one time it was suggested that King Tut himself had been killed by a hippo during a hunt.

Q: Did they have fortresses in Ancient Egypt like Ta-Senet?

A: Yes. The fortress of Ta-Senet described in the book is modelled after a fortress unearthed in Buhen. While the Buhen one is of much later construction (around 1860BCE), and even larger than the one described in Ta-Senet, it is possible that early-Dynastic fortresses were not so dissimilar from later ones.

Q: Did they have tattoos like Bey's, Ebrium's, Batr, and Makae's in the ancient world?

A: Bey and Ebrium's tattoos are modelled after the tattoos found on the bodies of mummies found in Siberia, dating back to 3rd-4th century BCE (about 2,400 years *after* this novel takes place). But I found the style intriguing and decided to include them on the off-chance such tattooing did exist in the ancient period. In particular, the tattoos described are like those of two mummies found in Siberia called the Man of Pazyryk (found in the 1940s) and the Ice Maiden (found in the 1990s). Batr and Makae's tattoos are described above, and are modelled after the Libu and Meshwesh tribes of Libya.

As for tattoos in Ancient Egypt, there is little evidence that they were common. There have been a couple of female mummies (probably dancers or musicians) found that had small tattoos of the goddess Bes, and some small figurines with marking suggestive of tattoos. How widespread tattooing was, and what purpose it served, is not apparent.

Coming Early 2015!

Book #2 of the Ancient Egyptian Romance Series,
In the Temple of Mehyt

Egypt, 2974 BCE.

The tranquility of the Temple of Mehyt is shattered when the high priest and priestess are found murdered. The queen calls upon Satsobek, the unruly daughter of an Egyptian nobleman, and Ebrium, a foreign former pirate, to investigate. Their partnership is complicated by the fact that Ebrium once saved Satsobek's life, yet the two have shunned one another ever since.

Follow Ebrium and Satsobek from the secret recesses of the temple to the seedy underbelly of Egypt's gaming halls as they uncover a series of intrigues, and a power struggle that threatens the tenuous peace of Kemet.

To stay up to date on publications, sign up for La Venta West Inc Publishers' mailing list at
www.laventawestpublishers.blogspot.com,
or Danielle S. LeBlanc at
www.DanielleSLeBlanc.blogspot.com

More from La Venta West, Inc.

A Single Girl's Guide to Greece
By Suzanne Bourgeois

(Book 1 of *Traveling Romances*)

For Ava, a travel writer, the best way to get away from a bad relationship is to head to Greece to hike medieval strongholds and tour the countryside. Two weeks later, however, she finds herself broke in a beautiful, yet remote, seaside town. When a handsome café worker tricks her into joining him for dinner, she has no idea she just might have found the answer to her problems.

To view the author's pictures of the seaside town, a recipe described in the novella, and to stay up to date on publications, sign up for La Venta West, Inc Publishers' mailing list at **www.laventawestpublishers.blogspot.com**

36305119R00149

Made in the USA
Lexington, KY
14 October 2014